JO MAY

Twice Removed

Curious rhythms in an off-beat town

This book was professionally typeset on Reedsy.
Find out more at reedsy.com

For Ian

Inveterate chuckler and nice man

I refuse to pray that you have gone to a better place,
because no god is deserving of my prayers.
No benign deity would have let you suffer as you did.

So, no prayers. Just my hope that somewhere
beyond the clouds, you are at peace.

RIP my friend.

A good walk is like a good book.
You want neither to end.
But if they must, be it in a pub.

Jo May

Contents

Preface

Thistledean is a town created by me. A place I would like to live.

In some ways it is a surrogate for some of the things that make our modern world such a frustrating place to be. Sometimes it feels that we're being swept along, manipulated and herded by things we can't control.

Jo May

A Star Appears

Tony met Julia when she fell off a bus. He was walking past, caught her when she stumbled, and they became friends. A simplistic view, but accurate. The fleshed-out version makes a compelling tale .....

Tony Mason was out shopping when a coach pulled up near the dentist. It was 'a pensioner's special', the like of which regularly deposits groups of senior citizens in the town square. They come to spend a few hours, mooching and eating, before returning home sated and happy. At least, most of them do. Mrs Marshall, Tony's 92-year-old friend, describes these elderly onslaughts as *'budget invasions full of precarious senior moments.'* That proved prophetic because Tony happened to be passing the tide of alighting passengers when a lady stumbled down the last step and toppled into him. Instinctively, he grabbed her, preventing a fall. 'Good catch,' she said, clinging to his arm. She hitched herself upright, then looked up and laughed. He laughed back.

'I'm a dizzy bugger,' she said.

Age? Well, let's not beat about the bush - she was elderly, somewhere over eighty, a generation older than her saviour. Her body was slim and angular and she had something of a stoop. She was wearing a blue woollen coat with low-heeled, black shoes. She carried a walking stick in one hand and a raffia shopping bag in the other. Her hair was light grey, slightly waved and windswept. She looked like she'd been walking the moors in a gale rather than sitting on a coach. The skin on her hands was liver-spotted and her face tanned and deeply lined, as if she'd spent years in the sun. Everything indicated a person who has lived a full life, outdoors and hard. Then, her eyes.

They were deep blue but gentle and sparkled with life, like diamonds in the sunshine after a shower of rain. They shone with youth and mischief. They were eyes designed to accompany a smile.

She finally got herself upright and obliged by grinning.

'Thank you.'

'You're welcome. Disaster averted.'

'At least for now,' she mumbled.

She gazed around slowly then looked up at Tony and cocked her head slightly to one side. 'Would you walk with me a while?'

He didn't hesitate. He wasn't sure what it was but he immediately felt relaxed with her. They were a generation apart and complete strangers – yet there was no threat, no uncertainty; just an instant friendship. Actually, it was deeper than that – it was a bond. He felt he wanted to be be with her in case she stumbled again. He wanted to know who she was, where she was from. He wanted to protect this frail old lady with the sparkling eyes.

'Of course I'll walk with you! Let me take your bag.'

She thanked him and took his arm as they began to walk slowly up the hill.

'Yes, that's right. Up brew first, that's the hard bit.' She blew a theatrical breath. 'Then we can walk down later at leisure.' She paused and looked at him. 'Of course, if you have other plans I'll walk down alone.'

He smiled. 'I have nowhere to be. I'm all yours. Tony Mason at your service.'

'I'm Julia. Julia Carter. Pleased to meet you, Tony.'

They smiled at each other. And there they were – friends.

She asked about Tony. Was he local? She presumed so. He told her he has lived hereabouts all his life, having spent fifty-plus years on a smallholding a couple of miles away in the hills before moving into town. He was about to explain why he had made the move when she suddenly stopped and looked up the hill. She appeared to be looking up at Tony's apartment and he swore she knew where he sits and gazes out from his sitting room window, directly below the clock tower.

Tony's apartment, above the chemist shop, is part of what used to be the offices of the urban district council before that was disbanded and incorporated into a regional council over thirty years ago. It has grand rooms, the grandest being the sitting room (formerly the council chamber itself) wood panelled with a large fireplace. Two bedrooms and bathroom are on the floor below. Although it was the previous owner who decided on this configuration, it all makes sense because when the chemist is open during the day he is twice removed on the second floor. During the night when the chemist is closed, the bedrooms on the first floor are quiet. Plus, by day, he has the advantage of that wonderful elevated view. The sitting room is rather unusual because it has a bay window, whereas there isn't one on the floors below. It juts out over the Square like a strong chin and is quite distinctive.

'Yes,' he said, following her gaze, 'I live there,'

'I had a feeling you did. How strange ...'

'Strange that I live there or strange that you knew?'

'Both, I suppose.' She paused. 'I mean, when I knew I was coming here I looked up Thistledean on the Internet. There is a photograph showing the exact view we're seeing right this minute. It could have been taken from this very spot. It's uncanny. For some reason I was drawn to that photograph. What are the odds that I would be on the arm of the man who lives there?'

A tear ran down her cheek. She looked at him and said, 'How often in life are things perfect, even for an instant?' She gripped his arm tighter and smiled. Tony didn't know how to respond. 'Come on,' she said. 'Let's move on.'

They drift and hobble, silently wrapped in their own thoughts, past the post office and the pet shop on their left. Julia paused and looked at the window, which was full of stuffed toys.

'I wonder if they are expensive to keep,' she said.

Tony snapped out of his day-dream. 'Could well be. They look well fed ... stuffed you might say,' he replied, smiling.

They walked on up to the chemist at the apex of the Square and began to make their way slowly down the other side, pausing to look in the windows. First the gift shop, then The Chocolate Box, before they stopped at Cobbles café for coffee and cake.

'Can't miss out; I've already paid for mine,' Julia laughed.

It was a pleasant day so they sat at an outside table. Along came Sniffy the Beagle, the town's canine mascot. He got a pat and a morsel of cake, and Julia got to smile at a happy-looking dog. She ruffled his ears and was rewarded with a tail wag.

'Cheerful little soul, isn't he?' she observed as the dog continued his rounds.

'He brightens up many a person's day, visitor and local alike.'

She smiled when Tony explained that Sniffy performs a daily round dishing out wags for treats. They sat for a while watching the world go by before continuing their stroll until Julia joined her fellow travellers for lunch while Tony ran a few errands. He'd agreed to accompany her back to the coach. 'To make sure I get there safely,' she'd said smiling. He'd hoped it was more than that, in that she wanted to spend a few more minutes in his company. It was peculiar but he felt they had unfinished business. He didn't want her to leave.

When they arrived at the coach she surprised him by announcing that she was indeed staying on for a while. She'd reserved a room at The Three Seasons B&B for a few nights and would take some time to explore the area. It had been recommended to her by Ron, the pub landlord. She asked Tony if it was OK.

'I've never heard anyone complain!' Then he smiled and admitted he'd never been asked before. Consequently, to say he never heard anyone complain before was accurate by default.

Julia patted him on the arm. 'You daft thing.'

It Tolls for Thee

O n a clear, sunny morning in early September, a single bell rang out. The bell tolled for Ivy Prendergast, a special lady, a heroine of her town, a representation of all that is good. For more than forty years, throughout her professional life she had been a midwife, one of two in the town of Thistledean. She worked alongside her lifelong friend, Elizabeth Marshall. Almost every family that lives and breathes locally has been touched by their ministrations. Ivy was the only person to call her friend Elizabeth; everyone else knew her as Mrs Marshall - formal, respectful.

It is five days since Ivy passed, aged ninety-four. The town council decreed that the church bell would ring until her funeral. For five minutes at a quarter past every hour, she would be hailed. Ironically, the bell was an electronic recording; the real one was away for repair after they'd found a crack in the bronze. A tiny thumb drive acts as surrogate, so the sound is played through a P.A. system and a large speaker placed high in the church's belfry.

It is ironic that Ivy should be heralded by modern means because when she and Elizabeth began their labours, pre-National Health Service days, things were comparatively primitive. A towel, a bowl of boiled water and an open fire in the grate, and occasionally arriving at outlying properties by horse and cart. Yes, Ivy would smile at the paradox.

Joan Bentley sat on a wooden bench facing the Square, listening to the bell. It was 07.16 on Friday morning and she was remembering her friend. She recalled the ready smile and ever-watchful eyes below an unruly mane of wavy white hair. The only other sound was the clackety-clack of a lady's heels as she walked her dog down the footpath across the Square. She and her black Labrador turned down a passage, leaving the bell as the lone sound on the pristine day. Every now and then a zephyr of wind ruffled the silence, and Joan heard the whisper of her dear friend. If she concentrated she could hear the faintest echo as the bell rang and the sound murmured back from surrounding buildings.

The sun had clambered over the hills to her left, bright and sharp, and began to dissipate the morning dew. Joan was sad but proud. Ivy's last months had been comfortable thanks to Joan's determination and foresight; not just her to be fair, she'd had support from friends and others who'd shared her vision. A large bungalow in the grounds of a local manor house had been transformed into a retreat specifically for local people. It had begun with a dream and incorporated a hard-won battle, but was ultimately worth the angst. The retreat was completed just in time. Ivy was the first resident, transferred from a state-run residential home in another town. She had lived her last days among friends, in comfort. She had died with Joan and Elizabeth, her two dearest friends, by her side and at peace.

From his elevated vantage point, Tony spied Joan sitting alone on the bench and knew she was reflecting on her friend. He felt he was intruding on his friend's private moment so he stood and backed away into his living room to sit on the sofa. He understood the energy Joan had put into the last months of the life of Ivy Prendergast. He knew, just for now, that Joan was out of fuel, but he also knew she could be proud of the way she had cared for her friend. He could hear the bell, but it was very faint. At 07:20, it fell silent. Tony knew Joan would leave, just as she had for the last few mornings. He returned to the window and saw his friend walk down the left side of the cobbled square, past the bakers and out of sight towards her cottage. Despite her bluster and strength (being known as The Colonel after spending 30 years in the British Army before retiring to run local scout and guide groups with a rod of iron), he felt sad for her because he knew she'd be hurting and lonely. She lived alone so her house would be quiet; but he also knew that Joan's spirit would not let her lie low for long.

Looking On

Tony returned to sit in his favourite wing chair to sip the day's first mug of coffee. When he moved in about five years ago, Tony had bought a pair of vintage wing-back chairs that were old but extremely comfortable. He sits in one of them to gaze out of the window and spends many a happy hour observing. He sees people he knows, friends going about their business; in fact, one or two wave - although it's not always easy for people to see him because the bright sky reflects off the glass of the bay.

For people he doesn't know, he tries to imagine what they are like, what they do, what makes them tick. He enjoys reading people through observation - how they walk, for example. Some are upright, some slouch, others look to have too many moving parts - as if their joints are a bit loose. There are limpers, shufflers, amblers and dashers. Some people look around as if wary, some are confident, oblivious. He observes how people dress, what kind of shoes they wear. Do expensive shoes mean a better person, or merely a richer one? 'Good' shoes, well polished, used to be a social calling card. Are they still? Or can you make your footwear appear expensive? These days some scruffy footwear is intentionally distressed. Sometimes the scruffiest people are the wealthiest. You can tell a lot if you take notice. Some people act as if they are being watched; others look to be in a dream, in another dimension even; some people look as if they would rather be somewhere else; Some look happy, others don't.

Tony looks down on the town from his second-floor bay window and mentally juggles this fascinating mix of humanity. He sees things from up on his perch that annoy him a little, like dog-handlers who fail to pick

7

up mess or people who throw litter. They often they look around furtively, believing nobody is watching. He imagines himself with a loud hailer, coughing pointedly as they ignore their responsibilities. He pictures their embarrassment as they are rumbled and smiles to himself.

But how would Tony appear to someone watching him? To start with, fairly short; certainly not tall, with receding grey hair (cropped short because of an unruly double crown). Pretty fit-looking for a man in his mid-late fifties, with a busy stride and upright gait. Usually casually dressed, on the scruffy side of smart - 'outdoorsy' to be polite. He's often in walking boots or chunky, dark-coloured walking shoes. He has a healthy, tanned complexion due to his love of the outdoors and he likes walking. He's also a good connector, with a ready smile; some people seem to actively avoid eye contact but Tony believes that consciously avoiding another person is actually more difficult than engaging them. For him, a brief glance and a smile is easy and natural. One thing he has always believed is that everyone has a tale to tell. He'd always been a watcher, but he decided that rather than imagine it he would henceforth show an interest and find out. Initially, he was a bit nervous in case what he intended could be construed as rather intrusive, but realised that if anyone wished to tell him to push off that would be their right.

Most people seem to give him the time of day although Lizzie the pub landlady reckons he's the archetypal curtain-twitcher, part-snooper and part-voyeur; the type you find on a street of terraced houses; peering out through a crack in the curtains; an all-seeing shadow behind a grimy window; the embodiment of the floral-pinnied guardian of urban tittle-tattle. A rather brutal summation, but amusing to everyone except Tony, who nonetheless takes it on the chin. It's true that Tony occupies much of his time by immersing himself in the fabric of Thistledean - because he loves the town and its people.

In his experience, most people find it a cozy, friendly place, but there are exceptions. He recalls one visitor (who had a misunderstanding with the local traffic warden – not the first person, nor will he be the last) who was inclined to voice his displeasure. He did so by writing on the visitor's page of the town's website: *'This infernal place sits at the end of an ill-maintained, badly illuminated deathtrap of a road. A miserable pustule of a town that reminds one of a decaying lump of meat held on a long fork over the dying embers of a fire. But the fire will go out, the fork will rust and the meat will rot away to nothing. Good riddance. J.J. Wilson.'* All that effort because of a parking ticket.

The lady who maintains the town's showpiece website thought the wordy assault rather descriptive. She described it as 'nasty but imaginative.' She removed the man's vitriol and re-wrote it: *'Thistledean sits in magnificent isolation at the head of a gorgeous valley. A succulent morsel cooked to perfection over a blazing, welcoming fire then nurtured in the folds of the lovely Northumberland Fells. Anon.'* 'Anon' is Felicity Winstay. She runs the gift shop on the high street and is the town's Publicity and Marketing Officer. At least that's what The Colonel calls her, believing a little flattery encourages the resident PR guru to ever greater endeavours.

Tony has a bird's-eye view straight down High Street, which is also called the Square. Technically, it's a long, narrow parallelogram. Well, that's how it was christened in a brochure promoting the town's market when the PR department went 'glossy' a decade ago. Then somebody jumped on the description and insisted that it is actually a rectangle. An argument ensued and a chap *'who knew a thing or two about geometry, thank you very much,'* said that a rectangle can indeed be a parallelogram. It all got rather heated, so in the end they called it a Square - in the generic, town planning sense, as opposed to being geometrically accurate. The 'public house discussion' continued but ended with geometry man leaving in a huff when someone pointed at the window and said, *'Anyone who thinks that square out there is actually a square is not to be trusted as a geometrist.'* Then someone questioned the word geometrist - surely it should be geometrician? So, a further pint or two was consumed while this was discussed, without satisfactory resolution. As Ron the landlord says, *'Unresolved discussions are the lifeblood of the Bull and Dog. My cash register glows red during a good wrangle.'*

'We'll ask Brian,' said Rob the Tax. 'He'll know.'

'Why should he know?' asked Joan.

'He's an educated man - I'll bet he's got an A-Level in mathematics.'

'You don't need maths A-level to know that that thing out there is not a square.'

'Go and look at the sign on the tourist office wall. It says square. S-Q-U-A ...'

'Alright, alright! Let's say it's a square *and* a rectangle.'

'And a High Street.'

'Oh, Lord preserve us.'

[To explain, Rob the Tax is an abridged version of his full nickname, Robert the Tax, due to his former profession working for Her Majesty's Government in some dark corner in the tax collection department of the Inland Revenue. Monkey reckons that Robert the Tax sounds like a merciless feudal excise man from the seventeenth century, while his shortened name, Rob the Tax, sounds more 1950s East End criminal. 'Either way,' he pointed out, 'he's someone not to be trusted.' Monkey is Tony's best friend - real name John Maynard. He is a semi-retired bricklayer and general builder, and known as Monkey because 'monkey' is slang for 500 and he claims to be able to lay 500 bricks a day *'with his eyes shut.'* Cuttingly, it's been said (often by Rob) that most of John's jobs look to have been done with his eyes shut.]

Whatever 'the Square' is called there are shops all round the outside fronted by a footpath, then an asphalt 'ring road.' Within the road, delineated by a post and chain fence, is a cobbled parking area accessed by four gateways positioned midway along each side. High Street is on a hill - or, more accurately, High Street *is* a hill, so perhaps it really should be called High to Low Street. However one describes it, it's apparently quite an arduous trek from bottom to top. You can tell by the huffing and puffing of the more mature, particularly those who have partaken of luncheon in the Black Bull public house down at the bottom on the right. When they've staggered to the top, below Tony's window, they lean on walking sticks outside the chemist debating whether to top up on their angina medication or re-charge their inhalers - or, occasionally, both. The hill is quite steep - Monkey reckons it's a one-in-five (not so much the gradient; rather, one in five don't make it to the top.)

If we think of the Square as a clock face, Tony sits at the top - twelve o'clock. The Black Bull, bottom right as he looks down, is about seven o'clock. By night the cobbled area is lit by sodium-yellow street lights. They are replica Victorian cast-iron gas lamps that provide a meagre light which is mostly absorbed by the old stone cobbles. What remains is dirty, off-yellow smudges around the perimeter of the Square.

The cobbled area is grid-delineated for parking, though the lines are worn and none too distinct. It is also dotted with trees. Locals who have debated the matter reckon there used to be many more, organised in parade-ground order. Over the years, residents who have knowingly regarded the scene, smoking pipes and shuffling from foot to foot below a variety of headgear, believe the majority of trees have succumbed to the vicious winters hereabouts, so we're left with a random dotting, like the skeletal remains of a forest in a nuclear winter. It's actually amazing that so many remain. From his perch Tony sees the unfortunate trees are regularly reversed into, either by gormless drivers or those full of the Black Bull's liquid hospitality.

Parking is 'first hour free.' An hour is an awkward limit if you're having lunch in The Bull (as locals lazily refer to it). Do you dash in and wolf down a meal within the hour to save yourself a few quid? Or, do you pop three pound coins in the meter to give you two hours to have a leisurely pie and chips? Going over time risks an unwinnable encounter with Peter Lord, traffic warden of the parish - an (often) unpopular character who lurks on the cobbles, slinking hither and thither, issuing unwelcome tickets. He's a merciless chap who recently issued a ticket to an elderly lady called Gertrude Harris whose car had obviously expired. Poor lady. On top of paying Dempsey (the local garage man) to tow the car away, she had to buy a new car AND pay a £65 parking fine. Gertrude is currently recovering from the ordeal with her sister in Dorset, a journey she undertook by train.

Three quid for a couple of hours parking seems a bit steep. However, it's not bad if you have a car full; seventy-five pence per person for two hours when four of you share the transport. That's OK even here, far up in the north of England where excursions are accounted for in pennies rather than pounds.

The thrifty visitor appreciates The Bull's marketing strategy: *Second drink half-price when you have an adult meal, Monday to Friday between midday and 4:30 p.m. (excluding bank holidays).* Bit long-winded but hidden within the verbosity is a fairly good deal - if you want more than one drink, that is. It's roughly akin to a 10% discount if you commit to a meal and a drink.

As Monkey points out, 'you need mathematics A-Level to understand the offer.' The deal is all about turnover. Offering tempters for the thrifty is one reason The Black Bull outlasted The Plume of Feathers which, until recently, was the only competition. 'The Feathers,' which was dead opposite across the Square (five o'clock), is now a charity shop - a peculiar choice, you would have thought, for what is largely a tourist town. Who the hell goes to a charity shop on holiday? Perhaps those who appreciate a *'second drink half-price ...'*.

Actually, the main reason for The Feathers' demise was rather sinister. The pub had barely recovered from a double whammy of a rat infestation and a culinary slating in *'Northern Life'* (an 'oop-markit glossie') when disaster struck. The pub's coup de grâce came when a bride stabbed her husband in the consummation chamber (as the locals in the bar refer to the bridal suite, which is directly above). Dust has been known to drift down from the exposed rafters when newly-weds are in town, but not on this occasion. The groom had allegedly been caught *in flagrante delicto* with a young lady - one to whom he was not married - in the beer cellar. One local (Brian) said the groom had been *'tapping a new barrel.'* The girl in question had been employed as a songstress for the evening to entertain the natives and was on a half-time break when the liaison occurred. Let's be fair, there was no allegedly about it - the pair had been caught straddled over a firkin of Theakston Old Peculier when Lizzy the pub landlady (called Fizzy Lizzy behind her back) went to change a barrel of lager. She, an unforgiving soul of upright morals, had informed the bride of her husband's infidelity. Two hours later after a brief but noisy skirmish and an unfortunate incident with a room-service steak knife, the police were called. A young groom lay supine and his bride was escorted to a nearby constabulary.

Tony happened to be there that evening and later recalled, *'My lasting memory is of an epilepsy-inducing kaleidoscope of flashing blue lights. Sundry emergency vehicles waited patiently in the Square while their owners tended the dead or interrogated the living. The whole hypnotic scene was accompanied by a mournful Leonard Cohen soundtrack in the bar. A miserable episode indeed.'*

The sad affair proved the death knell for both a marriage and the pub. Not only had the hostelry lost two future customers but word got round that the place was cursed and to be avoided. In an effort to revitalize the pub the owners launched a marketing drive to attract new customers, particularly aimed at hen parties. Who on earth decided on that particular strategy is anybody's guess. Happy hen partygoers were supposed to frolic in the bar just feet from where a new bride had stabbed her husband! Maybe it was to serve as a final warning to future brides not to get lumbered with some gormless entity. Anyhow, the strategy failed, trade plummeted and within two months The Feathers had closed its doors for good and became a charity shop.

The hospice fund-raisers moved in, for which the dying are eternally grateful.

Lizzy and Ron, who were only tenants in The Feathers, subsequently bought the Bull and Dog across the Square. They do have a few letting rooms but are diligent with who they allow in - and they learned from their experience and no longer entertain hen-parties.

Coaches are not allowed to park in the Square so they deposit their charges either near the tourist office (six-fifteen) or outside the dentist (nine o'clock) before heading off to a designated car park a few hundred yards away behind the supermarket. Nobody is quite sure why the dentist serves as an alternate dropping-off spot, but there we are. One day, two consecutive coaches dropped their incumbents there so the town, unusually flush with funds, installed two benches and a large flower tub. Thereafter the dropping-off point became 'official.'

It was on one of these occasions that Tony had rescued and befriended Julia. It's very rare for the elderly visitors to have a personal chaperone - the disgorged tourists usually bustle about, at random, like excited ants. At least some of them do. Twice a week during summer months a coach-load of waddling senior citizens arrive, most of whom don't bustle. For an all-in price

13

they get a coach trip to and from Thistledean, having been picked up from their accommodation (often of the sheltered variety), a morning coffee break in Cobbles café (three o'clock) and a pre-ordered lunch in The Bull. On arrival the seniors have an hour to hobble around before a mid-morning coffee and cake. This is followed by a further hour-long mooch before lunch. A nap on a park bench or a further stagger and it's back on the coach. These trips are limited to the summer months; the winters can be a bit harsh hereabouts and nobody wants the responsibility of shovelling up dead pensioners.

When Tony sits in his high perch as the dusk deepens and the street lights come on, looking down the length of the Square he feels like an airline pilot making a night landing, the runway below terminating in the arrivals hall at the bottom of the hill. Actually that's Smith & Sons the butchers (six o'clock), a place to meat and greet weary travellers. (Meat! Huh. Notice the gratuitous pun there? Don't worry, I won't make a habit of it). The former market hall takes up most of the bottom of the Square, save for an access road which exits past each end of the building. The market hall is about three-quarters of a furlong from where Tony sits (about 150 metres for the youngsters among you). The butchers is the centre of three shops. To the left looking down is Frampton's Bakery (five-forty-five), to the right the Tourist Information Centre (six-fifteen).

Since Edward the First granted a charter for the town's market way back in the thirteenth century, people have come to buy, sell and be convivial. The twice-weekly market has been the town's heartbeat for centuries. Once dominated by cow shit, the clatter of horses hooves and mead, it's now dog turds, sports utility vehicles and locally grown veg. But (largely) the conviviality remains, particularly when Peter Lord is on a tea break.

Above the roof line of the market hall Tony can see the peaks and dales of the northern moors (during daylight at least), at times calling for rather poetic reflection. '*I gaze upon the distant hills and see the wandering ghosts of those I've met down life's wrong turns. As summer exhales her last breaths, cool mists swirl among the valleys and sweep my memories before them.*'

14

House Guest

Tony was rather taken aback, but secretly very pleased that Julia decided to stay on a while; it's not often the fates surprise you with a morale booster. He'd been reflective of late and having a purpose with Julia was a healthy distraction, even if the endgame was just stopping her from falling flat on her face. He surprised himself rather when, on impulse, he offered her his spare room. He subsequently justified his decision by saying he didn't want her isolated on the edge of town, particularly as she didn't appear to be the steadiest on her feet. He explained that he had plenty of space and would welcome a house guest for a spell.

She told him that because she'd agreed to stay at the B & B she would stay there that evening - it was only fair on the proprietors - but if he was sure it wasn't too much trouble, she would love to come and stay thereafter for a day or two. She'd chosen that particular B&B because she was intrigued by the name - Three Seasons. The owner, Mrs Porter, had explained that she and her husband jet off to warmer climes, Malta in fact, for a few months over winter; consequently they are only open spring, summer and autumn. Besides, she'd said, the name did make it stand out and they'd had no end of business from the inquisitive.

'Not daft, these northerners,' Tony said.

And so began an extraordinary and enjoyable few days. Julia had no spare clothes so Tony took her to Laces, the ladies shop two doors up from the pub, then the chemist to buy a few essentials. She phoned her doctor and arranged to have a week's prescription serviced by the local chemist. Tony found out what she liked to eat and drink and stocked up accordingly. There are not many people her age who would do something like this on impulse, but he was to discover that adventure and the unexpected were part of her make-up.

His apartment's previous owner had become wheelchair-bound due to chronic arthritis so had installed a lift, at no little expense, accessed from the lobby of a private entrance at the rear of the building. Tony normally took the stairs for exercise, but he and Julia rode up together. The lift stops at a landing between the two floors and there is a wheelchair-friendly ramp up and down to each floor. Thus, it was easy for his guest to get around with the aid of her stick and the handrails. They walked down the slope and he showed her the spare room and bathroom. He left her to get settled and told her to treat the place as her own 'except for leaving empty beer bottles and takeaway containers lying around.'

Julia grinned and walked towards her bedroom with a 'humph.'

Tony said that he would wait for her upstairs in the lounge and asked if she would like tea.

'I'll be up presently,' she replied. 'Tea would be lovely.' Tony couldn't help smiling. Who says 'presently' these days?

When she joined him fifteen minutes later, Julia was particularly interested in the bay-windowed sitting room and it's view down the Square.

'Wow!' she said, looking out. 'What an aspect! Lord of all you survey. It's like being on the bridge of a ship.'

She walked slowly round the room as the floorboards creaked beneath her. She looked at the mahogany panelling and said she could smell the antiquity. 'I can just imagine the debate and squabbling in this chamber in days of old. How wonderful to be immersed in history like this.'

'All this wood is not everyone's cup of tea,' he said, 'but I like it OK. I painted the ceiling white and put this lighter carpet down recently, which brightens the place up a bit. It's airy enough for me. Or at least I've got used to it.'

'I think it's just fine,' she said as she settled on the couch and drank her tea. 'It's lovely. I feel so at home here. There's a wonderful atmosphere.'

He placed the second chair so Julia and he could gaze out together. They sat and chatted either side of a small occasional table upon which were two cups of tea and a small plate of assorted biscuits, the latter to be replaced later by aperitifs. The table, he explained with some pride, was made by 'Mouseman', aka Robert Thompson from 50 miles away in Kilburn, North Yorkshire. His trademark is a mouse, which he carves on the majority of his pieces; on this table it's on a leg.

Julia announced that she was a little tired, so she retired to the couch where she lay down to nap. She soon fell asleep. Tony covered her with a travel rug, pleased that she felt secure enough in his company just to curl up. She'd taken her shoes off, so he checked the size and while she slept he nipped out and bought her a little present. When she woke nearly two hours later he presented her with her gift – a pair of slippers in the shape of sheep, made locally on one of the farms and sold through the gift shop. They might be a novelty item, but they were genuine wool and very cozy. Tony himself owned a pair in the shape of cows; they were leather and designed for the male of the species, but probably not as cozy as the sheep variety. So they sat, both in their slippers, and grinned like children.

They spent many an hour before the window as Tony learned of Julia's background and fascinating life. He told her a little about his time on the smallholding and that his wife had disappeared. But when she told him her stories he realized what a restricted existence he'd lived. Basically, he kept quiet and listened.

Goodbye Old Friend

On Monday at 10.30 AM the town came to a standstill and Thistledean said farewell to Ivy Prendergast. The shops and business premises all round the Square were closed, every single one of them. A tide of people walked up the hill towards the small church, stone-built with a square bell-tower. It was full to its limit, and at least a hundred people gathered outside in the graveyard and down the steps into the roadway beyond.

The front pew on the right, large enough for six people, had been reserved. Ivy had no known relatives, but her two closest friends, Elizabeth Marshall and Joan Bentley, led a small party into the church following the coffin. Into her nineties, Mrs. Marshall looked tiny next to Joan, but her heart is strong. In the group were Arthur and Nelly Noble, long-time friends of Ivy. Also, Caroline Spears, Director of Thistledean's new Retreat and Joyce Melling, the carer who had spent many hours looking after Ivy during her last couple of years. Joyce herself is past retirement age but Ivy referred to her as 'young' Joyce. The two women had talked and talked, often late into the night, even into the following day on occasion.

Ivy, propped up on a mass of pillows, told stories nearly a century old, back to her childhood home in Wales where she lost her father to a mining accident and her mother to a travelling man. Her mother had travelled ever since and Ivy and her sister, Emily, never saw her again. She never really found out what 'travelling man' meant, just that he arrived one day and left the next with her mother. The sisters went into care at nine, and Ivy was fostered at sixteen with a family in Hereford. She did well at school and went into nursing from where she specialized in midwifery. She 'started afresh' in

Thistledean aged twenty-four and dedicated her life to her work. She never married.

Emily was also fostered but to a different family in Stone, Staffordshire. Aged twenty-one she married a local man, five years her senior. He ran a joinery business. Emily and her husband tragically died in a house fire three years into their marriage.

Ivy's foster parents were long dead so the nearest thing she had to family was Elizabeth Marshall. Later, Ivy and Joan Bentley struck up a friendship. Neither could really recall why they became close, they just bonded as some people do. Joan was a massive support when Ivy lost most of her savings to a conman who persuaded her to invest in a Ponzi scheme. She lived her latter years on a modest pension, so Joan was determined to bring her home by any means. After a stay in hospital following a broken hip, Ivy was 'shunted' off to a nondescript nursing home miles from 'home'. Joan set about rescuing her and brought her home to her friends in Thistledean.

Since 9.00 AM the electronic bell had sounded continuously. Ivy's coffin arrived on a horse-drawn cart. Mrs. Marshall had been approached by John Carlton, a hill farmer who had been delivered by Ivy, sixty years ago. She was credited with saving the lives of both mother and son after a difficult birth. All those years ago, Ivy had arrived at the farm on a horse and cart and Mrs. Marshall immediately agreed that her friend would have loved John's gesture. John was driving the cart himself, wearing a black suit with a borrowed top hat and carrying a whip. *'Splendid,'* was how Mrs. Marshall described his appearance. The cart itself was draped with green cloth and pulled by a wonderful jet-black horse, groomed to a sheen and sporting polished tack.

The bell fell silent the moment Ivy's coffin entered the church carried by six local pallbearers, including two of Joan's closest friends, Tony Mason and John Maynard. In the congregation were people Ivy had brought into the world; many with their children, some with their grandchildren and there were even a couple of great-grandchildren present. Reverend Rachel Billings led the service and the eulogy was delivered by Arthur Noble. His voice resonated through the church and was broadcast outside via the P.A. system. A natural orator, though his words were amusing, the hearers instinctively knew they were said with affection and deep respect. Joan read a passage from Ivy's favourite novel, *The Sea* by John Banville – a story about memories of childhood. Though ultimately it's about loss and regret, Ivy never tired of the wonderful prose and insightful narrative. Elizabeth believed the reason Ivy liked the book so much was that her friend could rise above any melancholy and appreciate the beauty elsewhere, much as she had done in life.

As Reverend Rachel and Arthur Noble spoke, Elizabeth Marshall drifted elsewhere to be with her lifelong friend one last time. She looked at the oak coffin, upon which was a bouquet of yellow and red roses, and recalled the wonder of what they had achieved together. She could hear the echoes of many hundreds of shrieks and happy smiles and all the nervous chatter. Snow in winter, sweltering heat in summer. She recalled the first cry of so many little ones making their entrance. Ever-present are the few awful moments when things went awry to the despair of bewildered parents. They were few, but enough to remind both Ivy and Elizabeth that, however hard they tried, sometimes things were beyond their control. Ivy always said that the disasters left dark corners within her for ever, but she'd said that they, as midwives, were lucky because they could go on to the next birth and rejoice with new parents. Those who lost a baby had to cope forever and try and make sense of what had happened, never to forget.

The service came to an end with the hymn *Bread of Heaven*, in deference to Ivy's Welsh origins. The pallbearers carried Ivy out into the churchyard where one half of a double plot had been prepared. Elizabeth Marshall looked on as her friend's body was lowered into her grave. Joan took her hand as they both threw a single red rose on to the coffin.

'Goodbye, love,' whispered Elizabeth. 'I'll see you soon.'

Joan and Elizabeth smiled sadly at each other and turned away. Tony was standing next to John and they each hugged the grieving ladies as they passed. The church had emptied and the throng parted to allow them to pass. Nothing was said as they went down the three steps out of the graveyard, between a pair of ancient yew trees and beneath the wooden arch. They approached a car that would take them the short ride to the pub and the wake. Joan helped Mrs. Marshall into the car then walked round the rear to get in the opposite door.

Standing next to the car was a man wearing a blue jacket with a dark green scarf round his neck and tucked into the coat. He stood with his hands clasped in front of him and looked intently at Joan as she passed. She made herself comfortable in the back of the car. Joan felt the man's presence and looked up, but he was gone. Was her imagination playing tricks?

Junta

'**N**ever thought it would come to this,' said Johnny Webster. 'Leaving my home in the hills, coming to live in a place like this. That was certainly not in the grand plan, I can tell you.'

Johnny Webster is Tony's friend. He lives in a retirement home in Holdean, Thistledean's larger neighbour about four miles distant. Tony calls in once a month for a catch-up, bringing a Chinese takeaway and a bottle of red wine with him. Today he was explaining about the new retreat in Thistledean. He tentatively suggested that Johnny might like to move.

'It was strange to start with; I was a bit resentful of my infirmity, frustrated as hell, but to be honest I'm lucky - I'm happy here. They are a nice bunch and I've made some good friends. We have a bit of a laugh, to be honest. And I can still get out and about a bit.'

Though he's only a year off ninety, Johnny's not the oldest - his friend Jack is ninety-five and calls him 'young Johnny.' 'Only yesterday,' he said, 'I met another inmate, Cindy, down in a café in town. We laughed like drains because she still had her slippers on - forgot to change before she went out!'

Tony felt he owed a lot to his old friend. Johnny had lived alone on the adjacent farm to him. He'd married but his wife died more than fifty years ago in childbirth, and their daughter had succumbed too. One of Ivy Prendergast's darkest corners. Since then he'd been on his own. The trauma of what happened prohibited him from getting attached again; he just couldn't risk the chance of further emotional despair.

Johnny had been there for Tony while he'd had a difficult time with his father. Much of Tony's childhood was a blur of poor memories. Sometimes he was beaten and there was no closeness, no real family. His father always seemed to be lugging a burden round with him which left no spare capacity for any meaningful relationship. Even Tony's mother had a difficult time; she was downtrodden and taken for granted. When she died soon after Tony's eleventh birthday, he was left alone with a distant father. Their smallholding was a couple of miles outside town. It fed and housed them, but not much more. The thing that has always frustrated Tony was why his father had been the way he was. He suspected something from his younger days had shaped the adult Tony knew, but never did find out. His father certainly never said anything.

Thirty years on, not long after his father died, Tony had sold up and moved to his apartment in town. A new start away from the mud and memories. But throughout his teenage years, the one bright spark had been Johnny, who had been there to listen and encourage. Teenage years are confusing enough without throwing in a dysfunctional family. Though a generation apart, they had been friends down the years and Tony always felt he 'owed' Johnny, to which he always countered, 'Nonsense, proper friendship is a two-way street. And you and I were friends.' That meant a lot to Tony.

'What's special about this retreat anyway?' Johnny asked.

'Not particularly special, except it's being run for locals and funded by locals, as opposed to the norm where they are council-run and financed, like this one. It's actually a large bungalow within the grounds of Harmer Hall, just outside town. It was Joan that came up with the idea of converting it into our own retreat. There was some opposition, quite a lot actually because of the cost, but Monkey and I got behind her and eventually we won the doubters over. It's turned out well, thankfully. There are only four suites, but enough capacity for residents of Thistledean, who otherwise would struggle to afford a comfortable place to end their days in relative comfort among friends in the place they love.

Not everyone is as lucky as you here. It's not the idea of a retirement home that's unusual, but the way it's funded is. To be able to do it you need to understand a bit about how the town operates. It's slightly unusual. Basically, Thistledean is run by a committee officially known as an Octad, which means a set of eight. Nobody is quite sure when it originated, but it's certainly over a century ago. Do you know anything about it?'

'Not really, I've heard of some sort of ruling council, but not how it works.'

Tony smiled. 'Huh, not ruling exactly - that sounds tyrannical, although these days the town council is colloquially referred to as The Junta! It comprises four women and four men, one of whom is me for my sins. We meet monthly, except for exceptional times like a Royal wedding or a foot-and-mouth outbreak, and each of us is chairperson for a month. These four-weekly assemblies are widely publicised and any issues are reported to that month's chair for discussion (and occasional resolution) at the next meeting. At the end of each gathering the following month's leader is chosen. Actually, not chosen - there's a rota, so it's more 'inflicted upon' than chosen.' He chuckled. 'It's not a popular position - too much hassle. I'm chair at the moment so I'll be glad to hand over next Tuesday.

The Junta is influential when it comes to local civic matters. It really has no official standing in the overall geopolitical structure, but within the town boundaries it has plenty of clout. Major decisions, for example on planning, are made at regional level here in Holdean, but before plans are even submitted they have to pass committee (Junta) stage. It's like the House of Lords but backwards. In other words, decisions are rubber-stamped locally *before* they go for regional approval. By extension, there's no point in going through an expensive planning process only to later have it 'knocked back' by The Junta.

The Junta is not spitefully regressive or argumentative; it just keeps development and the well-being of the town on the straight and narrow. '*Local for locals*' is the unofficial motto. It may sound narrow-minded but we are what we are and the good folk of Thistledean like it that way and believe the town is retaining its identity.'

'Blimey, it sounds positively Dickensian,' said Johnny, laughing.

'It's not really. How many places do you come across that are all exactly the same? Same shops, same precincts, concrete council offices etc., etc. All we try and do is retain our identity, keep it unique. It's sort of light-hearted but serious at the same time. Plans that are knocked back are rare, largely because people fear ridicule. If a plan is deemed unworthy, it is stamped in large red letters: *'Stick it up your Junta,'* and returned to the applicant. Not terribly funny really, and very childish if you're a victim, but mildly amusing for everyone else - and a deterrent for those who wish to submit a controversial application. Do you may remember the infamous headline in The Sun newspaper during the Falklands conflict? Well, back in the early 80s we borrowed their caption. Failed applicants are told they are perfectly entitled to appeal a decision - but nobody ever has.'

Tony poured another glass of wine for Johnny and half a glass for himself. 'Best be a bit careful, I've got to pilot the ship back home. Don't want pulling over by the rozzers.'

'Police are on thin on the ground round here - you'd be unlucky to get caught.'

'Nevertheless, I'll err on the side of caution.'

'You know, I called up to Thistledean from time to time,' said Johnny, 'mainly to visit the market. In fact the cheese stall took some of our stuff from the farm, but I never realized it was run like you say. I suppose the town being out on a limb gives you a bit of carte blanche with how you do things.'

There was a tap on the door and a blue-clad carer popped her head round and asked if they wanted a cuppa. She saw the wine glasses so smiled and disappeared again. 'Thanks anyway, Doreen,' called Johnny to the closing door.

'It's unusual but, as I say, the idea is to protect the town's heritage. There's a lady called Felicity who is a Junta member. In addition to being proprietress of the gift shop, she is also a part-time philosopher. She put the town's collective desire to retain its individuality like this: *'If you parachute into rural France, wherever you land you will recognize it as being France. There is a definitive national identity. If you parachuted into England, you feel like you've landed anywhere from Beirut to Beijing. I don't want to live anywhere - I want to live in England. I want to live here.'* Slightly convoluted perhaps, but you get the point. My mate John Maynard ... you've met John, haven't you?' Johnny nodded. 'Well, he replied, *'If I found out I'd landed in France I'd head north immediately, straight for the channel. Bloody awful country. The shops all close when anybody actually needs them and the bureaucracy is a nightmare. To cap it all, it's full of French people who can't make a decent ale and don't speak English.'*

'A good lad is Monkey,' said Johnny. 'I like him.'

'OK, I have to be away. I'll see you. Oh yes, I've just remembered ... there's a new article on retiring and care homes on the town's website. It's called Arcadia - it's amusing but poignant. It's called 'Retreat' and certainly worth a look.' He wrote down the details on a pad. 'Here's the address.'

They said their goodbyes and Tony promised he'd be back next month. 'Tell Celia not to forget her slippers. There's rain forecast.'

Johnny smiled and waved his friend away. With nothing more pressing to do, he opened his laptop and looked up the article ...

Arcadia

I am delighted to welcome a guest article written by a friend of mine, Roger Deane. Roger lives on a narrowboat in The Midlands so has a slightly unusual perspective on the conundrum of our 'senior' years. In his own way, he's addressing an issue that will affect all of us, whether personally, or with regard to family members.

The article is particularly relevant considering the recent transformation of part of Harmer Hall into our own retreat. The piece is easy-going but with a serious message.

Enjoy.

Felicity.

ARCADIA

By Roger Deane

We fret and sweat as we plan for our final thousand days. A lifetime spent preparing for the last bit that will see us ensconced in our retirement homes in faux-leather chairs watching daytime TV or doing jigsaws. Three years seems an optimistic estimate of the time we spend in our care home. But just a moment; before we go any further, allow me to address a bugbear with which I am particularly exasperated, namely the phrase 'Care Home.' It may be accurate but it is an awful term, as is 'Nursing Home.' In fact, anything with 'Home' in it conjures up a depressing image. We'll call it Arcadia from now on. Arcadia has various connotations - *'idyllically pastoral,'* for example. See, that's better. Albeit by definition it's a touch spiritual, it implies peace and serenity - which is probably what we're aiming for at the end of the day. Having said that, maybe we should focus on harem-scarem and barrelling into the next world in a fog of exhaust fumes. However we define it, Arcadia is better than 'Home.'

One thousand days is an approximate figure of course; some of us linger longer, others perish promptly. Naturally, it's health-dependent, but it's more than that. It's survival of the fittest (or survival of the least knackered) as we're forced to fight for the TV remote or sprint for the last lunchtime sausage. Sprint? Wrong word, perhaps. But there's a bit of a conundrum here – the fitter we are when we enter Arcadia, the longer we can expect to endure it! There's an argument for compulsory incarceration at 30. All those years, half a lifetime indeed, spent dashing for the last cream cake should keep us in tip-top condition.

Arcadia costs vary depending on whether we need 'rest' or 'nursing'; nursing is considerably more. Those with a medical issue sometimes need expensive clinical assistance to keep dribbling. Those who are fitter shuffle themselves independently round the circle of Arcadian life: bed to breakfast to television to lunch to jigsaw to dinner to sleep to nightcap to bed to breakfast ... to wooden box - eventually.

Bugger. I hate thinking about this, but it seems I must. It's an unsavoury but unavoidable part of my journey. The trick, I think, is to consider it briefly, yet determinedly. Quickly reach a conclusion and get it over and done with. Like a lightning strike as opposed to a full day's drizzle.

Crucial questions: how long have I got till the start of my thousand? How far in the future is selling my worldly goods and relaxing in somebody else's property at my own expense? The fact is I don't know the answers; none of us really knows. The period in my life when I leapt out of bed and went for a jog seems like a snap of the fingers ago, but it's quite a number of years - at the very least a couple of decades. See, I can't even remember. Back then, running shoes ran, unlike now when they act as comfort blankets for diabetic feet. All of a sudden it's not 'Tally Ho!', it's more '*Make sure I've taken the 75mg Aspirin!*' and "*I hope I don't get cramp putting my socks on!*' How the hell has it come to this? Where did the time go?

I'll work in £ / Day mode - please adjust for your own currency. The median cost of our new Home, ballpark figure, is £100,000 for our thousand days. If we want to flounder in a particularly comfy leather recliner overlooking an exclusive stretch of coastline, we might need considerably more - at least double that figure. A milking stool overlooking a power station in the industrial north of England (which is where I'm likely heading) will hopefully cost considerably less. With a bit of luck my frugal choice of location and budget chair will allow me to enjoy king prawns from time to time instead of mass-produced sausage.

Anyway, let's base it on a hundred grand (one grand = one thousand). Incidentally, have you noticed how casually the word 'grand' is thrown around with gay abandon these days in relation to money, in the UK anyway? In particular by large-breasted property experts referring to terraced slums up for auction in the ghostly shadows of northern Satanic mills. Like some towns close to where I used to live, for example, although our town wasn't one of the grimmest. Ours was leafy green (but getting bloated with new stuff, like houses, cars and people). We had a very good assortment of independent shops supplying a comforting range of food, medication and orthopaedic accoutrements. As I write, I live on a boat so few normal rules apply. But I still have to consider my future.

(By the way, when discussing Arcadian costs it's best to use a median figure rather than an average because some poor unfortunates can linger well over a decade and skew the figures.)

Anyhow, what it all boils down to is that (as of today) we need to save a hundred thousand pounds over our working lives to fund our 1000 bumper days at the end. £100k over an approximate 45 working years. That's £2,222.22 per year or £8 a day (£56 a week). For each of us. The country's biggest problem is that we can't trust people to save for their own demise. We've proved that because there's a care black hole, which apparently is growing exponentially. The shortfall is simply because we're surrounded by selfish bastards who refuse to save anything. They spend money on a variety of expensive 'in-the-moment' things like telephones and televisions. Incidentally, another relevant 'tele' is teleology, which is 'the account of a *given thing's purpose.'* Applied to Arcadia, it would mean the medium by which we go from active independence to inactive isolation in our eternal wooden box.

Then we've got the cars and holiday conundrum. In short, people actually want to enjoy themselves. Get something positive out of their lives, have fun. Which frankly is bloody ridiculous and utterly selfish. Goodness knows what granny would have thought as she saved a few pennies to buy something from the man knocking on the door selling dishcloths.

Credit is at the root of the problem. The drip. We can **'afford'** anything right now thanks to the benevolence of thousands of organisations willing to lend us cash. No need to bother about next year. As long as I can eat my extra-large pizza watching a soap opera on a sixty-inch TV, I'll be happy. At least I'll be happy until Josie pops round with the latest **i-thing** and I'll simply **have** to match that. But it'll be OK. I'll spread the payments over 36 months, by which time I'll be seventeen and should be earning a decent wage in a budget German supermarket.

Of course, there are plenty who don't (or can't) work who are unable to save, so they have be looked after from the public purse. My purse, your purse. The current proposal in the UK is to pop a quid or two on National Insurance Tax to cover 'contingencies.' Well, it might work, as long as all this extra dosh doesn't go on refurbishing the House of Commons lavatories. Laundering the seat of government, if you will.

But it's not quite as simple as that. In addition to saving for our final thousand, we need to fund the fun-filled years between retirement from work and the beginning of our retirement from life. We need financial reserves for golf, holidays, food, bingo, motor cars, vitamins etc., etc. Yes, they all need to be paid for, or at least some of them. The pension lump sum might help, if you've got one coming. Unless you've used that to pay off the second mortgage you took out to pay for your offspring's university education - or to pay off your own mortgage so you can downsize. (At which point you can, mercifully, tell your offspring to piss off as there won't be room in the new bungalow. And no, we're not putting a dormer on. Ugly damn things.)

We've probably looked forward to retirement, the day we can hang up our stethoscope or hammer. As we sail off into the gloom we have our retirement pot (hopefully) but it's under constant pressure. Also, in our twilight years things decline physically. Golf courses become longer and clubs heavier so we either bulk up or buy an electric trolley. Either way there's a cost. In our dotage we need less food (but of better quality). The amount we now spend on a couple of decent steaks used to fund half a trolley-load of budget stuff that would last a fortnight. Its rather a diet/cash dichotomy actually. All the processed crap we've ingested over the years has saved us a fortune, allowing us to maintain a relatively new motor car, but the chemicals in the ultra-processed pseudo-food has shortened our lifespan. Perhaps this nutritional mantra, dished up by a canny establishment, is a way to kill us more efficiently - enabling us to lessen the *'longevity burden'* on our various Arcadias. Blimey.

As we progress down the avenue of age we have a job hearing the bingo caller and if we do manage to tune our hearing aids to the correct frequency we have the devil's own job keeping up with the onslaught of numbers. Bad for the self-esteem and mental health. Consequently, an innocent hour or two in the company of *'two fat ladies'* inadvertently leads to a visit to a hearing-aid specialist and a psychotherapist for psychological 're-centering.' More drain on the resources. (Not sure I can say *Two Fat Ladies* these days? Tough, I have. For those that don't know, it's the symbolic representation of the number 88. Which, coincidentally, is also the weight in kilos of your average bingo player.) Another conundrum - by the time we can afford that smart little sports car we've always dreamed of, we can't get in it because we can't bend down low enough! At least without the unseemly expulsion of various gases. Besides we probably need to spend the car money on a new shed to store all the vitamins and potions required to keep us running (or shuffling) smoothly.

The challenges of our winter years lie ahead like a bombed-out runway, and it's daunting indeed. Bugger it. I'll think about it tomorrow. Or somebody else can.

Roger Deane

Relatively Speaking

'**I** have lived most of my life removed from reality,' said Julia, wistfully. 'For more than sixty years I've not been honest with myself. I need to start. I have only ever told one person this, a friend who has since died.' She looked at Tony. 'Aged twenty-one, I was adopted. But I tried to ignore the fact and begun to live my life as if everything I'd known to that point was actually true. I became a teacher, then a lecturer, but my leisure time and holidays were spent mirroring the life of the person I initially believed to be my grandmother. In effect, I wanted her to be my grandmother. But she wasn't. As far as blood ties and family were concerned, she was a stranger. And in effect, I went all over the world following in a stranger's footsteps. How peculiar is that?'

She sighed. 'Before I found out I wasn't actually related to her, she became my heroine. Before I knew it, it was too late to rid my younger self of her influence. I literally couldn't get her out of my head. My faux grandmother has been with me all through my life. She's part of who I am and admitting she's not flesh and blood is tough.'

She sat and looked out of the window and drifted away. Just as Tony himself had done on so many occasions, she gazed out over the distant fells.

'She was called Mary Roberts, but became Mary Roberts-Carter when she married Major James Carter in Vancouver. Mary was a mountaineer, adventurer and travel-writer, documenting her adventures in western Canada. She was a non-aggressive feminist and a woman who tackled challenges, physical or mental, in a tweed skirt. She wrote regular columns in the *New Westminster Times* and *Vancouver Island Guardian*. Soon her fame spread as stories and photographs of my doughty relative zipped down telegraph wires.

Mary and James travelled in Europe and Asia and it's wonderful to know she had such a happy marriage and lived a fascinating life. Sadly I never met her - she died in 1928, two years before I was born. She passed away at the age of sixty-eight from complications following a broken ankle sustained while trekking in Northern Pakistan. Allegedly her last words were, *"It seems my time is done, thwarted by a hill in the Hindu Kush. What a pity. Still, it's more dramatic than being run over by a tram in the rain."*

'As you'll gather, she was rather an inspiration for me. I've spent much of my spare time travelling. I literally followed her life. I began in Canada in my early twenties after university. Mary was born in Vancouver and lived there till she and Major Carter moved to a town called Golden in the eastern Rockies, not far from Calgary. It was a small place when they arrived towards the end of the 1880s, just getting going. But while they lived there the Canadian Pacific Railway came to town and the community flourished due to the logging boom. Their star seemed to grow with the town. But what suited Mary and James best was the environment. There were magnificent mountains to discover and explore and they would trek together for days. Mary kept journals and notes which she would transcribe into articles on her return home.

'When I went over I found a hotel called 'Mary's', would you believe, in Golden itself. Amazing. Go on ... look it up! I swear it's true.' She laughed. 'It wasn't exactly the height of luxury but how could I not stay there? What a beautiful area it is. There's a town nearby called Revelstoke and an area called Kicking Horse - wonderful names that seem to capture the amazing landscapes and culture. Then there's Golden itself, such an appropriate name for a jewel of a place, if you'll forgive the mixed metaphor.' She smiled. 'I spent a month trekking, with a guide, in the mountains and sleeping like a log. I could truly see the appeal of this wonderful country to Mary so many years before. Within this busy, bustling world, the silence of the forests is like no other. It's as if everything is absorbed by the trees and they become the keepers of age-old mysteries. If you listen very carefully you can hear the wind whisper their secrets far above."

* * *

Over the course of the next few days (the initial two-day stay was already up to four) she told Tony of her trips to Europe and then Asia. It was near the end of her European travels, about forty years ago, when Julia had her first accident. She fell from an ice-field, slipping and sliding hundreds of feet. She bounced off rocks and finally came to a halt when she reached the tree-line, wedged in the low branches of a spruce tree. She was badly injured but it could have been far worse. She suffered three cracked ribs and a broken leg. She was taken off the mountain initially on a sled, then a helicopter, and spent two weeks in Geneva University Hospital in the orthopaedic centre. She could have lost her life, but she was fortunate on that occasion. She was lucky to recover to the extent where she could continue her travels, albeit in a very restricted manner to start with.

'What my accident did, once again,' she continued, 'was emphasize the dangers Mary faced and the remarkable fact that she and James could undertake such adventures for so long in such isolated places. Had she suffered the type of accident that befell me, help (both on the mountain and while recuperating) would have been minimal. I don't see how she would ever have continued. I was pretty restricted to begin with after my fall and it contributes to my hobbling about today. Although I was to make a proper job of things a number of years later.' She smiled.

'But how can I possibly complain when I've had the most extraordinary experiences? One thing I could manage, slowly, was cycling and when I landed in India about six weeks after my first accident, I cycled many miles. That experience was like a story within a caper within a dream. There is an incredible variety of people, culture and vistas. All my senses were bombarded with sights and sounds and smells. I was followed wherever I went by my swarm, as I called them. Any time I slowed or halted for any reason my swarm would form. Warm, friendly, head-bobbing, jabbering locals fascinated by me and my machine. Where was I going? Where from? Why? Questions asked time and again by simple, wonderful people, many of whom had never seen a European, and certainly not full of dust and carrying her very existence in panniers.

'Where from' and 'where to' I could answer, but 'why' was more difficult. I was following in my grandmother's footsteps, I would say. It still didn't really answer the question; in fact it prompted more. You can't bamboozle a peasant and they won't be fobbed off – they require something simple to grasp. I said I was trying to find myself through my relative, what made me tick, what drove me on. Still unsatisfactory, the original 'why' still suspended in the dusty air stirred by scores of impatient feet.

'I never did answer them properly. How could I when the only following of relatives they do is into the fields to reap or sow, or walk to the next village to trade? Referring to them as simple peasants is disrespectful. Yes, they lead simple lives, but there is beauty in the people, and their generosity and benevolent spirit was almost unbound. My requests for a place to lay my head were never refused. This despite the incredible poverty I witnessed and the hardship. People died of the most basic diseases; there was no medicine in the vast expanse of the rural north. My travels were choreographed. I had bottled water and sanitized food and I rarely went more than two days without visiting a large town where my western sensibilities could be indulged. But the local people out on the farms lived the simplest, most beautiful and yet precarious lives.

'I was unable to climb anything but the gentlest slopes at first, but I was still to see first-hand the majesty and scale of the mighty Himalayas, at least from a distance. Mary, as a pioneer, led the way for us all to follow. Many of the routes and trails that are used today were broken by Mary and James trekking through unknown, unmapped terrain. Of course the vastness of the place meant that they only scratched the surface but it must have been as frightening as it was exciting. It was easy for me, you see. I knew that it could be done because others had done it before. On numerous occasions Mary and James would embark on something not knowing if they would return. Armed with only their courage and experience they would step into the unknown. That is very courageous. To my eye, for this alone, Mary deserves the recognition she has had.

'Part of the reason for me telling you all this is that her last climb shaped my life too, and it completes the circle. In an ironic twist of fate, the peak that did for Mary was nearly my undoing as well. I fell and injured my back. Mine was a simple slip, resulting in me tumbling down a shallow ravine. I don't know the exact cause of Mary's accident, but it was doubtless more dramatic than mine. I smashed my telephone in the fall. I was shaken and knew I was injured, but managed to walk as far as I could before I happened upon a group of Swedish trekkers. They sat me down and phoned the rescue services. I was flown out by helicopter. I had cracked three vertebrae and was lucky not to have been paralysed. That's why I'm a bit doddery these days. The nerves around my upper spine are a bit rumpled and my right leg is feeble, but there are plenty far worse off than me.'

****

It was early evening - the street-lights had come on in the Square and most visitors had left. There were only a few cars on the cobbles, mostly gathered down near the Bull. Julia and Tony sat in companionable silence and sipped gin and tonics. He had put together a casserole which was cooking in the kitchen below. The smell was making him hungry but he didn't want to break the spell Julia had cast with her story.

'I must go home tomorrow,' she announced. 'My pills are running out as my doctor sent a prescription for five days only. Plus, I don't want to outstay my welcome.'

He ignored that. She knew damn well that he enjoyed having her here. He turned, smiled at her and asked instead what had become of James.

'He died of pneumonia at home in Paris. He was part-way through a series of lectures when he fell ill. It's ironic that after all the dangers he had faced throughout his life he'd be doomed by an illness - a very unglamorous way for a colourful man to meet his end. Mary was heartbroken. Although she'd taken much strength from James, she did undertake two further trips after his death. From both the tone of what she wrote at the time and another account I came across in a magazine, she had lost a spark. I believe it led to a degree of recklessness. Perhaps that's too strong a way to put it, but she didn't appear

36

to take the same detailed precautions. Maybe she'd needed James' guidance for that, I don't know. At this time she was in Northern Pakistan. But on the day she was injured the weather was marginal and reports said that she appeared to have a devil-may-care attitude to the climb.'

Julia and Tony had a last meal together before she left the following day. Last meal sounds a bit drastic - they'd tentatively agreed that she would come and spend New Year with him, so hopefully there would be other meals. He'd book them New Year's Day lunch in the Bull and they'd retreat later to his flat for The Queen's Speech and a lengthy nap. Anyhow, for their last meal the casserole was worthy and they shared the bottle of Saint Emilion he'd been saving for a special occasion. He didn't have many special occasions these days so he was glad of the excuse.

Over dinner he asked if she'd ever married. She looked wistful.

'Oh, so nearly,' she said. She smiled and looked off to the side, lost for a moment in a memory. He didn't push her. If she wanted to tell him, she would. She excused herself and he watched her walk slowly down the ramp leading to her bedroom, one hand holding her walking stick, the other grabbing the hand rail. When they sat and talked she was bright as a button, but watching her walk he realized how frustrating her physical shortcomings must be for her. He really had developed a fondness for her. She'd a bit of everything - humility, intelligence, humour and self-deprecation accompanied an old-world style. He didn't know what he mean by that exactly, but there was just something classy about her - one of those people you could put in any situation and she'd just somehow fit in; someone who would always find the right thing to say. She also had courage. Courage to face her past and courage to battle through her infirmities and live a full, adventurous life, even at this late stage. Mind you, he reasoned, the alternative was not an enticing proposition.

The following morning they set off for her home in Keswick on Derwentwater in the Lake District. Tony's four-year-old Land Rover Discovery was a big, comfortable beast and they both relaxed during the two-hour trip. It was a bit of a climb up into the car so Julia had to use a caravan step to clamber in. They didn't talk much on the way down, each of them apparently consumed by their own thoughts.

She lived in a comfortable two-bedroom flat overlooking the lake. It was spacious, modern, well-equipped and serviced by a lift. The view alone must have made it expensive. She was on the first floor and wholly independent, but there were wardens on hand should they be required.

Julia introduced her neighbour across the hall, Agnes Duckworth. By chance, also a retired lecturer, the pair were good moral and neighbourly support for each other. Tony slipped Agnes a card. 'Here,' he said, 'just in case she gets in any more trouble.' He told her briefly about how he'd caught her and how she had decided to stay on. Tony popped into town to buy her a few essential groceries to see her through until she could organize a delivery from the nearby supermarket. Over a cup of tea, she thanked him for his hospitality and he thanked her for a fascinating few days. She looked up at him with those sparkly eyes and smiled. They hugged and he set off on the return trip to Thistledean.

As he drove, he felt he'd met someone who was rather more than a mere friend. Perhaps the stars were aligned. He felt they'd met just at the right time, just when they'd both needed a companion. He wasn't to know then, but the next time he saw her things would be very different.

Monkey Business

John Maynard is not a member of The Junta. What he is, is someone who regularly raises points for discussion. Most of the time he's just winding everyone up. It's probably because he's not a member of the hierarchy, although he insists he's not bothered about that. A couple of months ago he complained bitterly about fly-tipping. However, when the allegation was investigated, it turned out that the rooks had got into a rubbish bin and strewn stuff around the car park. Dilys Frampton, who's a Junta member and local baker, was instructed to go and tell John to put a lid on it to prevent further outbursts. We meant a lid on the bin, of course, but John took it the wrong way and an unprintable letter arrived the following month, the gist of which questioned why the hell we have a committee if valid complaints are going to be summarily ignored. The letter was read, discussed and 'filed'. Tony bought John a pint of Guinness the following lunchtime and peace returned.

There was recently a discussion in The Bull between a few locals and a visitor. The visitor, a chap all the way up from Devon on a walking trip, said, 'With the influence your Junta has, it sounds like a great place to live, providing you do what you're told.'

'It's not like that, really,' replied Archie Smith, local butcher and Junta member. 'We, that's the Junta, listen to the mood of the place and if anyone wants to object to things they get in touch and let us know. There are one or two who reckon to be more progressive who argue that it's high time the town had a new identity, time the pipe and slippers were discarded in favour of Vivienne Westwood and tofu. But those same detractors, almost without exception, are those who have had plans knocked back or been 'discouraged' from opening a coffee-shop franchise – which nobody really seems to want. They're quite happy with Cobbles café and, from the townsfolk I speak to, if you want fashion shops and fast food you can go to any other place in the country, nay Europe, but in little Thistledean we're offering a gentler, old leather and walnut alternative.'

Brian Elder, Golf Club Secretary, said, 'Of course, we want to welcome visitors and we have researched the matter. Visitors want to enjoy a market town with traditional shops rather than mobile phone outlets and three-for-a-pound emporiums. People come specifically because it's a throw-back. The thinking is that each visitor only has so much to spend so the goal is that their spare cash goes to local people and so back into the local economy. From time to time people come and try to exert undue influence on our antiquated system. They are invariably people with money, usually recently acquired, who drive big cars, have a limited vocabulary spoken with over-loud voices. They believe that cash is king and a wad can solve anything. Well, so far Thistledean has proved them wrong. And it's a collective effort.'

'Well, good for you if you can make it work,' said the man from Devon.

Brian went on. 'There is a legendary story which we all still laugh about. About three years ago, two visitors - a man and his wife - were in here picking holes in our way of life. They blustered that they would invest in some property, do basically what they wanted and knock some commercial sense into us locals. They boasted that no one could stop them. They'd said that nobody can interfere with commercial progress forever. Nobody took much notice. We had seen their bombastic, inflated type before and let them rattle on. John Maynard got a bit ratty with them after they said the town needed some sense knocking into it.' Brian in the telling of his story used Archie as a 'victim', standing right in front of him, pointing at his chest. 'He said something along these lines, "*I'll tell you precisely what this town is my friend, it's an antidote. An antidote to people like you. An antidote to the life most people lead, where pressure is the fuel by which they live and die, where respect is non-existent and society is driven by the beast of avarice. This town is exactly how we want it. If you don't like it, push off.*'

The man, somewhat startled it has to be said, had gone to interrupt but

John, who is quite a big chap, shut him up.

'*Be quiet, I haven't finished. We who live here are a peninsula, not an archipelago. We are a single, unified, friendly, caring entity, not a group of self-important islands striving to outdo each other. If you want the latter you can find it anywhere else. So, don't come in here with your shiny car and bulging wallet and try and tell us how to live.*'

Brian laughed at the memory. 'He's a builder is John, so I'm not sure where all this flowery stuff about islands came from, but it didn't half shut the other bloke up. When they left soon after, half-drunk and followed by a noxious cloud of budget perfume, they found the front seats of their Range Rover full of cow shit. They were livid, yelling all sorts to nobody in particular. They complained to the local constabulary (fifteen minutes away in Holdean). P.C. Warburton took up the case and investigated, rather half-heartedly. In fact, the case is still open and, if you ask him, '*investigations are ongoing.*' Have been for three years now. The authorities couldn't prove that anyone had actually broken into their car, nor that the owners failed to lock it. Dempsey, our local garage man, known to be quite handy with electronic kit and a Slim Jim, was 'interviewed' (meaning PC Warburton popped in for a brew) but witnesses swore he was working at the time of the incident. No fingerprints were found, nor hoof-prints, as Ron the pub landlord helpfully pointed out, and the Square's CCTV had mysteriously failed to activate.

The couple provide entertainment to this day. Their photograph is right there behind the bar' - he pointed to a framed photo - 'in that rather smart gold, blingy frame. There they are discovering their violated motor car. Immortalised for our entertainment, she with dyed blonde curls haloed in the murky street lights and he, tie loose, hands on hips, a face like thunder. If anyone gets too big for their boots regulars just point at the photo and have a giggle.'

The man from Devon laughed his head off. 'You're making it all up!'

'No, God's truth.' He pointed at the photo again. 'There's the evidence.'

Devon man smiled. 'Your town has this solid, old-world feel. No, not old-world exactly, it's as if it's stubbornly staying where it feels comfortable. Like it's sitting in a comfy chair in its slippers and doesn't want to get up. When you walk around here you automatically feel nostalgic, as if you're walking in your grandpa's shoes. But at the same time it doesn't feel restrictive. It just is. It's lovely, really.'

'You seem to have given this some thought.'

'I suppose I have. I came up this way for a day or two only, but have stayed a bit longer, purely because I like it. The thing that really strikes me is the contrast to where I come from - the whole area has changed beyond recognition. I tell you, sometimes I wish I could fill the cars of the second-home owners full of cow shit! It's ruined the way of life I grew up with. I understand absolutely your philosophy here. Local shops have disappeared where we live. Half the houses are occupied for only a few months a year so the shops can't survive. So they close and become fancy restaurants instead, which only open when the fancy people come with their fancy cars. How do you manage keep it like it is?'

Brian pursed his lips and said, 'We look after ourselves, I suppose. I mean individually and collectively. We have respect for each other and the place. To me, respect is key. It's disappeared in so many walks of life and the lack of it is killing communities. How do we keep it as it is? Well, here's one example. No shop changes hands without the Junta's approval and the Junta acts on behalf of us all, which we accept. Any new incumbent is grilled to make sure the best interests of the town are upheld and traditions maintained. Grilled is not the right word - interrogated is perhaps more accurate.' He chuckled. 'There was an occasion when a local chap, who had better remain nameless, got himself into a financial muddle. He owned a sports and leisure shop which, among other things, rented out and sold bicycles and issued fishing permits. Anyhow, it all went wrong so he sold his shop in a hurry at a reduced price to an outsider. Before anyone really realized what was going on the new owner had equipped the shop with glass-topped freezers and was on the point of opening a frozen food outlet. We've got some fabulous shops here, in addition to our regular market. They all would have suffered if the new shop had got a foothold, so, as we tend to do, we took action.

Before the stuff was properly frozen, the Junta was 'made aware' of a problem with the drainage outside the shop which necessitated digging up the footpath to conduct detailed investigations. Unfortunately this prevented entry into the establishment. The first ten days of the food outlet were to be the last ten days. No access, no customers, no shop. The new proprietor sold up to Mrs. Townsend, Tourist Supremo and independently loaded, who currently rents the building to Felicity Winstay. Some wag in the pub said that the shop was bought, opened, stocked and closed within three weeks. Now THAT'S fast food.'

'Looking at it, you'd have no idea there was so much going on.'

'Yes, you'd be surprised. The system appears draconian but works well. Admittedly the treatment received by the chilly entrepreneur was a bit over the top but it only takes one situation like that to discourage anybody else. There is only one charity shop and that was set up to raise funds for our local hospice - no longer, since it closed of course, so a new beneficiary must be decided by public suggestion and Junta approval. In all likelihood proceeds will go towards our retreat, but there's also our new visitor centre to consider near the stone circle. We only have one baker, chemist, gift shop and so on. Not good for competitive pricing, but the Junta keeps a close eye. The exception is the two butchers. Smith and Son's is down at the bottom of High Street, but Parker's is found halfway down the left-hand side of the Square, just up from the gift shop.

It's an amusing side-show, really. Rival butchers Archie Smith and Dolores Parker are both Junta members, as have been three generations of their respective families. There's plenty of bickering and banter between them, but all good-natured. Both have offspring so their presence could be guaranteed for another generation at least, providing there is no catastrophic indiscretion in the interim. Both businesses go back well over a century and actually provide a different product range. Smith & Sons are licensed for game and are the more traditional of the two, selling primarily to locals. Parker's do sell a small range of meat in-house to long-standing customers but have diversified. They now specialize in a variety of pies which are sold countrywide under the imaginative banner 'Thistledean Pies.' In fact, so well known have they become that people do visit specifically to buy straight from the horse's mouth, so to speak. That's great for them but also good for the town in general. We do OK, don't we, Colonel?'

'We tick along, yes. You'd think that we eight members of the Junta are persons of privilege. Uh, in fact we're not. There are no financial rewards; in fact there are no advantages whatsoever. Quite the opposite. In truth, whoever's turn it is to be chair usually finds it a pain in the rear end. Members anticipate the end of their term with relish. Then they can relax for seven months. People approach and grumble about all sorts of daft stuff, like John and his fly-tipping rooks, but whoever is chair tries to carry out their role diligently and with pride. Viewed from outside, the town could be seen collectively as a bit snobby or reclusive. Sure, we're a bit picky about who we allow to trade here, but you see the results. To be honest, it's nice for a visitor like you to say something nice. Sort of endorses our philosophy of our individualism.'

She chuckled. 'We only have one road in and out, called Hall Road after the big house just out of town. Although the locals refer to it as 'Get Lost Lane,' which has at least two connotations. It's single track with scallops bitten into the fields left and right as passing places, each one large enough for a bus. First to arrive at a scallop pulls in. At busy times, and there aren't many, you have to perform a sort of Scottish reel, like Strip the Willow, to get past oncoming vehicles. Left and right and around we go, yee haa!' She laughed. 'It reminds me of the nightmare that is driving in Malta in the Med, where everybody seems to aim for the shade, whichever side of the road it's on.

'In fact recently, because there's only one road, it was suggested that a barrier be installed on the edge of town, like a border post. Locals would have an electronic pass which would facilitate automatic entry, but all visitors would be quizzed by volunteer officials. Any unsavoury characters would be turned round forthwith. The vote was five to three against the proposal so the Junta were uncomfortably close to creating an independent state.'

Brian said, 'One of the real advantages about the way we do things is financial flexibility. Keep this under your hat, but we basically have two main sources of income. Firstly, all the commercial enterprises in the town donate - I say 'donate' advisedly ... actually they are contracted to donate - two percent of their takings to the civic fund. There's no formal contract between the town and donor businesses - just a handshake agreement. The two percent is stuck on the selling price anyway so it's a win-win. Two pounds in a hundred doesn't seem like much, but it adds up.

The other source is our smallish supermarket. I say smallish because it started small but has grown more than we expected. There was long and heated debate about it about eight years ago. It was such an important decision that the Junta decided that a communal vote was necessary, a referendum if you will. The main bone of contention was that a new supermarket would damage existing trades. Frankly, nobody wanted that. But we did need a general grocers, unlike the freezer centre that nobody seemed to want.

The whole thing came to a head because old Mr Ponsonby was retiring. He ran the grocers at the top of High Street. People grumbled but the poor old lad was 77 after all, and he was finding the fetching and carrying all too much. He owned the building, so paid no rent, and only made a modest living from the shop. It was damned hard work; in fact goodness knows how he kept going at his age. But for anyone buying the whole thing as a going concern, it just would not have been financially viable. Money raised by selling the property was Mr Ponsonby's retirement fund. It was a good-sized premises, double-fronted by dint of being two properties knocked into one, and it did sell for a respectable sum. Mr Ponsonby enjoys his retirement in a cottage down near the park.

His property was bought by a pair of investors who split it back into two independent units. One became a hair-dressers and beauty salon, run by a lass called Paula, with a rented out flat above; the other was taken on by Paul Broadbent, a local accountant, whose office is on the first floor. Incidentally, Paul is the guy who keeps a check on the town's financial interests.He subsequently leased the ground floor to a satellite branch of the Newcastle Building Society. Wins all round - except for the town, which now had no grocers.

Anyhow, we resolved the issue finally by deciding to open a shop outside the existing shopping area on a cooperative basis. It was built on the site of a former abattoir which closed twenty years ago. It was decided that the supermarket would sell anything not available on High Street, meaning largely non-perishables such as tinned goods, a limited amount of frozen food, cleaning products, paper towels etc., etc. There were actually quite a lot of things when we worked it all out. It also houses an off-license, because we didn't want alcohol on High Street - except the pub of course - and a launderette/dry cleaners. On this basis the plan was put to the vote and carried - not unanimously but with an overwhelming majority.

We even expanded a couple of years ago when we opened a small garden centre, which itself is in the process of being enlarged. Now in its ninth year, the shop is self-supporting. The town, via the Junta, controls the shop. It supports six employees and makes a healthy annual donation to the town's development fund. It's better than just self-supporting, actually; it's really rather profitable. There are no crippling overheads apart from wages, utilities, insurance and the like. No headline rent or lease, of course, which can be a killer. The supermarket books are overseen by Paul Broadbent who, as I've said, has an office in the former shop premises.'

Monkey had crept in and had been listening in. He added, 'We were talking about the supermarket set-up the other day. We reckoned it was almost as if it was all planned. The launch and profitability of the garden centre is unlike most of the things that happen around here - in that it works. In the normal course of events we seem to end up with an uncoordinated series of events dumped on an unsuspecting population by a ruling body juggling a set of random theories.'

'You're only bitter because you're not one of the ruling elite,' said Brian.

Monkey smiled.

Joan did a double-take, looking at Devon man. 'I saw you at Ivy's funeral the other day.' It was a statement, not a question.

'Yes, I was there. I'm sorry for the loss of your friend.'

'How did you know Ivy was my friend?'

'It was pretty obvious, actually. I know grief when I see it. I didn't mean to pry - I was just there to pay my respects and happened to be by the car when you came out.' It seemed a plausible explanation, but Joan looked at him with ill-disguised suspicion.

Polly

Tony left his flat to run a few errands. He'd received a text from Polly in her art gallery asking if he'd pop in and have a word. Being chairman of the Junta he was this month's target for grumbles and complaints, so he sighed and wondered what her problem was. He replied that he'd be there around eleven. He set out to buy himself a treat for supper, simply because he could. Since he'd lived on his own, he indulged himself from time to time. Whatever Polly wanted he would have something to look forward to later. He bought a fillet steak from Smiths and some fresh vegetables from Astrid's market stall - carrots, runner beans and cauliflower.

Astrid has been coming to Thistledean for twenty years or more and is an ever-present. She arrives in a old van, sells her wares and leaves at four in the afternoon. She is a fixture, but nobody even knows her last name. Whatever the season, she always wears a weathered woolen coat and fingerless gloves. She never smiles and looks to carry the weight of the world around with her. Tony has tried all sorts over the past few years to get a positive reaction but has concluded that it's impossible. He's made it his life's challenge to induce a smile, so far without success. He even feigned a trip once, a comedy stumble he'd rehearsed at home in an effort to provoke a reaction. He went down in front of her stall in a whirl of arms and legs. A circus clown would have been proud. But, reaction was there none.

He stood chagrined, like a comedian whose gag had failed. A poor sap left standing in the silent, smokey haze of a northern club, wishing the earth would open up and take him. Astrid stood po-faced, waited till he'd picked himself up and gave him a withering look. It was a look of pity. Not sympathetic either, more one of psychological commiseration. A look that said she knew he didn't have long before he'd be hauled away and incarcerated in an institution.

Mildred on the pet stall next door had watched the performance and understood what had gone on. She showed great self-control by not laughing. Tony jokingly bribed her to keep his antics to herself. He bought some dog chews, despite not having a dog. He'd give them to Sniffy.

'What is it with her?' he asked. 'What have I done wrong?'

'It's not just you, don't worry. She's been like that since I've known her. I think her face froze solid long ago during a vicious winter and never thawed out. You sure you want those chews?'

'Yes, sure. If Sniffy doesn't want them they'll come in if I burn my steak.'

It was time to face Polly in her gallery. He normally got on well with Polly, but because it was his turn in the chair he was rather wary. He just wasn't in the mood to be moaned at. He realized he was prejudging Polly unfairly, painting an unfair picture (to coin a phrase!). He liked her, actually, and as he entered the shop she smiled and bade him good morning. He relaxed seeing her cheerful demeanour, realizing that whatever she wanted couldn't be too burdensome.

The paintings on display are an eclectic mix illuminated by multiple mini spotlights strung from thin steel cables. Ivory walls and partitions house many paintings. She like to devote wall space to different artists, some local, others from further afield. She also takes work from art students at Newcastle University. Up two steps at the rear of the shop is a display of pottery. Polly has a potter's studio across the yard at the rear of the shop. She really is very talented and specializes in pieces made from porcelain and kaolin, which produce high-quality ware. Her pottery is relatively expensive and there is rarely anything for sale under three figures. She turns her hand to many designs - including figures, lamps, bowls and modernist abstracts. Most have a rouge/rose tint to them and are pretty distinguishable as Polly's.

Tony was about to complement her on the display but she started chattering excitedly.

'I've landed a big fish,' she exclaimed as she beamed and stared wide-eyed.

'Well?' he replied. 'Are you going to share your catch?'

'Oh yes, sorry! Of course.' She giggled. 'Betty Millard wants to show in my gallery. Can you believe it? Betty Millard, here in Thistledean.'

Tony had never been the best actor so his lack of enthusiasm probably oozed across the shop. He'd never heard of Betty Millard so when he said, 'Wow, that's great!' it must have sounded like a dead fish landing on a wet blanket.

Polly looked him over with a quizzical eye. 'You've no idea who she is, have you?'

'Uh, no,' he was forced to admit. 'Sorry.'

'There's no reason you should, I suppose.' She sighed. 'Unless you read the news regularly,' she added pointedly. 'She's a Brighton artist who was chosen by the king and queen of Belgium to paint portraits of each of their four children. It all made the national news about six months ago. I'm amazed you don't remember.'

'Again, I'm sorry, Polly. I'm hopeless when it comes to art. I appreciate it, but understand little.'

She sighed again. 'Well, now you know. Her profile has gone through the roof this past year. My sister, who lives in Shoreham, is a friend of hers.' Her enthusiasm was returning to its peak and she grinned madly. 'She bought Betty a piece of my pottery for her birthday a few months ago. Can you believe it? At a *'family-only price'* I might add.' She grinned again. 'Apparently she was really taken with it. She browsed my website and must have liked what she saw because she gave me a call yesterday. I could scarcely believe it, I thought somebody was winding me up at first. She's a very talented artist who paints more than just portraits. She made a recent tour of the north of England and Scotland and is basing an exhibition on that. She's 'touring' with some of the paintings of that trip. She'll display here for a month, then she moves on to a gallery in Newcastle. I can't tell you how excited I am. She'll also paint from sketches made on the Scottish trip while she's here, right here in the gallery. New things will be created here and people will be able to come in and watch her. And buy things. Not that buying is important, it's having her here that matters. Isn't it just fantastic? I may even persuade her to sketch the odd portrait.'

'Well, good for you. It's a real feather in your cap. And for Thistledean, too. How exciting! Do you want anything from me?'

'I just wanted to share my good news first of all.' She beamed again. 'But it would be nice to do some publicity around her visit, don't you think? I mean it could be a real money-spinner for the town.'

'I agree, absolutely. We have a committee meeting coming up and I'll certainly get the Junta on board. Perhaps you could ask around in the meantime and get some ideas that we can rubber-stamp at the meeting? As you realize, I don't know much about art galleries and their marketing but I'm more than willing to do what I can to help. Perhaps Millers in Holdean will print us a few publicity posters?'

'Good idea. I'll get on to them straight away. I can't tell you how excited I am.'

Tony smiled. 'It's great to see you buzzing. I'll start to spread the word. Keep us posted.'

It was now nearly midday. Polly had rejuvenated him and as he walked down to the Bull with his carrier bag of dinner items he was in a good mood. It's good seeing people happy and Polly's enthusiasm was infectious.

'Afternoon Rob, Colonel, John,' he said as he entered.

There was a muttered chorus of 'Hello,' 'Hi, Tony' and one 'Hello, Fergus.' Rob calls him Fergus sometimes, due to Tony's liking for Irish Whiskey. A little witticism that consistently fails to draw any appreciation.

Tony told them Polly's news, to mixed reviews. The Colonel was delighted while John was unsure about a *'hoard of luvvies wrecking the peace.'*

'Don't be such a heathen. It'll be great for the town,' said Joan. 'Time we pushed the cultural side a bit, and get you thinking about something other than bricks and soil pipes.' She laughed and pointed at Monkey.

'We'll have to get some champagne in … and Pimms,' said Lizzy. 'Stuff that posh folk drink. They won't put up with Ron's dodgy ale.'

'Oi! Who's side are you on?' called her husband from the other end of the bar.

Lizzy laughed and retreated into the kitchen.

Brian Elder came in, his palm held to his right cheek. Ron asked him what he wanted to drink.

'Whisthkee. Large.'

Ron grinned. 'What's with the swollen mouth?'

'Denthitht.'

'Oh dear, said Ron. Then he laughed. 'Isth ith a Bellsth Whisthkee you wanth?'

Brian stared at him furiously. 'Thstop thaking the pisth. Mithserable thsod.'

By this time everyone was in a fit of giggles, but Monkey had reached the point of no return. We've all been there, where the giggles take a life of their own and breathing becomes difficult.

'Geth lostht. Isth tshere no sthyhpasthy.' He downed his double Bells and stormed out muttering, 'Bollocsth to the loth of you.'

As the door thunked closed behind him everyone collapsed again.

'Very poor language for a golf club secretary, I must say,' laughed Monkey.

'Poor lad,' said The Colonel, wiping her eyes. 'He's not the first to suffer at the hands of old Tomasz.' She was referring to the local dentist, Tomasz Kowalski, whose name was Polish ('*a dentist of Polish extraction,*' as Rob had observed, quite wittily). Affectionately known as 'Tombstones,' he's actually a very good dentist and a popular chap. His grandfather settled in England, having flown fighter planes during the Second World War. Tomasz had returned to his ancestral home near Warsaw to train in dentistry and had practiced in Thistledean for three years since the retirement of Albert Daker, who had been a fixture for the previous thirty-five years. The town needed a dentist and Tomasz had actually been the only applicant; probably because the place is so out on a limb.

Despite the lack of competition he was put through a number of (largely unnecessary) interrogations by the Junta before he was accepted. He stoically answered all manner of intrusive questions about his beliefs, including his loyalty to the United Kingdom. Satisfied, the Junta eventually unanimously elected him the town's new dentist. Tomasz soon integrated. 'If you think about it,' Rob had commented, 'it's in everyone's interests to be nice because at some stage or other we'll be pinned in his chair and threatened by some very unpleasant instruments.'

'Not you, Rob. You've nothing to worry about,' John replied. 'You just take yours out and send them off for repair.'

'I'll have you know that both my teeth are my own,' Rob retorted, grinning.

There were no coach parties in town that day, but the pub was pretty busy with visitors to the market. Milly the young waitress was dashing to and fro and there was the pleasant aroma of fresh-cooked food.

After a nip of Jamesons Tony said his goodbyes and left. The sun was shining as he walked slowly up the hill. He sat on a bench across the Square from the café and ably assisted by his nip or two of whiskey, he nodded off.

Gone!

Tony woke with a start as a car spluttered into life nearby. With a stiff neck he clambered reluctantly off the bench and set off towards home. His mobile phone rang as he was walking back up the hill. It was Agnes Duckworth. They exchanged greetings but she sounded nervous so he asked if everything was OK.

'She's gone AWOL,' she said. 'Well, what I mean is that she told me last Tuesday she had to go away for a while and I haven't heard a word from her in over a week. It's strange behaviour and a little worrying.'

'What do you mean, gone away?' he asked, correctly assuming she was talking about Julia.

'Just that. When she goes away she usually calls me every two or three days. In fact I insist. She always laughs and tells me I can't insist, but she does call me. She rang at least twice while she was staying with you. But this time, nothing.'

He thought for a moment.

'How did she go? I mean she doesn't drive, does she?'

'No, Nick the caretaker said a taxi came for her at seven last Tuesday morning but he didn't know where they were heading. He had no reason to suspect anything was wrong, although he found it rather strange. It was about four hours earlier than she's usually up and about, but she was obviously in good spirits. He said she seemed fine the previous evening, too. She asked Nick to call at the newsagents to put a temporary stop on her newspaper. Am I worried? Well, I suppose I am a bit. She usually tells me if she's off anywhere.'

'No clues, no hints?'

'No, nothing really.'

'I know it's probably not ethical, but do you have access to her flat? Perhaps there's something there.'

'I do hold a spare key but I'm not keen on poking around.' She paused. 'To be honest there's no real reason to believe there's anything amiss. She's pretty independent-minded. She's probably just got a bee in her bonnet about something and set off. As you well know, she's not averse to having an adventure; she just normally tells me she's off somewhere, even if she does leave it to the last minute sometimes so I haven't time to try and change her mind. I suggest we leave it a day or two. I'll decide whether or not to have a look in her flat. If anything crops up or if I hear from her, I'll call you.'

'OK, that's good. Thank you,' he said, rather resignedly.

'Don't worry ... she'll be fine. I'll be in touch. Bye for now.'

He didn't sleep too well that night so in the morning he picked up the phone to call Agnes, as early as he dared, to see if she'd heard from Julia. As he was about to dial her number, he noticed an unread text. There was a number but no name attached. It read: *"Am following the only lead we have. Should have done it years ago. Agnes sent a text, tells me you've been fretting. Please don't. I'll call you soon, x J."*

He sent back: *"What on earth are you up to? I will help if I can. Please be careful. Love, Tony."*

There was no reply. The tone of her text implied that she wished to be alone so he respected that and didn't try to call her. Besides, it had been sent the previous evening - nearly twelve hours ago. He was relieved that she was OK but still alarmed that she'd apparently set off on some sort of mad crusade. He was intrigued, though. *'Following the only lead we have,'* she'd written. And 'we,' not I? And to where, or about what?

Instead he called Agnes to see if she knew anything more. It transpired that Julia had texted her the previous evening to apologize for disappearing, but wouldn't say how long she'd be away.

'Wouldn't?'

'Wouldn't or couldn't, I'm not sure.'

Tony sighed. 'Well, at least she's alive.'

'There is that. It is like her. Yet in a way it isn't,' Agnes told him. 'Historically she's set off here, there and everywhere, but she's always told me in advance. At least she did have the decency to text, even if it took her a week. She wouldn't elaborate though, or tell me where she was.'

'At least she's alright. That's what matters.'

They promised to keep in touch if either of them heard anything.

Jess

Apart from Tony and The Colonel, the remaining six Junta members are tradespeople or, as The Colonel puts it, 'actually have some purpose.' Tony doesn't really have a raison d'etre. It may be said he represents the retired people of the town - the folk with time on their hands to stroll and chat, and observe. They are the *'grey sentinels'* with time to keep an eye on what's going on. Monkey likens this 'malingering group' to the keen-eyed informants so prevalent in spy novels set in the darkest corners of the communist era - people who lurk in the shadows and peer round corners and report any subversive activity - or any activity.

Rob has been lumped into the grey brigade by dint of his early retirement. Apart from being the only golfer north of the English Channel worse than Tony, he bristles whenever he's associated with the grey lot. 'Besides.' he says, 'the only reason we appear to lurk in the shadows is because the street lighting is so appalling. The whole town is in shadow. In fact, it's amazing there aren't more pedestrian accidents - especially with all those loose cobbles in the Square. It's a jungle out there.'

Though his pedestrian reference was supposed to be amusing, there was a recent incident that certainly wasn't. A few days ago (a Saturday evening) Jess, the town's florist, was attacked while cashing up. Someone, believed to be male, cracked her over the head with a length of wood and made off with her days takings (about £500) plus her watch and engagement ring. Someone thought they heard a motorcycle around the same time, but wasn't able to give any specific details.

Polly had become concerned when Jess' lights were still on after seven, much later than usual. She'd gone in and found the poor lass slumped behind her counter. Her till was open and Polly could see a nasty gash on the side of her head. Jess was beginning to come round when Polly found her, but nevertheless she immediately rang for an ambulance. Thistledean doesn't have its own ambulance and the nearest is the best part of twenty minutes away in Holdean – that's if they are not already engaged on a call-out. This is when the town calls on its First Responders.

There is no doctor's surgery in Thistledean either, just a clinic open three mornings a week and staffed by one of the doctors from the practice in Holdean. Opening a new medical centre is on the cards but, historically, Thistledean has been medically isolated. Consequently, one thing for which the Junta has not been criticized is the setting up of a network of first aiders.

Thistledean is rather out on a limb so the townsfolk can be a little vulnerable to illness or accident. Consequently, it's important that they have someone on hand to at least stabilize a casualty before professional help arrives. The Junta asked for and received six volunteers about three years ago and the 'Civic Fund' chipped in to help fund some training for them and provide equipment.

Training was given by the North East Ambulance Service in Holdean and to be frank it has proved invaluable. At any one time there are two Responders on call, each of whom carries a mobile phone. The numbers are displayed in all shops and public buildings; indeed many residents have it on speed-dial. The First Responders carry a large kit bag with all manner of medical bits and bobs, such as bandages, creams, airways, even an AED (Automatic External Defibrillator). It's quite a responsibility and all the First Responders are held in high regard. It's not a job everybody is willing to take on.

Polly rang the number and the two people on call, Dilys Frampton (bakery) and Felicity (gift shop), arrived within two and three minutes, respectively. The main task is to stabilize and assess the casualty, having made sure in the first instance that they are not themselves in any danger. By the time they arrived Jess was conscious but dopey and confused. There was a real possibility of concussion, if not something more serious. There is a far greater awareness regarding head injuries these days, initiated in the world of professional sport. But initially, reassurance is one of the most important weapons in a First Responder's armoury. It's important to calm a casualty to be able to assess them. Panic helps neither carer nor casualty. Felicity took Jess' pulse while Dilys reassured and asked questions. 'You're going to be fine, Jess. Now how many fingers am I holding up? What's my name?' This helped to ascertain her state of awareness. Shock is a real possibility with a head injury, and sudden low blood pressure can be dangerous so it's important to be on your guard.

Jess gradually came round but complained of a thumping headache. By the time the ambulance arrived she was sitting up. The emergency crew took her pulse and blood-pressure and attached a portable ECG machine to check her heart. Nothing untoward was immediately found so they wheeled her gently to the ambulance to prepare for the short trip to hospital in Holdean.

By now the police had arrived and asked questions of the bystanders. Jess hadn't been able to tell them much. There was one attacker - short, not much more than five feet. Male, she was pretty sure. He wore a balaclava and gloves so she wouldn't be able to identify him again. Whoever it was never spoke and Jess only caught the merest glimpse as she turned round. She was struck before she realized anyone was there; the next thing she remembered was Dilys asking her questions.

Young Charlie, her fiancée, turned up as she was being gently questioned. He had a face like thunder as he climbed into the ambulance to accompany Jess to hospital. Charlie and Jess are childhood mates who got engaged the previous November; he'd scrimped and saved to buy Jess the very best ring he could afford. Charlie works with Jack Dempsey at the local garage - he's a good mechanic and well liked by everyone he comes into contact with. He and Jess are hard-working youngsters, saving all they can to buy their own house.

'I wouldn't like to be in the shoes of the person who attacked Jess if Charlie ever finds out,' said Monkey.

Tombstone agreed. 'It's a real violation. I'm not surprised Charlie's angry. He's not the only one.'

'No police, that's the real trouble. There's no visible deterrent. We get a couple of visits a week from a patrol car. It's bloody nonsense. Tony,' Monkey said, looking at his friend, 'bring this up with the Junta will you? Let's have a bit of inspirational leadership.' Then he added with a grin, '... for a change.'

'Suggestions?' asked Tony.

'More CCTV for a start, and a system that works. The archaic one we have now was knackered when John the Baptist was a lad. And we should have better lighting here around the Square. It's not surprising people feel vulnerable at night.'

'You could install a searchlight in your bay window,' suggested Tomasz. 'Then you could be a proper snooper.'

'I don't snoop and I object to the term 'snooper,' I'm an 'observer' - in particular an observer of human nature.'

'Snooper,' repeated Monkey, grinning.

'Shove off.'

The police patrol car drove away as Polly, who had a spare key, locked up Jess' shop. They all felt uncomfortable and as the police car pulled off the Square and out of sight it left a peculiar feeling of vulnerability.

'It's strange isn't it?' said Tony. 'Now they've gone I feel more exposed.'

Polly walked over to join us. 'It gives me the creeps all this. Poor Jess.'

'She'll be fine, I'm sure,' said Monkey. 'At least physically.'

Although frightened and groggy, Jess had feared for the reaction of Charlie. He'd be fuming and wanting to take revenge, and Jess worried he'd get himself in trouble by taking matters into his own hands. So despite being trussed up safely while being loaded into the ambulance, it was somebody else she thought of before herself.

This sort of incident was virtually unprecedented in Thistledean so it shocked the town to its core. It was as a result of this nasty attack that things did change in the way of some self-regulated security ...

Junta and Gilets

To learn a little about the workings of the Junta, a good example is the handling of the aftermath of Jess' attack. This was an emergency meeting; the regular monthly one was scheduled for a week on Tuesday, but the situation with Jess had resulted in much anger and some fear. People felt there was an urgent need for increased security. Basically, people were unsettled and the mood of the town was uneasy, so a show of solidarity was required. It may help to understand how the townsfolk are represented if we meet (briefly) the personnel. There are four men and four women:

1. Tony Mason (current chair), retired hill farmer and alleged town snoop
2. Dolores Parker, one of two town butchers (the pie makers)
3. Archie Smith, the other butcher (more traditional. 'Real meat'.)
4. Felicity Winstay (next chair), gift-shop owner, marketeer and philosopher
5. Simon Noble, chemist
6. Dilys Frampton, baker
7. Peter Flattery, café proprietor
8. Joan Bentley (aka The Colonel), ex-military and scout leader

Historically meetings have been held on a Tuesday for the reason that, as Monkey pointed out, *'Bugger all else happens on a Tuesday.'* He has a point. He is not a Junta member but, like a few other townsfolk, comes into The Bull on 'Junta Tuesday' to get an early report of happenings. Let's be honest it is just (another) excuse for a midweek slurp.

Meetings usually finish about nine-thirty, by which time most officials are well past the point of needing a restorative. Meetings are dry - the average age is mid-sixties and male bladders can't be trusted when burdened with a couple of pints. Why is it that women seem to have much better control? In addition, members have been known to nod off if the meetings drift on. Yes, the best way to get through the business of the day is sober and with haste.

At this extra meeting, they had a thorough discussion about security. The CCTV was indeed to be upgraded as was the lighting around the perimeter of the Square. Joan Bentley offered to oversee these upgrades and would start collating quotes the following morning. Everyone else thought it prudent not to argue with her, so summarily agreed to her self-election as security guru. Her cold-eyed stare round the table had all but ensured they voted for her. A sneaky smile indicated her satisfaction at this little battle having been won without bloodshed.

Most members had something angry to say about Jess' attack and Tony reported that the police were no nearer bringing anyone to account. Simon Noble pointed out that next time an attack occurred, and it was quite possible that another was likely, somebody could be really seriously hurt, or worse.

'It's all very well retaining our traditions and staying a century behind the rest of the world, but in certain aspects we must keep up, even lead. The safety of everyone must be paramount. I really think we should have some sort of local force, at the very least observing and reporting. Let's face it - the actual police are not going to help.' When Dilys Frampton pointed out that getting involved with vigilantism was dangerous ground, he clarified, 'I'm not talking about crazed lunatics with baseball bats, just a presence - particularly after dark. This was a very nasty robbery which I reckon may have been prevented if whoever it was had seen a couple of official-looking high-viz jackets. Nobody's asking anyone to charge in blindly and get themselves hurt.'

This was batted about for a while until Archie Smith piped up. 'I want to table a motion that we should see about setting up a volunteer force. Just a visual presence as Simon has said. Maybe half a dozen people to start with, patrolling in pairs. Lads, I reckon.'

'Ahem,' coughed The Colonel.

'Mainly lads,' corrected Archie, holding his hand up. 'I'm just not sure it's fair asking lasses to put themselves on the line.'

'It's up to them,' said The Colonel. 'I'd fancy myself against a wimp like Tony any day of the week.'

'Oi,' he said. 'You wouldn't have said that twenty years ago. I could run like the wind then - you'd never have got anywhere near.'

'I'll second Archie's motion,' said Dolores Parker. 'And I'll volunteer my husband Keith for duty. If nothing else it'll get him out of my hair for a bit. There we are, we're off and running.'

'You can send him on patrol with a couple of your pies, Dolores,' suggested Archie. 'They'll be a decent deterrent in addition to being lethal weapons.'

'Cheeky bugger!'

'OK, all in favour of a Thistledean defense force?' Tony said, looking round. 'Good. Unanimous. We can all spread the word for volunteers and pop posters on the pub notice board and tourist office.'

'Perhaps best not to advertise that we have a problem,' said Dilys. 'That's sure to put off genuine visitors. Word will soon get round, what with the internet and all.'

Everyone tended to agree with that so Tony suggested that word of mouth should be enough. 'Low-key recruitment, high-viz deterrent,' he said.

'Blimey, you sound like a real politician,' said Joan. 'Can't have that!'

'Thistledean Defense Farce,' muttered Peter Flattery, looking mournful.

'Look Peter, what else can we do?'

'I don't know, Flick. It just seems so inadequate.'

'I'm going to write to the police asking for extra patrols this way on,' said Tony, 'but apart from the steps we're taking, I'm not sure where else we can go.'

'You're right. I'm just sounding off. Thinking how I'd feel if it was my lass who'd been attacked.' He sighed. 'Come on. let's move on.'

'OK,' said Tony, 'I'll volunteer. Dolores sounds like she's recruited Keith. Simon, are you in?'

'Yes, I'm in.'

'Good. With The Colonel that's four. We need two more. I'll bet young Charlie will join up. He's as much incentive as anyone. I'll pop into the garage tomorrow and put it to him.'

'I bet Tomasz will do it,' said Archie. 'I'm seeing him tomorrow. I'll let you know.'

'Good. If those two agree, that's our half-dozen. Of course, more wouldn't be a bad thing.'

The Colonel piped up. 'I'll order some high-viz jackets. There's a place we use for the Guides' safety equipment and the like. They'll do us a good deal. At least they will when I've had a word.' She grinned. 'A few decent torches, too.'

'I'll put together some sort of rota,' said Peter from the café. 'What do you reckon - between six and nine PM for a start?'

There was a pause before Dilys (who was rapidly becoming the voice of reason during this discussion) said, 'It perhaps needs to be random, including daytime. If it's too predictable it's not much use. Anybody watching can suss it out if it's the same time every day. They'd soon pick out a routine.'

'You're quite right, Dil,' replied Peter. 'That's a good point. I'll draft something up on that basis and pass it round.'

Another positive murmur went round the table.

'Right,' said Tony. 'Other matters. Any planning issues?' He looked round. 'No? Good. Now, there are just a couple of other things ...' He mentioned Polly's art show, but most of the Junta were aware of it because the jungle drums had been beating. There were appreciative rumblings all round. 'We're getting some posters and flyers printed, hopefully at a beneficial price, and Felicity says she'll put a feature on our website. I was mulling this over and thought we could have a concurrent show of some sort above the tourist office. Something related, without treading on Polly's toes. Something craft-related, maybe? What do you think?'

Dolores said, 'We could get the History Society involved and display some of that meat you sell, Archie. Most of that's from way back when. Safer than shunting it out to your customers.'

'Ha, ha!' he replied, pointing at his rival. 'Anyway it's well-hung, not old. And at least you can recognize what I sell as part of a beast. Not like your stuff, which contain all sorts of mashed up bits and pieces.'

There was a communal chuckle.

'OK, enough of this butchery battling. Joking aside, I've been thinking about this for a while and thought a historical display about our town and surrounding area may be interesting - not least for the bus-loads of tourists who come. We have some interesting stuff lying about in boxes; perhaps it's time it was out on display. We could also do a feature on Keilder Forest and all the wonderful walking around here.'

There were approving nods so Tony said, 'I'll have a word with Barry Townsend, our history buff. His wife runs the Tourist Office after all, so it would all be quite a good fit. Besides, I'll have a bit more time on my hands when I hand over this chairman's ball and chain to Felicity after next week's meeting. Oh Lord, is it really a week away?'

'I'll speak to Barry; I'd like to be involved with that,' said Peter. 'Leave that with me.'

'OK, great,' said Tony. 'Paul Broadbent is coming to next week's meeting to update us on the supermarket and finances in general, so we'll skip that this evening. Right, is there anything else?' Head-shaking all the way round. 'OK, good. Finally then, I'd just like to read out a letter that arrived a couple of days ago ...'

Moss cottages
  Thistledean

Dear Mr Mason

As you are chairman of our town's committee (yes, I've checked), I am addressing you personally in the hope (rather than expectation) that you will raise my issue with your fellow Junta members at the earliest opportunity.

A philosopher (German I think, though his name escapes me) wrote: "Change is painful. But nothing is as painful as being stuck in the same place." I'm pretty sure he was musing about our journey through life BUT, due to an inconsiderate woman with a child in a perambulator, I was stuck in the same place in our town car park last Friday, a busy market day, as I'm sure you're aware.

My journey through life came to a temporary and frustrating halt. I wasted six or seven minutes. Time that is gone for ever. Time I could have used profitably – to invent a cure for a deadly disease, for example. Instead I was forced not only to listen to some Scottish bloke on the radio doing a quiz but also watch as the lady in question, probably out of spite, took a call on her telephone and discuss woolly tights with her friend.

Despite my gesticulations and polite protestations, I was summarily ignored.

Perhaps most serious of all is that the hot meat pie that I had bought for my elevenses cooled to listeria-breeding levels. In fact, as I write, a few hours after the incident, I am feeling decidedly peaky. Could you check the town's CCTV and ascertain the lady's address so, should it be necessary, I can send her a claim for medical expenses or (potentially more drastically) for my dependents to claim funeral expenses?

Finally, where on earth was our officious little traffic warden when we actually needed him? A reprimand is in order, I think. The other point here is that our traffic regulations should be amended to include inconsiderate mothers with perambulators who wilfully block public highways. Other suggestions that I hope the Junta will address forthwith include:

- *Put up a sign to deter unthoughtful parking.*
- *Paint more distinct lines on the cobbles.*
- *Issue me with a credit note for free parking for life.*
- *Write to my wife telling her not to block me in again. Silly moo.*

Yours faithfully
Tom Bradley

They soon adjourned downstairs to the bar, chuckling at Tom's letter.

Mercy Dash

O n Saturday evening, Tony's plan for the following day had included bacon and eggs, a read of the papers and a good walk in the hills. That all changed and Sunday finished very differently than he had envisaged. Overnight he had three missed calls and a text message - all from the same number he didn't recognize. There were no messages on the answerphone but the text read:

Tony. I have bitten off more than I can chew. I would ask Agnes but she's as doddery as me. I really could do with some help. Can you by any chance come? Hotel Le Florence, 48/50, rue Emile Zola, 02100 SAINT QUENTIN. J x
   P.S. There's a book on the cabinet by my bed.

He felt a surge of alarm. What the hell has happened? He called the number twice but it went to voicemail both times. The second time he left a message to say that he would come as soon as possible. Then he called Agnes to tell her that he'd heard from Julia and was going to France to join her in Saint-Quentin. He didn't tell her about the urgent tone of Julia's message; there was little point both of them worrying.

Book by the bed? Sure enough there was a hardback copy of Charles Dickens' A Tale of Two Cities. Poking out the top, being used as a book mark, was a piece of paper. Written on the sheet was:

1860 Mary born
   1885 M marries Major James Carter

1886 M & J move to Golden

1899 M & J have a son, John Carter

1900 M, J & J move to Paris

1902 on M & J begin travels round Europe for 2 years with 3-year-old John

1920 John moves to London

1925 John Carter marries Dorothy (nee wheeler)

1928 Mary dies. Hindu Kush

1932 J & D adopt J (age 2)

1940 October. J Sent to Grasmere, Cumbria as a child evacuee

1941 April. J and D killed in London bombing

1945 July. J to Uppermill. Foster?

Jacqueline Courtois. 1910. Saint Quentin

So here was why she'd travelled to France: Jacqueline Courtois. He wasn't used to jetting off; in fact the last time he had flown was nine years ago. The Internet told him there was a flight from Manchester to Paris (CDG) at 17:30 that afternoon - then trains from Gare du Nord, Paris to Saint-Quentin, at 21:34 or 22:34 and arriving roughly two hours later. He'd surely catch one of those.

It was an approximate three-and-a-half-hour drive to Manchester, so there was a chance he could catch the earlier flight at 14:30. But he figured something was likely to go wrong - traffic or whatever - so decided that the later one was the safer option. He booked the flight online and went in search of his passport and a few essential items, basic toiletries and a change of clothes. He packed everything in his small day-sack which he would be able to take with him on the plane.

He was acting in a sort of rushed, panicky way, and his adrenaline was pumping, the way you behave when you're nervous and something is not quite in your control. He grabbed the £300 he kept for emergencies (hidden in an imitation dog food tin in the larder) and set off the airport. (He wondered if he should change tins. He didn't even have a dog. Bit obvious for a savvy thief.)

In Holdean, he realized he'd not let Julia know what time he hoped to arrive so he pulled into the petrol station and sent her a text saying that with luck he'd be at the hotel late this evening.

He took the A69 to Carlisle and joined the M6 for the drive south. Cruising on the motorway he had further chance to reflect on Julia's predicament, but whichever way he looked at it nothing became any clearer. Much of the time all he could picture was his old friend getting herself in a muddle. Once again he felt protective and hoped she was fundamentally OK.

Remarkably, the budget flight left and arrived pretty much on time. It would have been far more 'budget' if he'd booked in advance, but of course that wasn't possible. He landed at 20:00 local time and changed some pounds for euros at the bureau de change and felt almost defiled by their paltry exchange rate. He managed to avoid the myriad of advertisements for perfume and lingerie and caught an airport shuttle bus to the RER train and the approximate fifty-minute trip to Gare du Nord in Paris. He jumped on the 21:34 train to Saint-Quentin a couple of minutes before its scheduled departure time and arrived at Hotel le Florence a little over twelve hours after receiving Julia's text.

Everything had gone pretty smoothly on his journey; it was as he arrived at the hotel that things looked a little rockier. He'd texted Julia from the train and told her he'd be there just before midnight. She replied that she would meet him in the bar, despite the lateness of the hour. He saw a woman who looked ten years older than when he'd last seen her, and she wasn't young to start with. She had dark smudges round her eyes and her skin was sallow and drawn. She looked utterly exhausted. She wore crumpled cream slacks and a dark blue blouse. She heaved herself up out of her chair and they hugged silently. Finally she broke off and smiled a weary smile. He knew then that basically she was alright; those eyes of hers tried to sparkle from within a face so tired she looked like a panda.

'What on earth have you been up to?' he asked.

'I've been looking for me.' She sat down on the twin sofa. 'Here,' she said as she took his hand, 'come and sit next to me. I'll tell you more tomorrow but in a nutshell I've been looking for my mother, or rather her family. In truth I'm too old for all this charging around. I've been rather foolish.'

Tony squeezed her hand. 'What you need now is bed. You look tired out. Let's get you to your room and we can talk tomorrow when you're rested.'

She nodded and she held on to his arm while shuffling to the lift. They said goodnight at her door and Tony went back down to the lobby to check in. As he waited he noticed the bar was just closing so nipped over and ordered a large whiskey and water.

'Fatigué?' asked the receptionist. *'Celine'* was embossed onto a blue name-badge. She was a plump, pretty girl of about twenty with a friendly smile.

He smiled back and nodded. 'Yes, a little. It has been a long day.' He held the glass up. 'This will help.'

She laughed. 'That will help you sleep, I think. Your friend,' she continued in slightly accented English, 'she has been very busy. She is an old lady but she must be very fit. Every day for five days she has left the hotel in the morning and not returned till after seven in the evening. She must be exhausted. Me and my colleagues are worried about her. Are you her son?'

'No,' he said, 'just a friend. I can see she is tired. I will try and look after her.' Then he asked, 'Has she booked an alarm call for the morning?'

'Oui. For seven o'clock.'

'Then would you please cancel it? She needs to sleep. It is already after midnight.'

'Yes. For sure. I am glad you are here.'

He smiled and took his drink to one of the easy chairs in the lobby and relaxed properly for the first time that day. Tony was exhausted but he was mighty relieved that he had found her. The next thing he knew, Celine the receptionist was tapping him on the shoulder, rousing him from sleep. 'Perhaps you should go up to your room, Monsieur?' she said, smiling.

'Oui. Merci beaucoup.'

Early Years

The following morning Tony woke at eight, showered and felt human again. He had a typical continental breakfast, including a croissant with butter and jam, some fruit salad with yogurt and lots of revitalizing fresh coffee. How he managed to avoid the bacon, sausage and eggs they'd included for foreigners he wasn't sure. It all smelled delicious. As he sat there, full of healthy stuff, his mid-section was gurgling like a blocked sluice. He wondered <u>WHY</u> he'd bothered avoiding the bacon, sausage and eggs.

There was no sign of Julia; he certainly wasn't going to wake her so he went for a stroll. The hotel was a large two-storey, brick-built building with slim dormer windows set in a steeply-pitched, grey slate roof. Ivy covered part of the front wall and three flags fluttered half-heartedly from poles in the gentle breeze above the revolving door. He recognized the French tricolour and the twelve stars of the European Union flag, but the third he could only assume was a regional one. It was a confusing blue, yellow and white affair with little obvious meaning.

He turned left and headed up the gentle hill towards a large square called Place Hotel de Ville – basically 'town hall square' in English. In one corner a market was taking place in the sunshine. There were stalls selling vegetables, cheese, meat, fish, olives and clothes. It was just after 9:00 a.m. and lots of locals bustled about chatting and bartering. He smiled at the thought of the little market in Thistledean and wondered how Astrid would cope with all these people. Peter Lord would have had a field day - there were cars, scooters and sit-up-and-beg bikes randomly abandoned all over the place.

He called at a chemist to supplement his stock of essentials and bought a couple of bottles of mineral water from a small épicerie run by a smiling Asian gent – plus ça change. He also called in at the Office de Tourisme just up the road from the hotel, where he picked up a street-map of Saint-Quentin, a more general one of the surrounding area and also a brief history of the city. On the front of the latter was a photograph of the magnificent Hotel de Ville.

Tony had visited a number of French cities whose showpiece centre was typically a large square surrounded by stately buildings, one of which is usually the town hall, with a French tricolour flying from the belfry or the balcony. This was no different. Whenever he saw the tricolour he imagined the singing of the Marseillaise at the start of a rugby international. He always thought it to be a wonderful, uplifting anthem and he could envisage players and spectators alike belting out the tune … 'Marchons, marchons…'.

The sandstone buildings are at their best either in the morning or late afternoon when they seem to come alive in gentle sunshine. Right now the frantic morning rush was over and, apart from the market, the city had settled into its working week as he made his way back to the hotel. Pigeons flitted and scavenged on the time-worn cobbles but come midday they'd all roost in the shade of the Square's colonnades and shelter from the fierce sun. Siesta time.

It was nearly 10:00 a.m. when he got back and Julia was in the dining room drinking tea. She pursed her lips and looked suspiciously into her cup as he approached. 'Awful,' she frowned. 'They can do many wonderful things, the French, but tea is a definite weakness.'

He smiled and told her she looked a bit less grey.

'I do feel better. I slept for nearly nine hours – that's unheard of.'

'Good. I'll join you for a coffee, if you don't mind.' He summoned a waiter. 'OK,' he said, 'first, you are going call Agnes and tell her you're alright. It's not fair to have people worrying. She cares about you, you know?' He passed her his phone. 'The number is up on the screen. All you have to do is press the green button.'

She made an exaggerated show of button-pressing and he heard one side of an apologetic conversation.

71

'There,' she said, handing my phone back. 'Happy?'

They smiled at each other.

'Right,' he said, pouring himself a coffee from the silver pot, 'what have you been up to?'

'Oh dear,' she said. 'It's all rather sordid and complicated.'

She sat and looked at her liver-spotted hands folded in front of her on the white cloth.

'Allow me to give you a start,' he said.

She looked up at me with a grim expression.

'You wanted me to find that list of dates and somebody to give you a nudge, didn't you?' I asked. 'Someone to kick-start your search.'

'Maybe. Probably. I suppose I did, yes. I've had the knowledge stuck in my subconscious for years, but never wanted to act on it. Felt frightened of what I might find, I suppose. It was as if admitting it was making it real, and I didn't want that. I've managed perfectly well with my surrogate families, had a good and interesting life, but things changed when we had those talks back in Thistledean. To be honest I've never found anyone to share all this with until you came along. For that I both liked you and resented you. But in the end I liked you more.'

'That's a relief to hear!' joked Tony, trying to keep the mood a little lighter. She smiled, reached over and patted his hand.

'The moment we paused and looked up at your flat that day, I knew something had changed. That prompted me to stay on for a few days. I tell you what it felt like - it was like I was standing with my back to a mountain. My past has loomed over my shoulder most of my adult life. But it's been indistinct - shrouded in mist, if you will. I have always known that at some stage I would have to turn and face it. I suppose I was leaving it a bit late but the moment came when I closed the door after you'd dropped me off at home after my stay. I knew then that it was time to try and unravel it all.'

She paused and took a sip of tea. She looked out of the window into the past.

'I found out I was adopted in 1951, aged 21. I'm sure you can imagine what shattering news that was. On my twenty-first birthday I benefited from a small trust fund set up by my adoptive parents, John and Dorothy Carter. They died when I was eleven. Had they lived and continued to supplement the fund until I came of age it would have been quite substantial; as it was, it was pretty small. I was also given the keys to a safety deposit box in the Jermyn Street branch of the National Westminster Bank in London. Here I found documents relating to my adoption. They were about me, that was not in doubt, but the documents were redacted – both mine and my real parents' names had been inked out. Whoever I had once been, I was now Julia Carter. I remember that day well. I mean, how could I forget it? Daniel Painter, my foster father, drove me to London. I asked to be left to my own devices, so he went off to meet friends.

'I went into that bank on my own but came out truly alone. I can't describe the feeling of isolation, of not belonging. It was awful. I remember walking in a daze to a small park – I can't tell you the name. I sat on a bench with my brown envelope and wept. On the way back up north I asked Daniel if had known. He admitted that yes, he had, but had been sworn to secrecy. He knew I had been adopted but not my original name. The awful thing is that I never suspected. I was an only child or, as I came to look on it later, the only child possession of my adoptive parents. They treated me OK, I suppose, but I'd nothing to judge it against so I didn't know any better. If there had been other siblings, adopted or not, perhaps it would have been different. I think they were decent parents and I never remember being short of anything. Did they love me? To be honest I've no idea. I can't remember one way or another. Isn't that awful in itself?

'Dorothy had a brother – Duncan. I called him uncle and I remember him being a big man. I was rather frightened of him, truth be told. I don't think he harmed me in any way, but he just always appeared threatening. Just his physical presence, I suppose. Since John and Dorothy died, I've discovered some things about Uncle Duncan. It was he, for example, that forwarded details of my trust fund and those bank details. It was only much later that I began to wonder what became of my parents' stuff – their house and personal belongings, for example. 'Our' house as I thought.' She sighed and shook her head slowly. 'I'll get to that later.'

The hotel restaurant was closing so they decided to freshen up and meet up again in a few minutes. They took a taxi down the hill towards the River Somme and canal. They were dropped off on the Avenue Général de Gaulle (Monsieur de Gaulle is a gentleman who seems to feature in the road plans of many towns and cities). They sat on a bench overlooking the Saint-Quentin Canal. A young River Somme was hidden from view down beyond the canal's far bank. The canal was broad and they saw a commercial barge come by, it's big diesel engine thumping out a low-pitch, steady rhythm. People live and work on these barges, often man and wife teams. The majority of the barge is cargo hold for carrying grain, logs or whatever. The rear portion behind the wheelhouse is where the owners live. It's home for the crews who are on the move the vast majority of the time. Tight margins dictate that these boats keep working - time idle is money lost. These back cabins are often brightly painted and some have a car on the roof, winched on and off by hydraulic crane. On the larger boats there may be a second cabin right at the front for a crew member, forward of the cargo hold and accessed by a deck-hatch and ladder.

They watched until the boat moved out of sight round a bend, leaving a thumping echo in its wake. Then they moved on, walking slowly. Julia had a walking stick in one hand and linked arms with Tony with the other. She talked all the while, voicing thoughts and fears, many of which she'd never shared before, never let go of. They crossed the canal and wandered into the memorial garden commemorating both world wars. It's situated at the head of a lake called Etang d'Isle - a peaceful, reverent spot. She told Tony that she had spent many hours in the library looking for clues to Jacqueline Courtois. 'I just couldn't seem to make any progress, even when I went on the Internet. GénéaFrance is a popular genealogy site. The blurb, translated from French, says: '*Today's children, curious about the past, go out to meet forgotten generations.*'

'Well, I couldn't find my forgotten generations,' she said forlornly. 'Not even a forgotten person. I also looked at the archives of old newspapers. Despite my speaking French pretty well, it was difficult because it's all so long ago and all I had was a name. Courtois came up a few times but there

74

was nothing to indicate that it was anything to do with me. I didn't even know if Jacqueline was a relative. Of course, my biggest hope is that she is my mother.

'How did you know to look for Jacqueline Courtois? Who is she?'

'Her name was on a piece of paper included in my bundle at the bank. Just her name and the date and location. It's all I have. Hard as I've tried, I can't get past hope. I sat there in the library and read till my vision blurred, but to no avail. I left my name and number with the librarian, a lovely young lady who spoke fluent English; in fact, when we spoke we did so in each others' language. We smiled together and it was a nice distraction from my frustrations. She said that she would contact a couple of local historical groups and if anything came of it she would phone me. I think she could sense my irritation and wanted to give me a fillip. She was very nice, very kind.'

They sat on a bench in the shade of a horse-chestnut tree. On the bench was a plaque:

Albert Mannion

4 Août 1919 á 14 Septembre 1942.

Mort pour La France

A simple memorial. Julia vocalised both their thoughts. 'Just 23. Dear, oh dear. We're left to assume that he was loved, that he fought bravely and that he will be missed. His family know all these things, so there's no need to tell anybody else, is there?'

'Just one of 70 million,' he replied. 'Each as important as the next to their family and friends.'

'Damn wars,' said Julia.

They sat and looked out over the lake for a few minutes.

Julia continued. 'I was sent to live with a family, a couple actually, in the Lake District in 1940. I was ten years old and can't remember saying goodbye to my parents (or who I thought were my parents.) Of course I wasn't to know that I would never see them again. I do remember feeling lonely and scared travelling up there on the train. There were quite a few of us getting off at various stops on the way and we were all apprehensive; well, I certainly was. I was told to get off at Penrith where I would be met. I had a small cardboard suitcase with a few clothes and my favourite teddy bear. I wore my best blue coat with a matching woollen bonnet; I also carried a rudimentary gas mask. There were perhaps a dozen of us who got off at the same time in Penrith. I remember we didn't talk much; we just smiled nervously at each other.

'The couple with whom I was to stay was called Pickles - Jody and Sam Pickles. I thought they were very old but they were probably only around sixty. She was a large lady who wore a flowery pinafore and sturdy shoes that thumped and clacked over the wooden floors in the downstairs of their house. He was stick-thin, only had one eye, and always wore braces to keep his pants up. Often his shirt would be untucked and he'd look untidy.' Julia chuckled. 'Funny what you remember. Maybe recalling trivia is a defense mechanism against remembering anything too unpleasant. I do remember being overwhelmed to begin with, but they were good people and they made me feel at home. I had my own room that looked out over their garden. I remember the apple trees and mountains beyond. It was so different to the bustle and noise of London, but I came to like it and, in time, to love it.' She looked over at Tony. 'I did retire to Keswick, after all.'

'I made friends there,' she continued. 'I became quite close to two or three of the London evacuees and, although it took longer, some local children also. My birthday is the third of November. I've wondered over the years whether that actually is my birth date or one just made up as part of my fake life - the latter, probably. Whichever, I remember getting a card from John and Dorothy and two £5 notes. Then I got a Christmas card, also with £10 inside. Those two cards, along with a brief phone call on Christmas day, were the only communication I had with them until I was told they were dead. It was the 19th of April 1941. Sam and Jody sat with me in their sitting room as Jody told me the news. I don't remember feeling too distraught but Jody hugged me to her chest. I recall the thump of her heart and the ticking of the mantelpiece clock. The two beat an unsyncopated rhythm that I remember added to my confusion.

'News of my parents' death spread and I received sorrowful looks from the adults and blank stares from the other children. But it wasn't just me who received bad news. My time in the limelight soon faded as other kids got their life-changing telegrams. We differed in that they lost their real parents. When someone else got their news it was my turn to stare, to not know what to say. I remember one little girl, a couple of years younger than me, who learned that her father had died. The poor thing was inconsolable and she cried and cried. She seemed to disappear away inside herself and became like a shadow in the half-light, grey and staring. She was taken away somewhere and we never saw her again. Memories like that stick, and in many ways they defined my childhood. To this day I wonder what happened to that girl. In a perverse way, her torment was such that it eased my pain. However bad I felt I would never be as miserable as her. Isn't that awful?'

Julia became silent and Tony looked over to see her weeping silent tears. She leaned on him and he put his arm round her shoulders.

'Come on,' he said after a few minutes, 'that's enough for now. Let's go and find a cup of coffee.'

He called the taxi company, having picked up a card on the way down. They were dropped at Place Hotel de Ville and found a seat under a striped awning outside a square-side café. The market had largely wound up and in the warmth of the late morning the pigeons seemed subdued, preparing perhaps for their midday roost. He checked his phone and there were a couple of text messages. The first from Agnes simply said *'Well done! X'* and the second from Peter Flattery from the café told him that he and Barry Townsend had drafted a plan to display the historical artifacts above the old market hall - and would he would like to pop in and have a look? In addition he'd persuaded a friend of his, who headed the craft/woodwork department at Holdean school, to have the youngsters build some wooden display cases as part of a project.

To Agnes he replied, *'Thanks, she's fine.'* Then he congratulated Peter on their efforts and told him he was away for a day or two and would be in touch as soon as possible. Julia looked over. 'Correspondence from the motherland,' he explained.

'I think I'd like to go home,' Julia announced out of the blue.

'Oh, good for you.' he replied. 'Can I come too?'

She laughed. 'Actually I was hoping to beg a bed at your apartment for a day or two,' she said with an inquiring look. 'If you don't mind, that is.'

'No, of course I don't mind.'

'Thank you.' She paused. 'To be honest I don't want to be alone just yet. I won't be a burden but I just need someone to lean on for a few days.' She looked over. 'I would never admit that to anyone else.'

'I'm flattered,' he replied. 'Even if you are a blithering nuisance.'

She laughed again and patted my hand. Then after a moment, she said, 'You've been so kind, I'd like to treat you. There's a little hotel I know in Paris, in the Latin Quarter. It's comfortable and pretty central, and there's a nearby restaurant that does really wonderful seafood. Will you let me treat you to say thank you?'

'You don't need to do that. It's a very generous offer but allow me to go Dutch. I must say a night in Paris does sound a lovely idea, though. Very jet-set.'

'I'm paying, I insist. Now, do as you're told for once.' She smiled as she thumped him feebly on the arm.

They booked the Hotel Monge in Paris for the following evening and reserved two first-class seats on the train. The Monge - unattractive name, great location. Julia insisted on paying for everything, even Tony's two nights in the Hotel Florence in Saint-Quentin. Then she retired to her room for what she termed a noontime nap.

Tony decided to have a wander. He looked at the Cathedral and it brought to mind one he had once visited, the memory of which had stuck with him for years - the Gothic Cathedral at Toul in the region of Lorraine (incidentally, situated in Place Charles de Gaulle - there's that name again!) That wonderful edifice can be seen from many miles distant, standing proud in the flat landscape. Presumably it's conspicuousness was partially the idea, but the scale and majesty of it somehow draws you in, makes you want to look closer. The nearer you get the more imposing it becomes; it is huge. However, when you get very close, you notice that the beautifully crafted carved stonework is crumbling. The faces on the gargoyles are indistinct as the years have taken their toll. Mythical beasts and foliate heads, angels and pagan figures vie for attention. Sadly they are fading into the past, losing the battle to time, battered by the weather, too expensive to restore, not important enough to preserve. The next generation may be the last to see them at all.

Tony was browsing the shops when his phone pinged. It was Julia asking where he was and telling him she had some news. He returned to the hotel to find her in the bar. She looked up excitedly as he came in.

'The girl from the library says somebody from a local historical society has some information for me. It's a woman and she's coming here in half an hour.'

'Ah,' he replied, 'this sounds intriguing. What has she to tell you?'

'Something about Jacqueline Courtois.' She looked at him wide-eyed.

Tony ordered a coffee while Julia had a small glass of Chablis. 'For the nerves, you realize,' she said with a smile.

He told her all about his walk but didn't think much registered; she was too excited. Forty minutes later a lady entered the bar with a hotel receptionist, who pointed in our direction. The visitor was around 70 years of age with coiffured white hair. She was immaculately dressed in a pale blue jacket, white blouse and black skirt. She walked towards us and extended her hand towards Julia.

'Bonjour Madame.' Then switching to accented English, 'I am Elsa Dupont. You must be Madame Carter?'

Julia nodded and said, 'Good afternoon.' She introduced me as her friend and Mme. Dupont shook my hand, 'Monsieur,' she said.

She looked back to Julia.

'My husband received a request yesterday from the library regarding information about Jacqueline Courtois. When he told me, I thought I may be able to help.' She looked directly at Julia, 'Now I see you, I am sure.'

Julia was wide-eyed.

Mme Dupont took a photograph from her bag.

'This, I believe, is the lady in question,' she said, pointing at the picture. 'The one on the left.'

Julia stared at the photograph for many moments. Then she passed it to

Tony. It was the eyes, unmistakably Julia's eyes. The photograph was black and white but, despite the age difference between Julia and the young lady in the picture, the resemblance was unmistakable. He passed it back.

'Oh my,' said Julia, transfixed by the old photograph. 'This is Jacqueline Courtois?'

'Yes, indeed,' replied Mme Dupont. 'That is her aged eighteen with two friends. It is the only photograph we can find. I had a great friend called Nadine Courtois who sadly died fifteen years ago. She was Jacqueline's cousin. Though Jacqueline was nearly twenty years older than my friend, I remember Nadine speaking about her and her mysterious disappearance. I do remember seeing other photographs of the two of them together, probably taken around the same time as that one,' she said, pointing to the photograph in Julia's hand. 'I can tell you that there was an unmistakable family resemblance. Unfortunately we are unable to locate the others. You will have to make do with the one you have there.'

'This is just wonderful. Thank you!' said Julia.

Mme Dupont smiled and continued. 'Jacqueline fell with child when she was twenty years old and was, how do I say, dispatched to England. Jacqueline's mother was called Simone Courtois. Shortly after Jacqueline left, Simone moved away. South, I believe, but I have no idea where.' She smiled wistfully at Julia. 'The word at the time was that Jacqueline had been sent to a convent, where she was cared for by nuns. Being with child out of marriage was a big disgrace in Saint Quentin back then, both for her and her family. Nothing was ever heard of Jacqueline, until now.' She paused. 'She is your mother, I think.'

Julia nodded and put her hand over her mouth to hide a sob. She reached over and grabbed Tony's hand, smiling sadly. 'Look,' she said, staring at the photograph, 'surely there can be no mistake?'

'No mistake.' He held her hand.

Elsa Dupont wiped a tear from her own eye with a monogrammed hand-kerchief.

'Thank you, Madame,' said Julia. 'You don't know how much this means to me.'

'I think I have a good idea, Mme Carter. Meeting you, and so unexpectedly, has rekindled a piece of my past I thought lost forever. In my mind I can see Nadine and her family as if it were yesterday.'

'Julia, please. Call me Julia.'

She rose and crossed to Elsa Dupont and kissed her on each cheek and hugged her.

'I can't thank you enough.'

They all took a few moments to collect their thoughts. Julia then said, 'Do you happen to know anything more about what happened to my mother after I was born? Assuming it was me with whom she was with child.'

'I am sorry, no. As far as I know, nobody heard from her after she went to England. Jacqueline was a young lady with no means of support. I fail to see how she could have looked after you on her own. I can't imagine the distress of giving you up, but I'm sure she would have made the decision with your best interests at heart. It is an awful situation but not uncommon, I think.'

'You have no idea where in England she went? Where the convent was?'

'Again, no. I'm sorry.'

Julia sighed.

'And what of my father? Is there any record of him?'

'Jacqueline never told anyone as far as I am aware. Nadine said there were rumours, but that is all. Small town gossip around the lavoir.'

'Lavoir?' I asked.

She smiled. 'A communal place people go to wash clothes. It is where local people exchanged news and digested the issues of the day. Gossip in other words. Much of it hearsay, made less believable by exaggeration. Most towns and villages have a lavoir, just as they have gossips who congregate there!'

Julia smiled. 'It sounds like your market, Tony.'

He smiled and acknowledged with a nod.

'Oh well,' said Julia, 'I believe I have the answer to my most important question. A question that has been nearly sixty years in the asking.'

Elsa and Julia exchanged addresses and phone numbers before the French lady took her leave. Each promised the other that they would keep in touch. Julia said across the room, 'Madame, please thank your husband most sincerely for me. I am so grateful he responded to my request.'

'Bien sur,' replied Elsa. 'Of course. He was excited to help. I will tell him your good news; I know he'll be happy. Goodbye.'

Insights

D uring our brief stay-over in Paris, Julia was a new woman and now even more ebullient than her most relaxed moments during that first week we shared in Thistledean. Despite the fact that she hadn't got all her answers, what she had learned had geed her up; one demon at least had been banished. It was lovely to see her ready smile. Tony caught her regularly looking at the photograph of her mother, Jacqueline Courtois. Her only problem was that her rickety body couldn't keep up and they had to take frequent pit stops. Not that it mattered; they both knew they were sharing something special and there was no rush.

The Monge Hotel was comfortable and she was right about the seafood restaurant; it really was excellent. Dover sole - what a treat that was. Simple, just grilled and served with butter. Julia had pan-fried sea bass which she said was also delicious. They shared a bottle of Chablis, or rather Julia had a glass out of Tony's bottle.

He was a little unsteady as they walked slowly by the Seine but it didn't stop them taking an hour-long river cruise, starting from Pont Neuf on Ile de la Cité. It was the only thing that Julia allowed Tony to pay for, and only because he beat her up the two steps to the ticket office. It was one of the best 50 euros he had ever spent and rounded off a beautiful evening. Apart from proposing a toast during the meal to her mother, they didn't mention Julia's family. Idle banter and a few laughs were what they both needed, and they retired to their rooms relaxed and contented.

The following lunchtime they were driving up the motorway towards the Lake District. Their flight had landed in Manchester at 10:45 a.m., once again just about on time. Julia began to tell Tony more of her story and explain a little of the research she'd done. Although she told her tale over the next few days, she had actually written it down years before. Here, reproduced verbatim, is the next stage of her tale. This is the crux of her story and the part she felt the need to expose - a blood-letting, she said, that made it real; she could see the whole mess in black and white and can be proud that she fought back to some degree. It's a fascinating insight, and all the more credible because it's in her own words:

'I lived in Grasmere till the end of the war. I made a few friends but we all dispersed as the war ended. Most went back to their parents. That obviously wasn't an option for me and, reading between the lines, Jody and Sam were finding me a bit of a handful. Hence, firmer and more seasoned carers were called for; also, I suppose, a support system that could offer ongoing continuity should it be needed. When all was said and done, they were virtually of retirement age and childless, and as such may have felt unprepared to shepherd a young woman into adulthood. I never resented them; I have fond memories of my time there, despite a troubled period after the death of my 'parents.'

So in late 1945, just after the end of the war, I left. I could feel the general mood was upbeat and optimistic. For me, I was largely isolated from the horrors to the south and east, and I had my own worries to concentrate on - so I just lived, drifting rather. I say I left Grasmere - perhaps more accurate to say that I was instructed to leave. I had no choice.

I said goodbye to Sam and Jody at Penrith station on a bleak winter's morning. Jody wept a little and wished me well. Sam patted me on the shoulder, an awkward gesture by somebody unfamiliar with intimacy. He looked down at me with his good eye and wished me luck. I thanked them for everything and smiled. They put me on the train bound for Manchester, from where I would connect to Uppermill - a small town in an area known as Saddleworth. I knew little about what was to be my new home. Sam had told me it was in Lancashire and the closest large town was Oldham. It was also not far from Derbyshire's Peak District. The rest I would doubtless discover.

I arrived at Uppermill station with only one suitcase, albeit a slightly larger one than the small cardboard one that had accompanied me from London five years previously. It contained a few bits and pieces such as the small (unrefined) water-colour paintings I had done and the few extra clothes Jody and Sam had bought for me. Most of the clothes were threadbare - money was very tight back then and I understood later that they must have stretched themselves to help me. I also had a few toiletries, my moth-eaten teddy bear called Douglas and six books. One was a well thumbed book written by Mary Roberts-Carter recounting her travels. The others, eclectically, were Jane Austin's *Pride and Prejudice*, *Typhoon* by William Conrad, two early Enid Blytons (*The Zoo Book* and *The Animal Book*) and a copy of the Bible.

I didn't even have a photograph of John and Dorothy, my adoptive parents, but I did cling on to a crumpled one of Sam and Jody; at least some slender evidence of my past. At that point in time I never considered why I ended up there; it never occurred to me to question who had made the decision. Basically, as before, I just went where I was told.

My foster parents were called Daniel and Sally Painter. They were a couple in their mid-thirties; he was an architect and she was a part-time teacher. They lived in a unique bungalow of Daniel's design up on a hillside overlooking Uppermill park. The main living area, kitchen, diner and lounge were open plan, divided only by a low-level island kitchen unit at one end. A wooden floor and open roof rafters gave it a Scandinavian feel. Huge glass windows opened out onto a wooden deck, which in turn looked out over the town. It was stunning, actually.

I had my own room and they made me welcome. I lived with them for six years. They were good years, happy. Looking back they seemed normal, and that I attributed to Daniel and Sally's governance. If there was a niggle it was that they withheld the fact that I'd been adopted. I know they were acting under instruction but it was rather galling. When I discovered the truth at the age of 21, I felt resentful that my foster parents had known something intensely personal about me and held it back. It was like a veil between us. Suddenly our relationship was less distinct, and it became them and me. Though I do love them, to this day a slight sour taste remains.

I found Uppermill itself a mixture of a place. Gloomy, yet pleasant at the same time. That sounds contradictory, but my impression of the main street that snaked along the valley floor was gloomy. It was wintertime when I arrived and the sun was low, often hidden by the surrounding hills or behind angry grey clouds. In corners the sun never reached, long shadows trapped the damp, leaving musty nooks like airless cellars. During my first few months the town never woke up, never got past a dull dawn. Rightly or wrongly therefore, my lasting impression was a dull one. Conversely, the stone buildings were attractive and the people friendly and chatty. There was a small-town feel to the place - in that respect a little like Grasmere, though Uppermill was bigger.

I made some friends but wasn't the most social creature. I preferred my own company to a large degree, despite encouragement from Daniel and Sally to go out and mix. But they could see I was contented enough and didn't push me too hard. I finished secondary school and I suppose I must have been reasonably bright because, much to the delight and surprise of my hosts, I won a place at Exeter University where I studied modern languages.

I was three years into a four-year degree course when I went 'home' to celebrate my twenty-first birthday in Uppermill with my foster parents and the few local friends I had made. I can't recall what presents I got because the only thing of importance was a buff envelope. It was from Uncle Duncan. He was Duncan Wheeler, my adoptive mother's brother - my adoptive uncle, I suppose. I vaguely recall meeting him briefly a few times in London, at birthdays or Christmas perhaps. I didn't like him; he was a brute of a man with a booming voice. I felt like he considered me a nuisance and I don't remember him ever addressing me directly. Bear in mind I was ten when I left, so most adults appeared big. But he was big, I'm sure of it.

The envelope contained a 'Best Wishes' card signed by 'Uncle Duncan.' It wasn't even a specific birthday or coming-of-age card, just a cheap generic one with 'Best Wishes' on the front. Also in the envelope were details of the National Westminster Bank on Jermyn Street. There was a silver key, too, to a safety deposit box. It was at this branch of the bank that I could arrange to draw down on my small trust fund and where I would open the box that blew my world apart, my Pandora.

Regarding my trust fund, I could take an annual amount or a lump sum. Neither was much, certainly by today's standards. That, combined with the news that I was adopted and rootless, made me realize that from this point on I was on my own. So I went to my nameless park and wept my woes away. It was a different me that returned to Uni for my final year. I felt ripped up and my work suffered. I got a 2:2 but it should have been so much better. It would have been if my past hadn't swept in.

During that last year I did some tentative research into my situation. Bear in mind it was now 1951, but I was adopted twenty years before that. These days, in the twenty-first century, the adoption laws are tight and detailed, geared up to the well-being of the child and protection and clarity for the adults. Now everyone's rights are covered. Back in 1930 it was very different. I'm sure things still go wrong. For example, it's impossible to predict exactly how various personalities will interact, but these days much of the gamble is removed in advance. Due diligence is carried out, if you will.

Child adoption had no legal status at all in Great Britain until 1926. Before that it was an informal and often secret arrangement offering neither parents nor child any rights whatsoever. Worse, pre-1926 the whole system was open to systemic corruption, including baby farming and child abuse. The whole thing was an unpleasant and dangerous mess. For example, unmarried mothers would hand over their baby plus a 'fee' of £15 (which was a good deal of money back then) in the expectation the child would be re-homed. It's probable that some babies were sold to childless couples for a good fee, or fostered or adopted for far less.

The whole system was rotten. Abortion was illegal, as was abandonment, and it wasn't unusual for babies - who'd been sold to foster/adoption agencies in the expectation that they would be re-homed - to be killed off because a suitable home couldn't be found. Killing babies was sometimes far easier that finding suitable homes for them.

In the years immediately following the 1926 legislation procedures were perhaps not fully understood; so in 1932, when I was adopted by John and Dorothy, it was unclear whether procedures had been followed correctly.

It was because of this uncertainty that Duncan Wheeler was able to muddy the waters and manipulate his sister and brother-in-law's estate. Duncan produced a document on their deaths stating that, henceforth, he was to be my legal guardian. Included in this was the management of my trust fund. I suspect, though I have no way of proving it, that my foster parents' estate should have been added to my trust fund, but it's obvious that it never happened.

Although today adopted children legally inherit from intestate adoptive parents, it was far less clear in 1932 when I was adopted. I think I should have inherited before Duncan. Although he was John and Dorothy's only close relative, it was really me that should have been the beneficiary by dint of being legally adopted. However, this is where the water-muddying came in. There were no official documents relating to my adoption. Well, there were, but none that hadn't been redacted. Useless for any legal purpose.

I challenged Duncan years later. Not because I needed or wanted the money, more because I needed to find out if my adoptive parents had been honourable towards me. It became important to confirm just how robust or fragile my foundations were.

It took me a while to track him down, but finally I did - to a large Victorian terraced house in Highgate, North London. I knew very little about the man but it looked like he had a business of some sort because 'Wheeler and Associates' was engraved on a small brass plaque to the right of the gloss-blue front door.

When the door opened to my knock it revealed my uncle. He was big, I hadn't dreamed that, but now he was running to fat too with a large belly and a double chin. He was probably in his mid-fifties and his hair was thin and grey. He wore an open-neck check shirt and dark grey trousers that may have once belonged to a suit; they were held up by a pair of red braces. Behind him was an elderly dog, a German Shepherd, who looked quizzically past his master's thigh.

He didn't recognize me. The last time we had met was 25 years ago and I had only been about nine years old at the time. Now in my mid-thirties I was, if I say it myself, a reasonably attractive woman. I was fit and tanned from my walking and was worldly-wise enough not to be intimidated like I was as a young girl.

I was wearing light-weight boots, jeans, T-shirt and waterproof jacket. I looked smart but casual, yet outdoorsy. I also had on a pair of tinted glasses. They disguised my eyes, which are my most distinguishable feature. My eyes would probably have given me away, even if he hadn't seen me for a quarter of a century.

I had decided on a third-person approach. A bit sneaky and oblique perhaps, but I hoped to catch him unawares. I told him I was part of a team doing research into the disappearance of six children born of French mothers, taken in by a Gloucestershire convent in the 1930s. Evidence had come to light, I told him, of financial irregularities. Also there had been allegations of abuse made by two of the children. I told him that we were having great difficulty tracking the other four children and that his name had been mentioned in relation to a girl called Courtois. We understand the child took the name of her adoptive parents, Carter, but all the records both from the convent and Hammersmith Adoption Agency had gone missing. Did he by any chance happen to know anything about Miss Courtois/Carter?

He said that unfortunately he was unable to help. He said he was busy, excused himself and closed the door on me. He hadn't actually lied, but he had certainly evaded my question. As you can imagine, I felt angry. Duncan Wheeler was being duplicitous. I had always disliked him, but now I had confirmation. Realistically I'd known in my heart that he was a bad apple, but to see him lie to my face was the last brick in the wall.

Had John and Dorothy been involved in the deception, too? I didn't know. My relationship with Duncan was pretty straightforward; we didn't like each other. My relationship with my adoptive parents was far less clear-cut. They had adopted me so must have wanted a child. But they hadn't really been warm or sensitive. Perhaps I was just a chattel to them. They had set up my trust fund but never visited me in Grasmere. They cared, yet they appeared not to. Contradictions.

As things stood I believed they were insensitive but not deliberately deceitful. I looked back and was sorry they had died young and sorry, too, that I never had chance to figure them out. My only connection was to Uncle Duncan and I'd made the decision to make life uncomfortable for him. In fact I dislike the term 'uncle' so decided there and then to stop using it. It personalised him too much and I didn't think he deserved it.

I decided on a course of action. At this time in my life I was lecturing at Düsseldorf University. I'd done a spell teaching, then lecturing in Lyon, but had moved to Germany three years previously. I had a close friend called Peter, a Dutch man with whom I worked. We were good mates, and friends only; Peter was gay. He had a tough time of his sexuality working in Germany, but Holland was much more liberal and he spent much of his leisure time on Kerksrtaat in Amsterdam, known as 'Gay Street,' when he went home. He took me there a couple of times. It was a fun place and I met some of his friends, who were lovely people. He was a great guy who sadly succumbed to AIDS in 1982. He had become a close friend and I miss him still.

Anyhow, it was Peter I asked to help me trip up Duncan Wheeler. Physically he was a pretty imposing chap, six foot two with muscles to suit. I sent him to visit Duncan posing as my brother. We'd created some false documents - adoption papers for both me and my 'brother' written on official-looking headed paper. Convincing to look at, yet utterly fictitious. We even distressed them by slopping a bit of tea on them and crumpling them up as if they'd been in the bottom of Peter's suitcase for years.

The papers listed John and Dorothy as my adoptive parents. Peter also stated that he had evidence that Duncan was Dorothy's brother. Actually he didn't, but we felt it wouldn't have been difficult to obtain them if necessary. Peter himself claimed to have been adopted by a couple from Galway in the west of Ireland, and who had subsequently been exposed as baby farmers under a litany of false identities.

The problem with this was that Duncan had probably seen Julia's original adoption papers. Indeed, he may still have had them or he may have destroyed them. What we were doing was letting him know we knew some facts. We had information, personal stuff, that only insiders would have access to.

When presented with this evidence Duncan Wheeler had no option but to deny any knowledge. He couldn't claim Peter's papers were false without admitting that he knew of the genuine ones. He admitted that Dorothy was indeed his sister, but they had been estranged since their early twenties. He knew nothing about any adoption and indignantly refuted the suggestion he was in any way involved. In fact he went on the bluster, threatening to take legal action if such scurrilous allegations were not withdrawn forthwith.

Duncan went to shut the door but Peter's boot prevented it. Duncan said he would call the police and have Peter arrested, then threatened to set his German Shepherd on Peter.

"Before you call the authorities or have me mauled," Peter had said, "I suggest you listen to what I have to say." The two men stood eye to eye. One fit and determined, the other fat and fearful.

At this point Peter became a little more unequivocal and a little less friendly, if indeed he had been friendly up to this point. Looking Duncan straight in the eye, he told him that he had evidence for all three of the following. He held fingers up as each point was made: "One. When your sister Dorothy and her husband John died in 1941, you took responsibility for Julia Courtois / Carter. Two. Julia had been sent to Grasmere then Uppermill. I have names, addresses and dates. Three. Julia visited a branch of The National Westminster Bank in Jermyn Street, Westminster in September 1951 where she found SOME (emphasising 'some') of the documents due to her."

Duncan said nothing. Peter raised his eyebrows and cocked his head slightly to one side as he asked Duncan some questions, to which he didn't expect answers. "Firstly, did Dorothy and John leave a will? We all know that tampering with such a document or withholding it is a serious offense. Secondly, is an adopted child the legal beneficiary of their adoptive parents' estate, even if those parents had died intestate? Thirdly, what had happened to Dorothy and John's estate, including their house on the their death? And finally, for now, who are Margaret Mooney and Mary O'Conner?

The last question was the clincher, the one that made him realize his goose was cooked. Duncan Wheeler blanched and appeared suddenly unsteady on his feet.

My knee-high leather boots, the ones with protective metal segs in the heels, make a distinctive and loud clicking noise as I walk along a footpath.

The noise is particularly noticeable on a windless day with little or no traffic about. I was wearing them that day as I approached Duncan Wheeler's front door. As I neared I could see Duncan look over to see who was coming. I walked slowly up the path stood next to Peter. We both stared unflinchingly at Duncan, who had partly recovered his poise and scowled back defiantly at us. Then I removed my blue-tinted glasses and we watched his knees buckle. He sunk to the floor and gasped. A ghost had returned twenty-five years on. I felt sorry for his elderly dog; I can still hear him whimper in the hallway, fearful for his master. I didn't feel a shred of remorse for Duncan Wheeler.

For the record, Margaret Mooney and Mary O'Conner are named as co-directors of Wheeler Associates. The company is listed as 'Import/Export.' We'd done a little digging with the help of Peter's mate Friedrich, a Dutch policeman. Import/export was correct as far as it went, but the trading of unwanted orphans from just about anywhere in Europe to wealthy, unscrupulous couples in the UK and Ireland was what they were about. 'A miserable, revolting organisation run by a disgusting man,' was how Friedrich described Duncan and his set-up.

Not every child that passed through Wheeler and Associates was trafficked. Enough were placed with either adoptive or foster parents to prove that they were a bona fide organisation if questioned. I suppose I was one of the lucky ones as I passed through early in their history. But even though my adoption by his sister and husband appeared authentic, Duncan couldn't help himself and used his inside knowledge to 'divert' my inheritance his own way - at least a good part of it. There was no way round the trust fund because it was in my name, but we think he falsified his sister's will and ended up with their house and chattels. There is record of the house being sold to a company in Hertfordshire but the company and proceeds are long gone. The house he lived in and worked from latterly is mortgaged to the hilt. Basically what you see today is a sham of a man within a shell of a life.

I would like to believe that John and Dorothy were not complicit in Duncan's duplicity, but I find it difficult. The only crumb I take is that they left me information on my adoption. Is that a hint there that they were ignorant of the goings on? Or was it a way to absolve themselves, at least in part, for their own cunning? I don't know, and to be honest I've largely purged them from my thoughts. Occasionally as I plough through my memories, my subconscious turns up an unpleasant nugget, but I cope with them now.

Despite all our efforts we were unable to find any more details about my mother. I looked, Peter helped, but we found nothing, no trace of Jacqueline Courtois. Presumably that part of my history was destroyed by Duncan and his associates.

My biggest regret in all this is that Mary and James were not my grandparents. I read of their exploits when I was a teenager in the Lake District and Uppermill and was so proud of them. In fact, it's fair to say that they inspired me. I could relate to their adventures because I was living in the country surrounded by hills and I dreamed of emulating them. In fact, when things got lonely those dreams picked me up. To have that sense of belonging ripped away when I was 21 was a real blow. But over time I came to convince myself that they really were my relatives. In fact there are not many people who know the truth. I based most of my free time on following in their footsteps and have had a wonderful life because of them.

JC 1961

Calm After the Storm

Tony's house guest soon bedded in - almost literally; she slept a lot, unwinding after her adventure. But she was pretty resolute and appeared settled; having said that, she hadn't appear unsettled the last time they met. She must have buried many things deep for them not to have affected her. She must have known she could open a can of worms when she set off to France. Tony treated her to a Wagyu steak on their first night home, grilled and delicious, 'even if it was me that cooked it.' It was accompanied by a glass of what he told her was his best Merlot; in fact it was his only Merlot, so he wasn't really fibbing. She didn't grumble, trusting soul that she was.

Leaving his guest to sleep in for as long as she needed, Tony decided to have a walk. He started out an hour before dawn, which he does occasionally. There is a different sound-track this early, partly because there's no white noise, those man-made sounds that bumble along in the background, stuff in our subconscious we normally never notice - such as a plane high up, or the whispered grumble of cars on a distant road. In their absence it's possible to hear rustling in the leaves, the cry of an owl, the high-pitched bark of a fox and the song of the day's earliest birds who seem to sing just before the first rays of light, enticing the dawn. He stood still in the dark, a gentle hiss in his ears and allowed this corner of the world to tell him it was doing just fine, thanks.

He headed south, this time along small lanes and tracks. He had a head-torch but kept it off where possible. The moonlight was just enough to light the way, except when he walked through an avenue of trees and was enveloped by the dark. Then he flicked the torched on and his world was confined to a circular pool of light on the roadway with blackness beyond. It's strange what the dark does. A small stream ran under the path at one point. During the day it has a friendly, burbling chatter; in the dark it is sinister, threatening even. He sat for a while on a log and drank tea from his flask as dawn began to break away to his left amid birdsong crescendos. Less intense than the manic mating calls of spring, but a wonderful chorus nevertheless. Perhaps they were discussing their impending departure for warmer winter climes.

In this southerly direction the landscape is gentle, less severe than the more rugged terrain of the other three points of the compass. He'd walked a couple of miles and now the day was fully awake. He continued through meadows and woodland and could see the golf course and a juvenile River Url snaking through the fields a mile or so away to his left. Beyond that, the hills deflate and the countryside flattens to become a patchwork of farm fields.

He pondered what had come out of his friendship with Julia, apart from enjoying her company. Partly her endurance, the fact that she's come through. You have to get past a person's husk to find the essence of the soul within. All too often in today's world we talk to a protective shell, a brittle husk built of material veneer. Why are we so fearful of others seeing the real us? Are we such poor specimens? So few people know who we really are and that is a tragedy because it's inside we find anything remotely interesting. Ultimately, what car someone drives or how large their house is unimportant. Sure, let's have some comfort and a little luxury, but not at the expense of our very selves.

What endures when he thinks about Julia is her fun, frailty, strength and endurance. In fact, all the things that make up a loving relationship. Talking and listening is how our race has developed over millennia, and what Julia has shared with Tony will be with him for ever. Likewise with whom he shares her story. He is directly involved with her and will remember most of her story; others may remember snippets, but everyone will be affected to varying degrees.

Tony's family life wasn't great, but at least he had roots; he knows where he's come from. Julia's tale is not exclusive, of course, but to discover your parents are not who you thought they were must be like having your heart torn out. How must it feel to look back on those first 21 years realizing it's all a mirage? Looking back now, it makes Tony question people a little more, to look for the why. Maybe not to directly seek it out, but at least be open to the chance that there may be a why, a reason why someone is as they are.

We all arrive at a particular point in time as the sum of our experiences. The first time Tony saw Julia he saw an old lass who nearly tumbled, her rickety body letting her down. That evolved when he looked into her sparkly eyes, then it changed again as she told her tales. He could just have walked away after he'd prevented her fall, to carry on with his business. But he's glad he didn't.

* * *

Tony popped into The Bull at lunchtime and was handed his security guard outfit - a yellow gilet and a torch. Monkey reckoned the jackets look like the sort of thing road-menders wear. That received a filthy look from The Colonel, who had in fact done a terrific job getting them organised. They'd arrived lunchtime on Wednesday, about fifteen hours after the Junta meeting ended. She had even managed to persuade a promotions company in Holdean to print *'Thistledean Security Officer'* on the back.

'Should have got, 'Danger - Men at Work', quipped Monkey.

'Shut it,' said The Colonel. 'And thank you for offering. I'll have a gin and tonic.'

Tony was walking through the Square after lunch when Arthur and Nelly pulled up beside him in their golf buggy. Arthur is sometimes referred to as the Baron, due to his imposing stature and stately disposition.

'I hear you've got the old bird stopping with you again,' he boomed. 'Tell her if she wants some sensible company for a change,' he raised his eyebrows at Tony, 'she's welcome to come and have some supper with us this evening. We've got Mrs. Marshall coming round and they might be good company for each other. Besides, she's probably sick of the sight of you.'

Tony grinned. 'How did you know she is staying? We only got back last night.'

'The walls have ears, dear boy. The walls have ears.'

'They've got mouths, too.'

'Yes, I suppose they must. I never thought of it like that.'

'Anyhow, on Julia's behalf, thank you for the invitation. I'll pass the message on with appropriate warnings about accepting invitations from a dodgy old alchemist.'

'Fair enough,' he laughed. 'We'll expect her at six unless we hear different. If she needs a lift, let me know and I'll pop up in the buggy.'

'Don't worry, I'll run her down if she's coming. I have to nip into Holdean this evening anyway.'

'Righty-ho,' he said.

And with that Arthur and Nelly they shot off with a crescendo of electric motor towards Frampton's bakery, the wheels of their buggy chattering over the cobbles.

'It's working,' said a whispered, fevered voice from behind him.

It was The Colonel. Tony jumped.

'Don't creep up like that. Blimey O'Reilly!' They laughed.

Then he whispered, 'what's working?'

'Our anti-crime directive. We haven't had a single terrorist attack since we started. It must be the new jackets.'

'I know you're jesting, but don't tempt fate for goodness' sake. Anyway, Brian tells me he's only ever seen you patrolling. What about the others? I know I've not done much but I've been away for a day or two.'

'Oh, they've all pitched in. The lads do more in the evenings. I quite like mooching about during the day. I slip my jacket on whenever I'm off shopping or whatever; fits in quite well, really. I had my photo taken with a group of tourists yesterday! We had an Orient Express in and they seemed fascinated that we have a private army.' She laughed.

The 'Orient Express' referred to is one of many coaches that bring Far Eastern visitors to experience Thistledean's history and the treasure trove of artifacts on display (and for sale) in the shops. Felicity has been 'creative' in promoting Thistledean as a hotbed of Roman history. There is some evidence they were here, but perhaps not to the extent Felicity claims.

'I'm not sure the main threat comes from our beautifully behaved and respectful visitors to whom you refer. Besides, if they saw the full extent of our army they would be amazed we keep such good order. Particularly if our troops have just had an hour in the Bull.'

'Visible presence, that's what counts.'

'The irony is we won't know if we're having any effect, will we? If nothing happens, all well and good, but nothing might have happened if we hadn't been here. The only way we'll be judged is if something goes awry - then we'll be castigated. Bit of a lose-lose, really.'

'Be optimistic for God's sake. We ARE doing some good. Full stop. Look at it this way - if there was another incident and we'd done nothing then we would have reason to feel miserable.'

'Yes, you're quite right.'

'Oh, and better have a word with that mate of yours ... Monkey. If I hear him call me Rosa Klebb again I won't be responsible for my actions.'

He looked a bit blank.

'Don't tell me you don't know what I'm taking about ...'

'No, seriously.'

'Rosa Klebb was a James Bond villain who wore a tweed suit and had a poisoned blade concealed in her shoe. A surly, miserable woman.'

He laughed. 'I do remember. He's living dangerously, that's for sure. If I see him on crutches I'll know what's happened.'

It was nearly 3.00 PM so Tony decided to call in for a coffee. Besides, he wanted to catch up with Peter and inquire about the history project. It was Thursday so there was no market; the Square was pretty quiet as he took an outdoor table next to the café's door. Sniffy, who appears to have an incredibly sensitive radar where treats are concerned, wandered up wagging his little tail. Tony leaned over and called to Peter to kindly bring him a slice of fruit cake with his coffee.

When it arrived he laughed. 'This dog is superbly trained. He must make you a fortune getting customers to order cakes just so he can have a nibble.'

'He's on a percentage.'

The beagle bade me farewell and sauntered over to a couple of visitors on a nearby table where he was fawned over again.

'It's amazing he isn't fat as a pig.'

Peter sat in an adjoining chair and explained, 'It's all that walking between treats.'

'Doesn't seem to work for me.' Tony asked about the historical display. Peter was really enthusiastic and said there was an enormous amount of stuff; in fact the majority would have to be stored somewhere. Barry said they'd be able to rotate exhibits and display different things from time to time to keep it all fresh.

'I knew we'd had a bequest,' said Peter, 'from an historian in Holdean, but never realized the extent of it. It's been sitting around for the best part of fifteen years. It's actually been an important spot historically for centuries, backed up as it is against the Northumbrian fells. There is a lot to its advantage; pasture for crops, fells for grazing livestock, water, some shelter from the worst of the north winds and a good defensive position.'

'Maybe Felicity is not so far off with her outrageous PR campaign.'

Peter smiled. 'It's going to make an interesting exhibition. The long room above the shops is ideal. We're getting some cabinets made and I've lined up an electrician who lives in town who won't over-charge. What we do need is the go-ahead for a plumber to fit some central heating, it's a big drafty room up there. We've had a couple of unofficial estimates and we reckon it'll cost about three thousand for a sensible basic system. Not cheap, but these days you can't get away with bodging it, especially where the public are involved.'

'Well, there shouldn't be a problem there. I'll email the Junta and I'm sure they'll rubber-stamp it. I can pop up and have a word with Paul Broadbent now. Last time I spoke to him he said our finances were healthy, so I really don't see that as an issue; I'll pop down and have a look when you're around. I look forward to seeing all your efforts. Just drop me a text and I'll come and join you.'

'Saturday morning, we'll be there. Barry would have been in today but he's away.'

'OK then, till Saturday ...'

Tony wandered up the hill fifty yards and called in to see Paul. He waited a few minutes till he finished with a client and was ushered in by his secretary.

'How's the golf swing, Tony?' he asked enthusiastically.

'Oh, you know,' he replied, 'it's difficult to find the words to describe it really.'

He laughed. 'I feel your pain.'

'In fact, the next installment of operation hack is on Saturday. No doubt I'll discover something else that's gone awry. One of the benefits of being, er, unpredictable, is that I visit parts of the county no one has set foot in before. Found a rare butterfly in a gorse bush last week.'

Paul laughed. 'Every cloud, and all that.... anyhow, what can I do for you? You got a lottery win to invest?'

'Unfortunately not. This is town business. We're going to need a few thousand to do up the room above the old market hall for an exhibition of the town's history. Last time we spoke you said we were in decent shape. Is that still the case?'

'Yes, we're fine. We have about eighty thousand sitting there doing not much. It's in an interest-bearing account, but available at seven days' notice. We'll have to get the say-so from the Junta; they're trustees, as you know.'

'Yes, I realize that, but I'm sure it won't be a problem. I'll contact them later. That's quite a wodge,' I continued. 'Where's all that from?'

'Profits from the supermarket, largely. It's doing well, particularly at this time of year. The garden centre is buzzing. It'll slow in the winter of course, but overall, you're right, we're in good shape.'

'Great. By the way, did The Colonel come to you for her cash? She forked out for the security team's clothing.'

'No, haven't seen her.'

Tony paused. 'I'll have a word. No doubt she'll be holding court in the Bull later.'

They bid farewell and Tony popped home to email his Junta colleagues and check Julia was alright.

Sporting Prowess

I t was time to put the golf swing, referred to by Paul Broadbent, to the test. It was Saturday and Tony set off for his weekly game of golf. On the outbound journey he was always full of optimism; however, it was rare for him to return home with his self-respect intact. Usually, at some stage during his six-hour foray to Eastvale Golf and Country Club, four miles down the road, something (or a number of things) happens upon which he looks back with some disappointment. Last Saturday, for example, he lashed a ball into the club car park off the tenth tee and broke the passenger window of the club secretary's Jaguar XF. He was a bit unlucky, in that he'd unwittingly picked out such a high-profile target. Yes, Brian Elder's car, the man previously seen having suffered at the hands of Thistledean's resident dentist, who was not best pleased. As you may imagine, Tony was mercilessly ribbed during the subsequent post-round inquest over a pint. Incidentally, the club used to be called Eastvale Golf Club. Then they added a tennis court and sauna and added 'and Country Club', upping the fees in line with its change of status.

The previous week he had been having such a difficult time that he'd actually run out of balls during the monthly medal. On a round-by-round basis his problems are compounded because there is no consistency of swing defect. In other words some days he hooks the ball to the left, on others he slices off to the right. Sometimes the putter develops a life of its own and he's quite unable to get the ball in the hole. That day everything seemed to be disappearing off to the right. So on the twelfth he aimed way to the left to compensate. For some unaccountable reason, the ball failed to slice and it sailed straight over the perimeter fence into a local farmer's hay barn. Anyhow, embarrassingly he'd had to borrow a ball from Pat Lancing, his playing partner. That became two when the very first shot with the new one one plopped into the River Url.

Now, normally he'd consider the Url to be a pretty, chattering brook that meanders through the course, but a week ago he was less than complimentary about it. He is on record as saying, *'Who the bloody hell put that there?'* A totally irrational thing to say as the river has been there for some time, but he was in a state of inner turmoil. He was unlucky again, in fact, because in times of little rain it's very difficult to lose a ball in the river. There is often so little water flowing that balls are found sitting on sand bars awaiting rescue. It may be out of bounds, therefore a two-shot penalty, but at least balls can be retrieved. But not after a downpour, like two weeks ago - oh no, not when he happened to stray. The babbling brook had become a foaming torrent and it took his ball. That single shot cost him about two pounds. His one-shot-old, almost pristine, dimpled sphere is likely thirty or forty miles away bumbling along the bottom of the River Tyne and making its way past Newcastle towards the North Sea. So he had to buy a second new ball from Pat. Not good.

Every time he gets home he locks his clubs in the closet by the lift and swears that he will never touch the confounded things again. But he always does. He has too many friends at the club. He pays his expensive dues and spends a few hours a week in the company of some good people, only one of whom is worse at golf than him - Rob the Tax. Rob's game has one huge advantage over Tony's, in that he rarely hits the ball far enough to lose it. In general, hitting the ball very little distance is considered a shortcoming; not, however, from a financial standpoint because he's unlikely to lose a ball. Most of his shots end up a short stroll from point of origin - very short.

Tony watches him hacking around and wonders how on earth he can get any pleasure from the game. It's usually possible to pick him out on the course. Each swing is accompanied by a distressed grunt, as if he's wielding an over-heavy axe at an unyielding sequoia. His grunt draws attention to anyone close by and it's not uncommon to hear an accompanying 'thunk' as his club is driven into the turf. By the time you look over to investigate the commotion a divot the size of a dead otter is flying through the air. In fact it's not uncommon for his otter to go further than the ball. On more than one occasion Tony has seen Rob's ball remain perfectly motionless as his otter flies overhead.

Instances like this are part of the reason he keep coming back - the uncharitable opportunity to laugh at somebody else. But Rob always has a smile on his face; in fact, he's often chuckling. Maybe he tells himself jokes or recalls comic sketches to counter any frustration. No one knows his secret but he remains perpetually cheerful as he plots his way round the course accompanied by his pre-shot mutterings: *'Right, you dozy old fool. Keep your head still.'* Then ... Grunt, Thud, Chuckle.

That morning there was no official competition so they were playing a friendly four-ball; which is a misnomer if ever there was one. They all might be friends in the pub or pottering round the market but out there on the battlefield no quarter is given - no putt is conceded, no duff escapes acerbic comment and no tactic is deemed too savage to distract the opposition. Tony's partner was Monkey and they were playing against the Gates brothers, Martin and Gerry, who run an estate and letting agency in nearby Holdean. They are both fierce competitors and play off handicaps of six and eight, respectively. They see Thistledean residents as inferior beings. Not exactly the back-woods folk of Deliverance fame - more dilatory, pottering ruralites.

During the golfing season Tony's handicap varies between 24 and 28, depending on how effective his practice sessions have been. They usually fall in the utterly ineffective category, so more often than not his handicap is the male maximum of 28. Monkey plays off single figures so is actually reasonably proficient. The Gates brothers see Monkey and Tony as easy meat, a way to collect a tenner a corner without too much effort. As they stood on the first tee the Gates brothers were bubbling, verging on cocky at their forthcoming conquest.

Team Gates won the coin toss and elected to drive first. Gerry settled over his ball, waggled his posterior and glanced down the fairway. Then it all got a bit tense as Monkey helpful pointed out, 'Whatever you do, Gerry, be careful of the river on the right. We've had a bit of rain recently.'

Gerry paused and pursed his lips. He looked up at Monkey.

'Thank you,' he said through gritted teeth. But of course the seed was now sown. Doubt is a horrid thing in a golfer's mind, particularly when a river lurks.

Gerry swung. He inadvertently leaned away from the hazard, but this is exactly what not to do because it opens up the body position and promotes a slice. This sent the ball to starboard and it landed flush in the Url.

'Dear, dear, what bad luck,' said Monkey with vast insincerity.

Gerry was furious. Martin, in an effort the avoid the river, overcompensated and hoiked his ball into the gorse down the left.

'You might want to play a provisional,' advised Monkey helpfully. 'It's nasty territory out there.'

Team Thistledean won the first hole, and the second. In fact, assisted by a few well-chosen and well-placed interjections from Monkey, the match was won by the fourteenth and they were each ten pounds to the good. They were in a good mood and strolling up the 18th fairway, just enjoying playing out the round. Tony's ball was about 150 yards from the green. He said to Monkey, 'do you think I can get there with a seven-iron?'

Monkey thought for a moment. 'Yes, I would think so. If you hit it a few times.'

They collapsed with laughter which did nothing to improve the mood of their opposition who stormed off into the locker room.

Tony was combing his hair after a long and satisfying shower when Monkey came up behind him. He looked at Tony in the mirror and whispered, 'I don't normally resort to underhand tactics like that, but I really dislike cocky smartarses. I hope you don't mind.' Tony smiled and shook his head. No, he didn't mind.

They graciously bought their opposition a drink with their own money. Team Gates were a bit frosty at first, particularly with Monkey, but did calm down after a couple of pints. In fact, being fierce competitors, they appeared to grudgingly appreciate Monkey's strategy - 'Monkey-business' as Martin termed it. They all smiled at that, and with two of them, the smiles reached their eyes.

Tony went home with a very rare victory under his belt. In fact, he was so ebullient he almost decided to retire from golf there and then. What better way to depart than right at the top – with a victory and freshly minted prize money? However, as he locked his clubs in the cupboard he dismissed the idea. He would miss laughing at Rob too much. How could he possibly deny himself so much pleasure? Besides, one day he may win another match.

That Old Chestnut

Tony was 'on patrol' in his road-menders' jacket. He was taking a well-earned rest on a bench when someone crept up behind him.

'Oi, you can't just sit there! What the hell are we paying you for? You're supposed to be on patrol. You're not much of a deterrent slobbing around on a bench!'

Tony laughed. It was Brian Elder who'd been in the Bull at the post-Junta inquest, so was aware of the patrol scheme.

'Slobbing around?' said Tony indignantly. 'I'm doing nothing of the sort. I'm watching covertly … for free, I might add.'

'Covert, my backside! You stand out like a daffodil in a rubbish dump.'

'Ooh, very poetic.'

'And if you got any more relaxed somebody could come along and take the bench from underneath you without you even noticing. I'd call you the thin yellow line but that would be considerably overestimating your significance in the war on crime.'

'I'm blending in, surreptitiously. Chatting with anyone who joins me on this bench, gleaning crucial information about the layout and activity on the Square. I'm so deeply under-cover, it's almost like I'm just an ordinary citizen. If it wasn't for this bright yellow thing I would be part of the infrastructure instead of an eagle-eyed sleuth.'

'God preserve us.'

Tony turned and looked up at his friend. 'Anyway, what brings you into town? Haven't you got a country club to run?'

'Dental follow-up.'

'Oh, Lord. Best of luck with that.'

'I'm hoping all last week's discomfort is behind me.' He frowned in mock anger. 'When you all took the piss, I might add! No, this is just a check-up.'

'Pity,' Tony commiserated.

'What do you mean, pity? Pity I won't be in agony again?'

'Uh, pity that you were in so much discomfort last week. But glad you're better.'

Brian looked at Tony cock-eyed and grinned. 'You just like seeing me suffer, don't you?' he moaned.

'No, no. Not at all.' Tony tried to look all innocent but it didn't work.

'As if launching a golf ball through my car window wasn't enough? You have to take the mickey out of my poor teeth. Speaking of which, I'd better go and see Tomasz. While you,' he said pointing at Tony, 'should start marching up and down the Square looking for ne'er-do-wells.'

Tony chuckled. 'Did you hear about that fantastic new golf club Rob bought?'

'Yes, I was there at the club when he tried it out. He did look at bit brow-beaten when he came back in. Poor lad. If anyone deserves a medal for fruitless endeavour, it's him.'

With a wave, Brian said goodbye and disappeared into the dentist. He was of course referring to Robert the Tax who bought himself a wonder golf club that was guaranteed to hit the ball further and straighter than ever before. Cost him a hundred and twenty pounds, including delivery. Turns out it didn't work as well as advertised - which may have been largely Rob's own fault if the truth be known. Anyhow, when he rang up to claim on the money back guarantee, just two days after buying the thing, the company had gone out of business. The pub was in uproar as he told his story. Tony was still chuckling at the memory of the tale when he heard a bit of a commotion.

Peter Lord, dictatorial traffic warden and all-powerful parking overlord, was having a heated discussion with a lady in a red Mercedes.

'One minute!' railed the woman. 'That's all I stopped for, sixty miserable seconds to go and get some toothpaste. The chemist is the only place I can get the sort I need. Recommended by that Polish git,' she pointed, 'over there, masquerading as a dentist.'

'The length of time you were away is unimportant, madam. Likewise your choice of toothpaste,' said Peter with calm authority. 'It's the fact that you failed to display a valid ticket – that is the issue.'

'It says quite clearly 'First Hour Free.''

'It also says that you must display a valid, current ticket. The first hour is indeed free, but how am I to tell if a motorist has been here for one minute or six hours if they don't display a ticket indicating their time of arrival?'

'This is perfectly ridiculous. I will be complaining in the strongest possible terms.'

'That, Madam, is your prerogative,' replied Peter. He finished writing on his pad and slipped the ticket into a waterproof wallet. 'Excuse me,' he said, easing the lady out of his way so he could reach across and pop the nasty little package underneath her windscreen wiper.

'And who the hell put these damn trees in the middle of a car park?' said the lady, getting increasingly flustered. 'It's absolutely fatuous. I demand that you remove that ticket from my car immediately.'

'I saw you hit the tree, madam,' said Peter, smiling.

'What?'

'You reversed into that tree, madam, when you arrived. I saw you. It is an Aesculus hippocastanum, commonly known as a horse chestnut. You precipitated a shower of chestnuts. The tree has been here for at least fifty years. If it can avoid the attentions of incompetent drivers like yourself, we very much hope it will survive for a further fifty years.'

'I've never heard so much nonsense in my life. I will see you lose your job over this.'

'May I suggest you review the CCTV footage before you take your embarrassing and expensive complaint down a blind alley?'

The lady looked up at the nearby faux gas lamp and could indeed see a camera peering down into the Square.

'You are an insufferable little man,' she said as she ripped the ticket from the windscreen and threw it across to the passenger seat. She clambered in, started her car and sped out of the car park.

'And you, madam, are £65 worse off,' muttered Peter with a smile on his face.

He saw Tony and waved. He wandered over.

'Ascelus what?' asked Tony.

'Horse chestnut ... conker tree,' he replied, laughing. 'I do love my job sometimes,' he said cheerily as he sauntered off to snare another unsuspecting victim.

Tied up with String

From up in his eyrie, Tony had been watching an old guy come into town over a period of about three months. Every Thursday he parked his ancient Land Rover in the same spot, by a horse chestnut tree near the top of the Square. The wizened old lad, with dirty brown boots and an old tweed jacket tied round the middle with string, appears to struggle just to walk to the chemist. He takes what looks like a prescription back to his car, then hobbles over to the café for a cup of tea.

One day, as Tony sat and watched, the old guy in the Land Rover arrived. This time, however, there was a change in procedure. He hobbled to the chemist carrying a package; a few minutes later he emerged empty-handed and walked slowly over to the café. Rather than collecting he was delivering. He sat outside in the sunshine and spoke to the waitress, then stared at his hands folded on the table in front of him. It was difficult to tell if he was happy or not because he always looked lugubrious. Tony got the feeling the old guy could do with some company so left the flat, crossed the car park and asked if he could join him. The man looked up, nodded and waved airily to an empty seat.

'Thanks,' Tony said, and introduced himself. The man was still looking down at his hands so Tony was speaking to the top of his head. He ordered a coffee from a passing waiter. The man surprised Tony by saying, 'I know who you are ... old Mason's lad. You lived up at the farm.'

'Yes, that's right. I left about five years ago. Uh, sorry, but I don't know you. At least as far as I can remember.'

'I knew your old man.'

Tony's coffee arrived. Milky white - they know how he likes it.

'A real character, he was.'

The man paused and looked at Tony, who, to be honest was rather dumbfounded. The old man looked down again. They were silent for a few moments. Two cyclists rumbled by over the cobbles.

'I lost Nel last night.'

Having no clue to whom he was referring, Tony simply said, 'Oh, I'm sorry to hear that.'

The man looked up at Tony. 'My missus. She'd been struggling for a long while. It's a blessing, I suppose, but I'll miss her.'

'Oh no, that's awful. I'm really sorry.'

The man nodded slowly. Tony just sat, unsure what to say to a man he'd only just met. He was in the habit of chatting with strangers but this was a new situation and not a nice one. He asked the man if he'd like to be left alone.

'No, you stay if you want.' He looked over and inclined his head. 'Drink your drink.'

Tony obediently took a sip, not sure if he should talk or not; but as he was uncomfortable with the silence, he asked, 'Were you married long?'

The man nodded again. 'Aye. Fifty-five years last month. It's going to feel strange without her,' he said, shaking his head.

'Will you be alone in the house?' Tony asked.

'No. I've my daughter and her son staying. We'll manage.' He looked at an old wristwatch. 'I need to be getting back.'

Tony begged some paper and a pen from a waitress and wrote down his phone number. 'Here...' he said, passing it over. 'Please call me if there's any way I can help.'

'There's not much to do. But thanks.'

'Will you keep coming into town?'

'Aye, like as not. My lass needs stuff from here.' He indicated the chemist with an incline of the head. 'I've just brought a load of Nel's tablets back. Didn't want 'em lying around the house, what with the youngster stayin'. But yes, I'll be back.'

'If you want to talk, I can come and have a brew when I see you. If you'd like to chat, that is.'

He looked at Tony with a sad expression. 'Aye, if you want. Suit yourself.'

With that he got up and walked back to his muddy Land Rover. His boots clunked on the cobbles and he fished in the pocket of his string-tied jacket for his keys. As the vehicle fired up with a puff of dark grey smoke, Tony realized he still didn't know the man's name. He was reminded of a man he'd met in France many years ago as a late teenager, when he and his family were staying in a farm cottage in the middle of nowhere – a rare family holiday in very rural France, on the edge of a hamlet that was just a dot on the map. Goodness knows why they ended up there, but anyway ... the French guy who helped look after and service the cottages was an old man, too, and dressed similar to Tony's new acquaintance. Everyone, including Tony and his family, addressed him as Monsieur – no name, just Monsieur: *'Monsieur will deliver the milk in the morning, Monsieur will bring you some eggs for lunch,'* and so on. It was most peculiar and it had driven Tony potty over the years that he never discovered the man's name. Rather irrational perhaps, but he didn't want the same to happen with his new friend. He vowed to find out.

Then something else struck him. He had only seen this guy over the previous few months, yet he knew Tony had lived on a small-holding – so why hadn't he seen him before? And how did he know of Tony and his father? Now he was properly intrigued. He paid for his coffee and went over to the chemist and asked Diane Noble if she could tell him the name of the man who'd just dropped off the tablets. He explained that he'd been speaking with him, that he'd just lost his wife and he wanted to help if he could. She told him the man was called Frank Lattimer and he lived at Slate Mill Farm. Diane told Tony she wouldn't normally give out personal information, but in this case ...

When he returned home he looked at an Ordnance Survey map and found that Slate Mill Farm was at the head of a valley. It was about nine miles north, as the crow flies, of where Tony had lived on his farm. He was amazed he'd never heard of either the man or his farm, despite its isolated location. In fact, the town of Otterburn was nearer to where he lived than Thistledean, so why didn't he use the chemist there? It was all very odd.

Intruders

Julia, who'd been having a rest, came huffing and puffing up the slope from her bedroom. She appeared rather fraught.

'What on earth's the matter?'

'Firstly, I wish I could cope with that uphill climb better. Second, Agnes sent me a text, then phoned within a couple of minutes to see if I got the text.' She paused at the top of the slope to get her breath back. 'She says my flat had been ransacked. According to her, it's a right old mess. What the heck is that all that about?'

'I've no idea. Here, come and sit down I'll make you a cuppa.'

'The police were called this morning and were asking Agnes all sorts of questions she couldn't answer. She passed my number on, and your address here. I hope that's alright.'

'Of course it is.'

'I'm expecting a call from them at any moment.'

She accepted her coffee with a thank you. Tony said that logic dictated it was related to the French trip. Julia was about to reply when the doorbell rang, surprising them both. Via the intercom system and camera above the external door, they could see two uniformed police officers, one female, one male. The female identified herself as Sergeant Day and asked if Julia Carter was there. Tony confirmed she was and the officer asked if she and her colleague could have a word with her.

'Yes, certainly, come on up,' he said as he buzzed them in.

'They got her quickly,' said Julia, 'it must be serious.'

'Agnes passed my address on so they've had time to get organised.'

Sergeant Day was tall and dark-haired. She introduced her colleague as Constable Singleton. He was even taller, well over six feet, and also dark-haired. Both wore white shirts with black trousers, with various pieces of equipment strapped round their waists.

Thistledean no longer has a police station and is covered by Holdean - at least nominally. To be honest, the police are not seen very often, which is part of the reason for the new security force. The police officers know the town is being short-changed, but there's very little they can do with their man-power and budgets cut to the bone.

Sergeant Day addressed Julia. 'Ms. Carter, we'd like you to answer a few questions about a break-in at your home in Keswick. Would that be convenient?'

'Absolutely,' she replied, 'please go ahead. Although it seems over the top you coming here when you could have just phoned.'

'The thing is, Ms. Carter, the caretaker of the property was attacked and badly injured. It's more than a simple break-in, I'm afraid.'

'Oh goodness!' She covered her mouth with her hands. 'Poor Nick. Is he going to be alright?'

'He's been taken to hospital, but we don't yet know the extent of his injuries at this stage.'

'Dear me, how awful!'

'Ms. Carter,' continued the sergeant, 'can you tell us why your apartment should be the focus of what appears to be a targeted break-in?'

Julia looked at me then up at the officers. 'No, I'm afraid I can't.' She frowned. 'At least not specifically.'

The sergeant raised her eyebrows. 'What do you mean by that, Ms. Carter?'

'Well, my friend and I,' indicating Tony, with a sideways nod of her head, 'have just returned from France where I'd gone to try and trace my mother's family. I'm an orphan, you see, and have spent half a lifetime wondering about my past. Before it was too late I took a trip to France and a few days ago I did discover my mother's family, at least vestiges of it, in a town called Saint-Quentin. I realized I'd bitten off more than I could chew so asked Tony to come and join me, which he kindly did. But why, as a result of that, anyone would break into my home, I really can't say.'

'Could you give us the name of anyone you contacted over there? I think my colleagues in Keswick would like to speak with them.'

Julia rooted out Mme Dupont's address and phone number from her handbag and copied them on to a notepad on the kitchen table. 'Here,' she said, passing it over. 'The link to my family is rather tenuous, even now. This lady had a friend who was cousin to the person I now believe to be my mother. Blimey, hearing myself say it out loud makes me realize just how disjointed and convoluted the whole thing is. I didn't actually meet any relatives of mine. But I can categorically state that Mme. Dupont, that lady,' she said, indicating the number on the piece of paper, 'is certainly not the type to get involved with something like this. She was nothing but a help to me and a very respectable lady. Please don't go upsetting her.'

'I'm sure it won't come to that, Ms. Carter. Nevertheless, we'll probably need to speak with her. Could you also tell me the names of your relatives?'

'I'm only 95% sure, but I believe my mother was Jacqueline Courtois and my grandmother was Simone. I have no way to trace them - or if there is I don't know it. I wish I knew more, to be honest.'

Julia explained about how her mother had left France in 1930, possibly heading for a convent here in the UK, although she'd been unable to find any record of that. Her grandmother had either died or left the Saint-Quentin area. She also told them about her searching in the library and on the Internet. Julia told the officers that she had stayed at Hotel Florence, with a stop-over in Paris at the Monge Hotel.

Tony said, 'What about Duncan and your adoptive parents?'

She looked at me with pursed lips. 'I don't see how that can be relevant today. It was an awfully long time ago.'

'Nevertheless, Ms. Carter, we do need to look at everything to rule it out.'

'I have written it all down. It's on my computer. I could send you a copy - that would be much easier than trying to explain it all. There are various names, dates and what went on. But it was about fifty years ago.'

'There is an email address on my card. Yes, please send it over. There may be something of relevance.' She handed Julia a business card before they took their leave, saying that officers from Keswick would no doubt be in touch. In all likelihood, they would require Julia to return home to see if anything was missing. Julia gave the officers her phone numbers and they left, telling Julia to expect a call in due course.

As Tony closed the door on the police officers Julia sighed noisily. 'It's like a bad dream, all this.'

'Well, let's cheer you up then. You've been invited out to dinner by Baron Arthur and Baroness Nelly. They're the fun couple who drive about in their golf buggy. Mrs. Marshall is going as well, and I think you'll have lots in common.'

'We're both old gimmers, you mean?'

He laughed.'No, I didn't mean that. But I suppose you are,' he added cheekily.

'Oi, watch it you!' She laughed.

'Mrs. Marshall's a really interesting character. You'll like her. She was the town's midwife with another lady called Ivy for about 30 or 40 years. Ivy sadly died recently, so maybe the Nobles are trying to cheer Mrs Marshall up. I'm sure she's got plenty of tales to tell. She's got a wicked sense of humour, too.'

'It's very kind of them, but I'm not sure I really feel up to it.'

'Nonsense. You'll love it when you get there. If you can charge off to France you can go down the road for dinner. Besides, I told them I'd drive you down. I'll be on my way out anyway; I can pick you up on my way back about ten o'clock. We'll leave here at about six so you've plenty of time to get organized.'

She smiled and said with mock resignation, 'Oh, very well then.'

'Good. Right, I'm off to the pub for a swifty. I'll see you later.'

Tony walked down the left side of High Street and called in at Paula's Hair and Beauty Salon. He'd decided Julia needed a bit of cheering up so he booked her a hair and pamper session for the following day. It was just up the hill from Cobbles café so she could nip in there for a cuppa afterwards. Fifty quid for an hour's pampering was a bit steep but, well, hang it. After all, it wasn't though he exactly spent much on his own hair. Nothing, in fact – just a self-administered hack with the clippers and number two comb. He reckons it makes him look like a 1970s football hooligan but it's easy maintenance. Besides, because of that infernal double crown, if it grows longer than very short it looks like a hedgehog with its finger in an electrical socket.

Simon and Diane, chemist proprietors, were having a meal in the pub when Tony arrived. Simon waved and beckoned him over. 'I got your email and replied in the positive. It's fine as far as I'm concerned - just the sort of thing to splash our cash on. That room has needed sorting out for years.'

'Good. What brings you guys in here?'

'Wedding anniversary,' said Diane. 'Twenty-two years. Not bad, eh? We're having a day off. Lunch then a drive out and a gentle walk, perhaps.'

'Congratulations!'

Tony looked at Simon. 'Your mum and dad have invited Julia down for dinner this evening, along with Mrs. Marshall. Should be a lively do.'

'They enjoy their dinner parties. Neither of them is that fleet of foot these days, but they don't half have oodles of energy. They have loads of tales and can talk for England.'

Tony smiled. 'I'll leave you to it. Enjoy your walk.'

Rob the Tax was at the bar sipping away on a pint of bitter and reading a newspaper. The place was pretty quiet - no coaches in today.

'Bloody French are at it again,' he muttered. He was reading the Holdean Observer. 'They're always on strike for something. It's surprising the country doesn't grind to a complete halt. It's the dockers this time.'

'It's not exactly going to affect you too much, is it?' said Brian. 'Unless you're thinking of a booze cruise ... to avoid our crippling taxes,' he added pointedly, 'the like of which you probably instigated during your miserable tax-officer days.'

'Damn socialists,' Rob went on, ignoring Brian. 'Hand me a couple of hundred euros and I'll give a man a job for a week. That's how it is. I'm amazed anything gets done.'

'Write to your MP,' said Brian.

'What good will that do?'

'It'll keep you out of our hair for a few minutes.'

'Never you mind, Rob,' said Ron. 'You carry on. Have a moan.'

'Thank you. I will.'

Brian asked, 'How's that old banger of yours running, Rob?'

'You've changed the subject ...'

'I have, haven't I?'

'But since you ask ... it's fine, thank you. And don't be rude. It's a quality motor car. You're only jealous. It just keeps going and going. Touch wood.'

'Why on earth don't you get something more befitting a man of your moderate standing? That thing looks on its last legs.' He paused. 'Having said that ...'

'Oh, ha ha. It's just flown though the MOT, I might tell you – not a single thing to do. She had an oil change and a check over, and Dempsey has pronounced it A1. I have another twelve months of driving nirvana. At least twelve months. It's economical and nippy; what more could you want? And now it's had a service it flits from pot hole to pot hole like a new-born cantaloupe.'

'Cantaloupe? Isn't that a melon? asked Ron.

'Antelope then ... or gazelle.'

'Stick with cantaloupe,' muttered Brian. 'Besides, it looks more like an ageing warthog that's been through a particularly intense breeding season.'

Tombstone Tomasz came in.

'Could I have a pot of tea and a pie and peas, please Ron?'

'Sure thing, take a seat.'

'I'll sit here at the bar if that's OK?'

'Fine. Be with you in a minute.'

'Blimey, what a morning!' Tomasz said. 'No names, but I've had a family in from a farm near Holdean. Well, a dad and two kids. Fair to say they are not regular dentist goers. Both kids needed multiple fillings and Dad's set looked like a building site. I'd have been better off with a JCB than my finely-tuned instruments.'

'You're lucky,' said Brian, 'you could have been in here listening to Rob rambling on about melons.'

Tombstone looked confused and Rob looked sideways from his newspaper and scowled.

'Right,' said Brian, reckoning he'd suitably upset Rob, 'I've got a raft of membership renewals to get out so I'm off to the club. See you anon.'

'You're quiet, Tony,' said Ron. 'You OK?'

'Yes, fine thanks. Just pondering. And to be honest, fruit and motor cars are not my strong suits so I left it to the experts.'

'How's the old lass doing?'

'OK. Well, I say OK but she's had her flat broken into in Keswick so she's a bit perturbed. Waiting to hear more from the coppers down there to find out what's what.'

'Oh dear, that sounds unpleasant. Give her our best.'

'I will.' He finished his whiskey and held his glass towards Ron. 'I'll just have one more in there and I'll be off.'

Half an hour later he was strolling through the park, looking up towards the hills. He was thinking about the old man on his farm. He made his mind up to try and find him tomorrow. In the children's play area off to his right, a young mum held the hand of a little girl as she slid down the slide with a screech of joy. A little one just starting out. Wonderful.

Keswick

Tony got back home to find Julia on the phone to the police. She'd obviously been on for a while because she was looking a bit frazzled. She finished the conversation, 'Yes, I'll do that. I'll try and be there around lunchtime tomorrow.'

She disconnected. 'You heard? They want me to go and see what's missing. To be honest, there's nothing I'd miss if it has been pinched. Dear me, what a faff.'

'I'll drive you down. We can leave after breakfast.'

'Are you sure? It's messing you around, isn't it?'

'Worry not. I have nothing to do tomorrow that can't be postponed for a day or two.'

'Well, if you're sure. That's kind. Thank you.'

'Besides it's either a taxi, which would cost a fortune, or public transport ... and goodness knows where you might end up.' He smiled. 'Reminds me, I had a mate once who told me about a train journey his wife took in France. They had to get from near Dijon to Lyon airport. She had to make two changes of train on her journey. Problem was she was prone to nodding off. She was a good napper - could fall asleep for queen and country. Now, some of these French trains cover huge distances and don't have many stops. I can't remember the exact details but one train she took terminated about 300 miles past where she needed to change. If she fell asleep she could be in a right pickle. So my mate had his wife's itinerary to hand and he would ring her ten minutes before each change. He'd keep her on the phone till she actually got off one train and onto the right connection. That's how I see you mucking about if you took public transport!'

She laughed.

'Right,' he said, 'why don't you go and have a nap so you'll enjoy your evening with the Nobles?'

He phoned Paula's and postponed Julia's pamper session for a few days. Then he texted The Colonel, reminding her to go and get reimbursed by Paul Broadbent. While Julia took to her room he went up to the lounge and sat in the window. He checked his Ordnance Survey map and worked out a route to the old man's farm. It was a dot on the map and he wondered again why he'd never come across it. He decided he'd go looking when they got back from Keswick. He looked down over High Street to see if the old guy's Land Rover was there, but it wasn't. It was quiet generally; no market, no tourist coaches. He saw Jess busy arranging flowers on her outside display. She was chatting with Polly who was sitting in the sunshine on her shop's front step, taking a breather with a cup of tea. He made a mental note to ask her how her plans were going for her distinguished visitor.

The following morning they left Thistledean just after 10:00 A.M. Julia said that she'd slept better than she had for ages after a lovely dinner with the Nobles.

'They are fine hosts, I must say. Nelly is quite a cook. We had Beef Wellington and it was delicious. She made the chicken liver pate and pastry herself too. Wow, I wish I could cook like that!'

Tony smiled. 'I wouldn't trust myself with expensive ingredients like that. My Beef Wellington would end up with a dish perfectly synonymous with its name.'

'Nonsense! You cooked a delicious steak on my last visit. Don't do yourself down.'

'Beginner's luck. How did you get on with Mrs. Marshall?'

'Oh, she's quite a gal. She was telling us about her midwifery and the struggles they had some days in winter. A lovely lady, and overall it was a thoroughly enjoyable evening.'

They had just come off the M6 and joined the A66 that would take them to Keswick. Tony's Discovery was eating up the miles.

'It feels peculiar coming home knowing there's been a break-in.'

'I'm sure it does. You may have to find somewhere to stay if the place isn't fit. Unless you want to drive back with me, that is.'

She was silent for a spell.

'I'll come back with you I think, if that's OK.'

'Sure it is. It's a lot of travelling, that's all. Let's see how we feel after you've spoken to the police.'

'Yes, good idea. There are one or two nice hotels if we need one. What took you to Holdean last evening anyway, if you don't mind me asking?' Tony could tell she was looking to re-direct the conversation.

'Not at all. I went to visit an old friend, a guy called Johnny Webster. I go and see him roughly once a month. Very nice guy, to whom I owe a debt of gratitude for helping me through a difficult adolescence. And beyond. He used to live nearby when we had the farm but he's now in a residential home on the outskirts of Holdean. We talk about the old days over a glass or two of wine, and chat about cricket, golf or soccer, depending on the season. He seems to enjoy hearing about my golfing debacles, too.' He told her Celia's slippers story.

'Oh, I can sympathize with that!' she exclaimed.

They swept down into Keswick and pulled up outside Julia's apartment block. She'd phoned an Inspector Birch on the way and it was presumably him waiting for them with a colleague in the car park. The inspector stepped forward to greet them. He was average height with silver-rimmed glasses and swept-back hair, dark turning grey. He wore a conservative charcoal grey suit under a voluminous fawn overcoat.

'How is Nick?' was the first thing Julia said, dispensing with the usual introduction and pleasantries.

'He's in an induced coma, Ms. Carter. I'm afraid the outcome is far from certain. He was savagely beaten. It was a severe attack.'

Julia was silent.

'That's partly why we're keen to talk to you. See if you can help shed any light on this. Thank you for coming so promptly.'

He turned and shook Tony's hand and they formally introduced themselves.

He turned back to Julia.

'Let's go and have a look inside, Ms. Carter. Would you mind waiting here, Mr. Mason? We'd like to talk to you as well.'

Tony nodded. While Julia accompanied the two officers inside he went into the garden and sat on a wooden bench overlooking Derwentwater. He was reminded of Albert Mannion's memorial by the étang in Saint-Quentin. It seemed like a lifetime ago. He reflected on the beauty of the location, incongruous against the misery of the attack and break-in. As a man who was merely doing his job fought for life, unconcerned ducks quacked feverishly and little waves washed up upon the gravel shore.

He was startled back to the world by a summons to Julia's apartment to Sergeant Appleby - an attractive blonde lady with a neat bob cut and ready smile. Despite her smile, Tony noted, she had a piercing glare. She wore a blue trouser suit over a white blouse but no coat as it was warm and sunny. Tony remarked by way of conversation that he was surprised her colleague was wearing a coat.

'He invariably does, Mr Mason. It's welded on. He has all sorts of unpleasant things secreted away in his pockets.'

As they walked towards the main entrance she turns to Tony, game face on, and looked at him with those piercing eyes, 'So what actually went on in France, Mr. Mason?'

He was taken aback by the sudden change in demeanour. He walked a few paces before saying, 'As far as I'm aware, nothing untoward. I was merely helping an old friend search for her lost relatives.'

'A respectable lady is not burgled without reason. And a man is fighting for his life. These are not run-of-the-mill events. It is more than a simple chance robbery, I am sure of that.'

Tony hesitated. 'Did you read her account of her younger years?'

'Yes, I did. And frankly the whole thing is mired with supposition and half-truths.'

Tony stopped walking so she turned and looked back. He looked directly at her as he said testily, 'If you seriously think that Julia had some reason to deceive you or had anything to do with this, I'm afraid you are deluded.

Maybe you're just trying to intimidate me, and by association Julia, but you're barking up the wrong tree. I assure you that trying to frighten us won't get you anywhere. Now, I'm going inside and if she has been subjected to this kind of slur you'll be sorry. I don't care who the hell you are.' He stormed inside.

He wasn't sure what to expect, but inside the apartment all was calm. Julia was sitting at the kitchen table, nursing a cup of tea, while Inspector Birch talked quietly on the phone. Tony asked if she was OK and she replied that she was fine.

'You look red in the face,' she said. 'What's the matter?'

'Oh, nothing ... just rushed up the stairs.'

She looked pointedly at him and cocked her head, but let it go.

'I can't see anything missing. My papers are all over the place but I don't think they've taken anything. Chances are that if they have I'll only find out when I need something and can't find it. Go and have a look. It seems more destructive than anything - wilful damage and pretty violent. I have to say it's rather disturbing.'

Tony wandered through into the lounge where Sergeant Appleby was standing by Julia's desk looking through papers. Chairs were overturned, table lamps smashed, wall pictures thrown on the floor - even the carpet was pulled up in one corner.

'Well?' asked the inspector, who'd come in behind him.

'Do you need to speak to me, inspector?'

'My sergeant has spoken to you, I believe. That is all for now.'

'You've trained her well if you wanted somebody aggressive and unpleasant. Her attitude doesn't encourage help.'

The inspector raised his eyebrows then looked quizzically at Tony before walking away to join his colleague across the room. Tony returned to the kitchen.

'Have they finished with you?' he asked Julia.

'I think so. I can't tell them much.'

'Right, let's get out of here. Are you ready?'

She pursed her lips and nodded.

'They want an official statement, I think.'

Tony called to the inspector and asked him. He requested they call at the police station either later that day or in the morning.

Julia said, 'When you've finished here, inspector, please leave the key with my neighbour at number 6, Agnes Duckworth. We'll be staying at the Inn on the Square if you need us.'

Tony and Julia knocked on Agnes' door but there was no reply. They scribbled a note to say they'd call in the morning and posted it through the letterbox.

Two things of note happened later that day. Inspector Birch phoned to say that Nick Saxleby had died of his injuries. Then an email arrived from Monsieur Dupont in Saint-Quentin addressed to Julia and copied to Tony.

A Century On

J ulia called Tony in his room and asked if he'd heard the news about Nick. He confirmed he had and went round to her room, where she was weeping. 'The poor man,' she repeated over and over. Tony helped her onto the bed and covered her with the counterpane. He sat in the chair by the window until she fell asleep, then went back to his room.

He signed into the hotel's WiFi, browsed through the news and then checked his emails. He'd received replies from all members of the Junta except The Colonel, who he knew to be away for a couple of days. To a person they endorsed the release of funds for the exhibition room. In another email he was offered ironmongery at rock-bottom prices and another from his bank offered a £100 bonus for opening a weekly saver account - new customers only. Not existing customers like me, he thought, who'd endured virtually zero interest rates for years. Bloody cheek.

Then he noticed one with a French heading, including the word 'histoire' - history. It was from Monsieur Dupont:

Rue Emile Zola
   Saint-Quentin

Cher Julia et Monsieur Mason

Forgive my English. A colleague has translated for me so I hope it all makes sense. I think I have found some useful information for you about your family. I believe it is very interesting. I think your father may be Jean-Claude Batiste.

Here is some information that will help me explain ...

Jean-Claude Batiste was a founder member of a group called 1919, which was an ultra-secret organisation based in the north of France. It is named after the year in which it was founded following the signing of the Treaty of Versailles (28th June 1919). Its raison d'etre were three-fold: to win back France's respect, maximize France's European influence and protect France from future German intrusion.

It was alleged that General Marshal Ferdinand Foch was the brainchild of 1919. He became supreme commander of Allied forces in March 1918 towards the end of the war. Known as a sometimes reckless and always aggressive commander he coordinated the French, British and US troops that stopped the German offensive and took the fight back to them in a war-winning counter-attack. He accepted the German cessation of hostilities and was present at the armistice on 11th November 1918.

However, the following year Foch was scathing about the terms of the Treaty of Versailles. He believed that Germany had been too leniently treated and had basically been left intact. He believed this to be an unsatisfactory and dangerous state of affairs. He said prophetically, *"This is not peace. It is an armistice for twenty years."*

Though the group 1919 was shrouded in mystery the organisation is alleged to have been involved in many activities throughout the inter-war years and, perhaps equally importantly, subsequently. It grew to legendary status, all the more unfathomable because nobody could actually prove it existed. They operated either in the shadows or so high up that they were unreachable.

They were fiercely protective of their homeland and they were fervent nationalists. They carried out acts of sabotage on anything they believed to be of foreign origin. Some of these acts appeared to be little more than mindless bloodshed. But the fact that I am writing about it now indicates that they might well have achieved one of their objectives, notably notoriety. One such act, believed to be the responsibility of 1919, was the sabotage of British airship R101 in 1930. R101 was on her maiden flight and was overflying France en route to India when it crashed near the city of Beauvais. Jean-Claude Batiste was an explosives expert and it is alleged he was instrumental in the downing of the airship.

Beauvais is less than one hundred miles from Batiste's home town of Saint-Quentin and 1919 operated throughout northern France. Geographically the allegations stood up. It was thought that the sabotage only took place so 1919 could prove its influence and create an aura of fear and invincibility. However, it could have been a public relations disaster because of the appalling loss of life. Forty-eight of the 54 people on board died, more dead than the Hindenburg indeed. Many British dignitaries died with the destruction of the R101, including Lord Thomson, the British Secretary of State for Air.

The official cause of the disaster was thought to be a tear in the outer cover, causing one of the gasbags to fail. The ship would then become nose-heavy and the elevators unable to correct the pitch. There was also a fire. Several hydrogen-filled airships had crashed without catching fire, but R101 did. It was the uncertainty of the official cause and the fact there was a fire that pointed to an 'outside influence.' Suspicion fell on 1919. Nothing was proved, of course, and there was even speculation that the organisation had instigated a false rumour themselves. Whatever the truth, it added to the mystery of the group. Numerous other acts of sabotage were attributed to them, usually involving companies or entities foreign to France. Indeed, there is a school of thought that 1919 continued to operate throughout the Second World War and that it is still influential to this day.

So, Julia, why is this important? We in our history society (I have asked some friends for help) have uncovered tantalising clues indicating the possibility that Jean-Claude Batiste was your father. Most notably a letter has been discovered. We believe it to have been from Jacqueline Courtois following the birth of her child. The letter referred to a photograph, though this was never found. The letter is brief and (translated) reads:

My love
  Here is our daughter.
  She is born healthy but taken. I will never see her again.
  My heart breaks.

I think of you often dear Jean.
Do not forget us.
J. xx

It is sad and we can only presume that it is from Jacqueline to Jean-Claude. His powerful associates provided means for Jacqueline to be spirited out of the country when she became pregnant. The fact that she wasn't killed is extraordinary in itself, and supposition was rife that Batiste was unwilling to sacrifice his younger lover. It also indicated to some people that Jean-Claude held enough sway within 1919 to ensure her survival. He would have been 35 years old and married when he and Jacqueline had their liaison. She would have been barely 20.

Jean-Claude Batiste was a well-respected figure in Saint-Quentin and had two sons with his wife Annie. The elder son was killed towards the end of the Second World War but the younger of the two, Jean-Pierre, married and had a child of his own, a daughter called Marie. We have discovered that Marie Batiste is a colourful, well-known political figure tipped to run for leadership of the ultra-right-wing communist party next year. The party's share of the vote has diminished in recent years, but with the twin issues of immigration and austerity, nationalistic feelings are running high in France and Marie Batiste is saying the right things to regain her party's lost ground. It is an important time for her country, her party and herself. Scandal in her family would not go down well, either in the form of the unmasking of her grandfather as a reckless saboteur (which is how he would be portrayed by her opponents) or the existence of an illegitimate child.

I will send further information if we find any.

Sincerely
Maurice and Elsa Dupont

Tony read the email through twice more and struggled to believe what he was seeing. He logged on to the Internet and searched for Marie Batiste. Sure enough, there she was - entry after entry supporting this, condemning that.

Vocal, outspoken and striking - and in a position of power. The photographs showed a woman with jet black, shoulder-length hair with prominent black eyebrows. She had fiery green eyes and in every photograph wore bright red lipstick. Were she and her supporters ruthless enough or frightened enough to reach out across the decades? Whoever was responsible, if there was any doubt about how serious it is, surely none remained. A man was dead.

The more he thought about it the less sure he was. Surely a politician, or those with a vested interest, would not be so reckless? Not in this day and age where every move is microscopically analysed by both opponents and the media. But it appears that Julia's probing had set off an alarm somewhere. So, was there an alternative? Perhaps it was just a break-in. He tried to think it through. What prompted the police to think Julia had been targeted? He presumed it was because the robbers had approached the caretaker for access specifically to Julia's property.

Was it all being skewed because of the attack on Nick? In other words if Nick hadn't been attacked would the police had even bothered with the break-in? Except perhaps for the most cursory investigation. As it was, a possible theft became an aggravated burglary which in turn would become a murder inquiry. Could the attackers be linked to Marie Batiste or was it merely a robbery gone horribly wrong? And at the end of the day, did the perpetrators find anything? If they knew what they were looking for and didn't find it, would they try somewhere else?

There was in fact a third alternative, in the form of relatives or former business associates of Duncan. Could it be that the network they had opened up in the late 1920s was still active? Would the unmasking of Jean-Claude Batiste threaten them about ninety years on? A peaceful chap at heart, Tony was finding all this increasingly bewildering. Despite his initial enthusiasm, he didn't want to overly alarm Julia. Presumably she had a copy of the email he'd received from the Duponts. He was sure she would elect to focus on the identity of her father. The problem was that they'd have to approach him through his descendants and that meant Marie Batiste. If Maurice Dupont's allegations were true, poking their noses in there would likely be asking for trouble. Julia could be a stubborn mule at times, but he decided to try and stall her while the police made further inquiries.

* * *

'Whether or not she is involved with this break-in is irrelevant,' Julia said after Tony had roused her and she'd read the message. 'The fact is, she and her relatives are the only ones who can confirm or deny whether Jean-Claude Batiste is my father. So contact them I will, with or without your help.'

The stubborn mule had spoken with, he had to admit, a certain undeniable logic. Tony nodded.

'Come on,' she said. 'Drive me down to the apartment. I'll call from there.'

'The police may still be there.'

'I doubt it. Anyway, if they are I'll phone from the kitchen.'

'Why not phone from here?'

'Home turf. I feel comfortable there. Besides, if I feel the need to get forceful, seeing the aftermath of the robbery will charge me up.'

As soon as she got home, Julia placed her phone on speaker and dialed a Parisian number listed on the Communist Party website, prefixing it with 0033. The call was answered promptly.

'Oui, bonjour.'

'Parlez-vous Anglais?'

'Yes, a little. Who is calling, please?'

'My name is Julia Carter. I would like to speak with Marie Batiste, please. Perhaps she would know me better as Julia Courtois.'

'May I ask the reason for your call?'

'It's a family matter. Urgent and private.'

'One moment, please.'

There was a minute's pause before the telephonist returned. 'Mme Batiste is not available just at the moment. Could you please leave your phone number and she will ring you back as soon as she is able?'

Tony shook his head vigorously but Julia ignored him. She gave them her number and hung up.

'They will know exactly where we are now,' he said, exasperated.

'They would have known already, or they could soon find out easily enough. Besides, I find that in instances like this it's always best to be forthright. There really isn't any point beating about the bush. I'm too old for that.'

'I suppose you're right,' he conceded. Nevertheless, he was the naturally cautious type, and couldn't help feeling she was being rather reckless. He was seeing a steely side to his friend, one that he'd not really seen before.

She smiled and patted his hand. 'I can be forceful sometimes. But the instances are becoming fewer and further between. I haven't the energy these days.'

She paused. 'Make us some tea would you, Tony? That always helps.'

Exactly how it would help he wasn't sure, but he filled the kettle nevertheless. Before it boiled, the phone rang. Julia put the call on speaker. The line was rather fuzzy but quite audible. 'Ms. Carter, I am Marie Batiste. What is this emergency of which you speak?'

'Madame Batiste,' replied Julia, strong and confident. 'I believe I am your grandfather's illegitimate daughter.'

There was silence.

'And why would you think that?'

'I believe your grandfather fathered a child by a young lady called Jacqueline Courtois in 1930. I am that child.'

There was another pause. Longer this time. Tony frowned at Julia, who put a finger to her lips.

'I think perhaps we should meet.'

'Does that mean that you believe me?'

'It means I think we should meet.'

'I assure you, Madame Batiste, I am not trying to interfere with your life. I am not after money or anything like that. My only desire is to ascertain whether Jean-Claude Batiste is indeed my father.'

'One moment, please.'

Julia looked at me and raised her eyebrows inquisitively.

He shrugged.

The phone clicked. 'I am speaking at a conference in Manchester on Tuesday, the day after tomorrow. I will be staying at the Lowry Hotel and I will be free after seven that evening. Perhaps we could meet then?'

Julia replied immediately. 'I will be there. Thank you, Madame Batiste.' She disconnected the call. 'I'm shaking,' she said. 'Look.' She held out her liver-spotted hand, which was indeed trembling. 'Will you come with me?'

He smiled and shook his head slowly. 'You know I will.'

She took his hand and smiled. 'Thank you. Again.'

They returned to the hotel for dinner and the following morning went to the police station where an officer took their statements, plus fingerprints for elimination purposes. They had discussed over dinner whether to pass on the Duponts' email to the police and concluded that they had little option. They reasoned they couldn't withhold information that may help their inquiry; they'd find themselves in trouble. Besides, for Nick's sake and that of his family, they wanted the police to find those responsible. But they didn't tell them about the meeting with Marie Batiste. Julia thought that if she could demonstrate some trust and discretion the politician would be more amenable to share information.

Julia was getting pretty subversive here. She said, 'Forwarding Dupont's email is an *'in the event of my demise'* contingency, in case anything goes wrong. But let's not give too much away, eh? Actually,' she said on reflection, 'demise is over-egging it, hopefully, but I think that having something in place could be a bargaining chip.'

He was dubious but couldn't come up with a counter-argument so went along with her logic. Released from the police station they returned to Julia's flat where they tidied up. One or two small bits of furniture were broken but nothing too bad, and in a couple of hours the place looked tidy enough. They dusted off dark and light fingerprint powders, depending on the surface, and decided to grab a sandwich in the Red Lion pub down the road. Before they went they called on Agnes across the hallway. She was pretty flustered; one might have thought it was she who had been burgled. She soon calmed down when they told her everything was under control, which was actually stretching the truth somewhat. But there was no point everyone being agitated. The two elderly ladies hugged in mutual support over the death of Nick Saxleby.

Over lunch they both relaxed properly for the first time in a couple of days. Julia wasn't ready to spend the night in her apartment so they had a second night at The Inn on the Square.

French Connection

The following afternoon they checked into the Lowry Hotel, address Dearmans Pl. Was that Plaza or Place? They weren't sure, but being Manchester and not Mirabel, it was probably Place. They both had rooms overlooking the River Irwell. The Lowry is comfortable, clinical and 'reassuringly expensive,' as the old TV advert goes. But for five stars, you pay. Tony wasn't too worried what it cost because Julia footed the bill.

'It's the least you can do,' he told her, grinning.

Julia picked up a message from reception as she checked in. From Marie Batiste, it confirmed their meeting in the hotel bar at 7:15 p.m.

The politician was even more striking in the flesh. She looked stylish in a black knee-length skirt, black stockings and light grey jacket over a white blouse. Very businesslike. Her jet black hair, lightly waved, had such a sheen that it reflected the overhead lights. She was around forty years of age and very toned, physically fit. She looked like a panther, with vibrant, dark green eyes, like lasers.

She walked towards them looking Julia in the eye, unblinking. They shook hands. 'Madame Carter.'

Julia smiled faintly and nodded. 'This is Tony Mason,' she said.

Marie Batiste turned her gaze on Tony and nodded. 'Monsieur Mason.'

Tony shook her hand and said hello. She offered to buy them a drink. Tony accepted and asked the attendant waiter for a Jameson whiskey over ice. Julia declined.

'I had a call at lunchtime,' began Marie Batiste, 'from a policeman. It came just before I was to leave the hotel for the conference centre where I was to deliver my speech. It was rather unsettling, I must say.' She spoke with barely an accent and was obviously fluent in English. 'They wanted to know my whereabouts five days ago. I asked what it was in connection with. It was only after I told them I was in Paris they told me it concerned a man's death in Cumbria. I had to check where Cumbria was. In fact I appeared on television twice on the day in question, both live news programmes. Once at lunchtime, once in the early evening. That seemed to satisfy them, at least for the moment, but I am to be interviewed by video-link tomorrow morning. Is there by any chance a connection between your theory that my grandfather is your father and the death of this man? Can you explain it to me?'

Julia told her that the dead man was in the employ of her apartment block. He was a caretaker, a friend to many and a decent family man. He was attacked by someone wishing to gain entry into her apartment and subsequently died of his injuries.

'I'm sorry,' replied Marie Batiste, 'but I assure you that it had nothing to do with me. In fact the first time I had even heard of you was when you called our office in Paris two days ago. I also fail to see what I would have gain by having someone break into your apartment.'

Julia replied, 'Should news emerge that your grandfather was a saboteur, apparently a merciless one at that, would it not affect your standing as a public figure? Indeed if it emerged that I was his illegitimate daughter, would that not have similar consequences?'

'I presume you are trying to threaten me, Ms. Carter. Unfortunately for you, that will not work. My public standing, as you term it, would not be affected. That's presuming that either of your two allegations can be proved. And if they can't, I would be careful what you say if I were you. So, no, I would be wholly unaffected.' She paused. 'Let us be clear on this. Perhaps you or somebody else is theorising that I, or someone in my employ, attacked a caretaker and broke into your apartment. With a view to what, may I ask? What would I hope to find? What would be so valuable to me that I would be prepared to risk my entire career? It's quite ridiculous. Besides which, people know about the legend surrounding my grandfather and he isn't thought of as a pseudo-terrorist; he's more a folk hero. People love him and love what he stood for. And to be frank, if he did conceive a child out of wedlock, it would only enhance his legend.'

'And furthermore,' she continued, 'I have survived this long in politics because I am honest about who I am. If it emerged that we are related through my grandfather, I would embrace that, not bump you off!' She laughed a practiced laugh.

Tony thought she spoke in such a confident, clear manner that she made you want to listen and believe. That is a gift, one that not many people have. More importantly, what she said also made sense. Julia said nothing; she just looked at Marie Batiste, who returned the stare.

After a moment's reflection, the French woman continued. 'Now that I have convinced you, hopefully, that I have nothing to gain either way, I will tell you that I do recall two photographs. I remember them clearly from our family archives. They were among my grandfather's papers, found after he died. One is of a group of three young women. One of them does indeed look like you.' She laid her first and second fingers of her right hand on her upper cheeks. 'It's the eyes. The second shows the same young woman, now apparently a mother holding a new-born baby. Without doubt it's the same young woman, but there is no way of confirming if that the baby is you. Furthermore there is no actual evidence, that I am aware of, that my grandfather is your father. I honestly don't know one way or the other if he had an affair with your mother. My parents told me there were rumours at the time, but there are always rumours.'

'Would your father know any more? Or any other family members?' asked Julia.

'What I've told you comes from my father. It was he who showed me the two photographs I mentioned. We discussed our family history when I was at university and I looked deeper when I entered politics. I couldn't afford any unpleasant surprises, so I learned all I could. So the answer is no, I don't believe he could add to what I've told you.' She paused and sipped her orange juice. 'I'll tell you this, though, and I have theorised about this over the years. If what you allege is true, then yes he, that's Jean-Claude, made a mistake, a big one. He cheated on his family and you can argue that that is inexcusable.

But what happened happened, and he found himself in a difficult situation. Don't get me wrong - Jacqueline Courtois was also in a very tough situation. What happened next was not, in effect, her choice. She was completely in the hands of her baby's father.' She paused again.

Julia noted the phrase 'the baby's father'. Maintaining a little distance.

'I realize I am speaking here as if there is little doubt. Although there is no proof, I think it likely that you are his daughter.' She stared at Julia again. 'I will of course deny saying that if it becomes necessary.'

Julia looked at her sadly. 'We come from very different worlds, Madame Batiste. Your first instinct is not to trust anybody. Mine is the opposite. Sadly that leaves the likes of me open to deception. But you don't need to threaten me. All I want is to hear what you have to say. I hope I will leave here believing what you've told me. I am trusting you to tell the truth. I am not out to make trouble.'

'Indeed, yes. I assure you, I am being straight with you. I think we partly have to consider the uncertain times in which they lived. That and the fact that my grandfather was a powerful man in a dangerous and ruthless organisation. I truly believe that he set things right in the best way he could. If you are indeed his daughter, you are living proof of that. Human life was cheap back then and it was well within his capabilities to have ...' she paused, '... arranged a different outcome. He couldn't allow her to stay. The fact that Jacqueline was allegedly sent to England by someone seen as a passionate French nationalist is ironic indeed. If it's true, I don't condone what he did but I forgive him.'

'Sadly,' said Julia, 'I cannot prove that Jean-Claude did not arrange an alternative outcome, as you put it. I cannot find trace of my mother after my birth. She may indeed have been the victim of an 'arranged outcome.' I have no way to tell one way or another.'

Everyone was quiet for a few seconds.

'The photograph,' said Julia, 'the one of mother and baby. May I see it?'

'It's not here. I merely recall seeing it. If it still survives it will be in our archives in my father's study. I have not seen it for many years. I will ask my father.'

She turned to me. 'And you, Mr. Mason. What is your interest in this matter?'

Tony smiled. 'You don't trust me either, do you? What a world you live in.' He shook his head. 'I am Julia's friend. I'm here to support her and try to ensure fair play.'

'Forgive me. I have been blind-sided before - strangers have to earn my trust. It is how I survive.'

'After today, we will remain strangers,' he promised.

She smiled thinly. She told them she'd had a long day and must freshen up before dinner. She asked for Julia's address in case she found the photograph then shook them each by the hand and bid us good evening. She turned heads as she crossed the lobby towards the elevators.

'It's funny,' Tony said. 'I now realize that I don't trust people who don't trust me.'

Julia laughed. 'That's a bit of a conundrum.'

'People like that, it's like they're always hiding something.'

'Mmm, I actually think she was being straight with us. That or she's a very convincing fibber.'

'We came here in the hope that you could confirm that Jean-Claude Batiste is your father. That didn't happen directly, although it's fair to say there is now more anecdotal evidence to suggest he is. Short of some sort of DNA test I don't see how we can get any closer.'

'We could try and talk to Marie Batiste's parents. We only have her word that her father told her everything. Maybe they are hiding something?'

'But why? According to Marie Batiste it make no difference to her if Jean-Claude is your father.'

'It matters to me.'

'Of course it does, and I'm not suggesting it doesn't. What I'm saying is that she appears to have no reason to avoid the truth.'

'I know, I know.' She sighed. 'I'm 95% sure who my mother is and now 70% sure who my father is. That's better than when I started, but not exactly perfect.'

They were silent for a few moments. The bar was pretty busy. Some looked like tourists, of these a smattering of overseas visitors. Most of the rest looked like business people relaxing on their way home.

'Would you like a drink?' he asked.

'You know what?' she replied with a big grin. 'I'm famished. How about we go out for dinner? I fancy something oriental. How about you?'

To be honest, the last thing he really needed was to go in search of dinner. But he didn't want to spoil her mood, so a Chinese it was.

Home for a Breath

'Y ou did what?' asked Inspector Birch the following morning. 'You actually met with a suspect?'

'Suspect? She told me you'd ruled her out; she was appearing on television on the day in question. I don't think she had anything to do with it,'

'Oh, you don't, do you? It's very reassuring to hear you say so. Look, Ms. Carter, we are investigating a very serious crime and I would appreciate you not interfering.'

'There is no need to be sarcastic, inspector. I was following a lead to try and discover who my parents were. A brief window of opportunity opened, giving me the chance to do something about it, so I took advantage. I'm sorry if I've trodden on your toes; my intention was not to get in your way, I assure you. Furthermore, I'm too old to be dithering about waiting for permission for this and that.'

We heard an infuriated sigh over the speaker.

Julia changed the subject. 'Have you officially finished with my apartment now, inspector?'

'Yes. I don't suppose anything useful came out of your meeting with Marie Batiste as regards my investigation?' Then he added pointedly, '<u>Our</u> investigation?'

'I'm sorry, no.' Julia chuckled. 'But, neither Tony or I believe she was responsible.'

'Oh, really? My God, it's amateur hour,' muttered the inspector. Then louder, 'Thank you, Ms. Carter, Mr. Mason. If you think of anything else, please get in touch via the Keswick station. And if I have any other tricky cases I need help with, I'll be sure to give you a call.'

Julia disconnected.

'At least he appears to have something of a sense of humour,' Julia grinned.

They drove straight up to Thistledean, finding no reason to call in at Keswick. Julia phoned her neighbour from the car and told Agnes she would be away for a few more days. They got back to Tony's apartment mid-afternoon. Julia excused herself and went to her room. She was quiet for nearly an hour before emerging to announce she was popping out to post a letter. Tony caught up with some correspondence. The Colonel had replied to his email and confirmed that she endorsed the funds for the exhibition room. He emailed Peter and let him know, then Paul Broadbent to advise him he could release funds as and when necessary up to £8,000, which should give them plenty of leeway.

He was about to close his laptop when an email pinged in. It was from Charlie, Jess' fiancée, titled *'Security Patrol.'* It was addressed to The Colonel but copied to all Junta members, plus Keith Parker and Tombstone Tomasz (the two members of the patrol force who, in addition to Charlie, were not Junta members).

'Tomasz and I copped three young lads at 11:35 PM last night. We saw them first on CCTV trying car doors in the car park near the Bull. They smashed two windscreens and overturned two benches near Cobbles Café, breaking the back of one of them.

We ran out and chased them. One got away but we tagged the others. We photographed the pair and emailed the photos to the police. The police sent us a crime scene reference number which should help any insurance claims. One car belonged to golf secretary Brian (who was bloody livid when we told him); the other owner we didn't know so gave the registration number to the police. They said they will try to contact them.

Police asked us to take names and address of the two lads, which we did, although they wouldn't tell us the name of the one who ran off. We heard a car speed off but the CCTV is very poor quality. (NOTE: We must upgrade cameras soonest).

I have copied you all in below with their photos, names and addresses.

Tomasz and I don't think the two we scragged are the ones who attacked Jess. More's the pity!

Police advised us to let them go and they would follow up. Cops were otherwise engaged in Holdean late that night. Familiar story!!?

Charlie

Since the recent Junta meeting, the software on the CCTV had been upgraded so that anyone with the password could access the live feed from the cameras. Remote access was how Charlie first spotted the three lads. Although a step in the right direction, the picture quality was poor. However, an upgrade was imminent.

The lads in the photos looked like two typical hoodlums, both big lads who had cropped hair. One had a hood, which Tomasz had pulled back for the photograph. Charlie was right, though - actually identifying anyone positively from the CCTV was nigh impossible as the picture quality was so poor. From their photos they looked like they were in their late teens and both gave addresses in Holdean. Hoodlum number three was obviously shorter than the others but no distinguishable features were apparent.

Tony emailed everyone back, congratulating Charlie and Tomasz, and expressed the hope that the police would indeed follow up. Just as he pressed 'send' another came in from The Colonel saying that replacement upgraded cameras plus six extra ones were due for installation the following Monday. She also said, '*Superb job, Charlie and Tomasz. You probably saved a lot more damage last night, hopefully in the future too. Well done.*' She continued by saying that the security company upgrading the system would be giving a demonstration of the new cameras and upgraded features in the function room in the Bull at 7:00 p.m. on Monday. She asked that, if possible, all members of the security patrol group, plus any Junta members if they wished, come along. She also said that attendees should bring their lap-tops or other mobile devices along so they could synchronize them to the new system.

Julia came back from posting her letter, excused herself and went straight back to her room for a nap. Tony looked out of his window. A bus was pulling in, ready to pick up its load of day-trippers. The day was sunny and warm and Thistledean was being seen in its finest livery; hopefully local businesses had had a decent day. The café and pub always do well, as do the gift shop and charity shop. Rare is the visitor with at least a few pounds in their pocket who comes and spends nothing. There's usually a little memento of a visit, even if it's returned to a charity shop in a different town a month or two down the road.

Soon, he reflected, there would be another attraction up and running, the historical exhibition. And it was only a week or two till Polly hosted her famous painter friend. Yes, he thought, little Thistledean was doing alright.

He noticed a lady sitting on her own on a bench near the top of High Street, close to the hairdressers. She'd looked up in Tony's direction a couple of times; now she got up and walked quickly down to the café. She went inside and disappeared from view. He made a note to ask Peter about her next time he called in.

His phone pinged. It was Monkey telling him he'd put their names down for a foursomes competition on Saturday, 12:40 start. He texted back in the affirmative and thanked him. He wondered, not for the first time, why the hell his pal put up with him as a partner. He suspected it was a friendship thing, a sort of Black Bull drinking-buddies' loyalty. And foursomes is alternate shots, which means Monkey was going to find himself in some mighty unusual spots after some of Tony's misguided missiles. Perhaps that's all part of the challenge he enjoys. It's certainly fodder for him taking the mickey in the bar afterwards. Whatever, Tony was looking forward to the fresh air and company.

Stranger in Town

A couple of days later, on Saturday, Tony and Julia had come out for some fresh air and they wandered slowly down towards the market. Eight youngsters were out entertaining the shoppers, Thistledean's fledgling brass band. They stopped and sat on a bench to listen for a while. Tony could see Julia was entranced. She smiled. 'I love to see innocent fun like this,' she said. 'What an antidote to all the mess we create for ourselves. There really is nothing to compare with the bright-eyed smile of a child.' She gently bobbed her head in time with the music. It was good to see her relaxed and happy.

As Tony looked round he swore he saw the woman who had scuttered into the café the other day. She was peering between two market stalls but disappeared the instant he looked in her direction. He excused himself and went over to the café where he asked Peter if he remembered a small lady with glasses who called in the other day.

'Now you mention it, I do,' he said. 'She asked me about Julia. She said she thought she recognized Julia as a friend of her parents.'

'I saw her again just now. She's being furtive. Very strange behaviour. I'll ask Julia and see if she's noticed anything.'

'I got your email, by the way. Thanks for that. We've chosen a plumber for the exhibition job. They start in the middle of next week.'

'Good, let's hope we can get it all well established before the tourist season winds down.'

'We're just about ready to go, really. Just waiting for this work and we can lay everything out and get cracking. I've spoken to Felicity who's getting our section of the website up and running.'

Tony gave him a friendly pat on the arm and left.

Julia said she wasn't aware of any lady creeping about so they strolled off and picked up some fresh supplies. She said she fancied a salad for tea if that was OK. It was, so they stocked up on cooked meats, a couple of pies and plenty of greens. Tony said he'd pick up a bottle of wine on his way home from golf. He left Julia watching the musicians back on the bench as he took the shopping home. Keith Parker was patrolling in his yellow gilet, and Peter Lord was also on the prowl. Because, as Traffic Warden, he was constantly out and about, Tony asked him to keep his eye out for anything out of the ordinary.

Peter asked, 'what does out of the ordinary mean.'

Tony thought for a moment. 'I not sure if I'm honest,' he chuckled. 'But you walk around every day amid familiar things, seeing familiar behaviour. When you see something that's unfamiliar, then it's out of the ordinary.'

'That,' he replied, 'is the most confusing set of guidelines I've ever heard.'

They grinned at each other.

'To sum up,' he continued, 'when I see something unfamiliar I need to decide if it's out of the ordinary. If it's serious enough to be called out of the ordinary, I shout 'Keith,' or whoever else is on duty. Then Keith dashes over and arrests the perpetrator.'

'That about sums it up,' Tony said, laughing. 'We have nothing to fear. We're safe in your hands.'

He went home before it got any worse.

* * *

Despite buying a Golf Monthly magazine and reading an article by former Open Champion and golfing legend Nick Faldo about swing tempo, Tony's golf game that Saturday remained at the lower end of the proficiency spectrum; although he later claimed that his tempo was better - a claim questioned in some quarters. Repetition is the cornerstone of consistency for the sportsperson. Not having been blessed with much natural ability, Tony had pondered long and hard to find 'the edge' - a way for him to compete; not at the highest level (or at any level). He devised a numerical system to try and develop a regular rhythm.

During the back-swing it went: ONE, TWO, THREE, pause at the top.

Then the downswing: ONE.

Strike of the ball: WHACK (hopefully!)

Follow-through and poised finish: TWO, THREE.

The idea was to accelerate through the ball and finish with balanced grace. So, with his newly-discovered routine he waggled and settled: one, two three, pause, one, WHACK, two, three.

'FOUR,' yelled Monkey as the ball headed towards a group of unsuspecting victims on the sixteenth green. They ducked en masse. Fortunately the ball cleared them by a few feet before skipping over a drainage ditch and bounding into a hedge.

'I really think it's all to do with tempo,' said Tony, as he crawled into the bush.

'Your ball does seem to be travelling faster, I'll admit,' replied Monkey. 'Now it's just the direction we need to sort out.'

'I appreciate your patience, really I do, Monkey.'

They smiled.

'And I admire your perseverance,' he said. 'And I can see you are trying.'

They were playing foresomes where one on the partnership drives and the other plays the second shot. Next hole the other person drives off. Because Tony had fired their ball into an unplayable spot, Monkey had been forced to take a penalty drop. He played a beautiful shot up onto the distant green. 'Not so bad,' he said. 'If you can just knock that putt in we'll save par.'

As it was, the putt Tony had been left was a sneaky one, down hill across a slight slope. He hit it a fraction too hard, only a fraction, and the ball dribbled lamely off the green into a bunker. 'My, these greens are fast today,' he mumbled.

'Yes,' agreed Monkey. 'Good job we have these bunkers as back-stops.'

The ball had disappeared from view. Simon Pinker, one half of their playing partners, said, 'It's not often you lose a ball while putting.'

Monkey was smiling to himself as he splashed the ball out of the sand back onto the green. By chance Tony holed the putt and they ended up with a six on that hole – one of their better ones. As usual the whole experience was a bit of a curate's egg. Some mediocre, some considerably worse.

'Another triumph of endeavour over ability,' said Monkey as they mounted the slope at the back of the eighteenth green en route to a well-earned pint.

'At least I'm a single-figure ale drinker,' muttered Tony with a healthy moustache of froth on his top lip.

Tolling of the Bells

O n Sunday morning there is a rather nice tradition in Thistledean - the church bells ring and the church-goers, as the nomenclature suggests, go to church. Perhaps twenty-five in number, most are in their seventh decade or older; the cynical may say that the good folks of Thistledean are trying to bank some points and make peace with the Lord before a face-to-face meeting with their saviour. But for most it's a pleasant social gathering with a spiritual overtone.

Sunday morning is when fancy hats appear. There is a mixture. Even late in the year, some ladies wear a gay assortment of colourful headgear adorned with flowers and ribbons. Others, expecting a cold snap later in the morning perhaps, wear fur hats to keep their ears warm (or faux-fur to be socially sensitive). The gents sport trilbies or fedoras, and very smart they all look too. It's a sort of parade where (mostly) senior townsfolk promenade. It's Thistledean's version of the continental promenade where the Cypriots, Italians or the Spanish show off their finery on Sunday mornings up and down the sea-fronts of the Mediterranean.

Actually, for those who live down the bottom of town the café is a welcome pit-stop en route to the church. Mid-point between the tourist office at the bottom of the hill and the chemist at the top, Cobbles is a half-way house, like camp three on Everest. Worshipers stop for a whiff of oxygen before a final push to the summit. The bell-ringers provide a theological backdrop to the serious business of tea-drinking and treat-eating. To be honest there isn't much rhythm to the campanologists' efforts. It's as if each pealer is competing to perform the loudest clang at the most irregular interval, hauling furiously on their ropes while bounding around the lobby below the bell tower, utterly out of control and hanging on for dear life.

A pair of visitors were sitting at a table outside the café, man and wife by all appearances. They were dressed in walking boots and waterproof jackets, despite the day being clear and sunny. Gradually they were joined by a number of smartly attired people. Some stayed on the patio as others went inside. The male visitor asked an elderly lady at a nearby table what the story was regarding the pre-service gathering of the clans. The local woman, wearing a lemon dress and ornate, flowery hat bade them good morning and told them her name was Margaret, as if a formal introduction was required before engaging in conversation. She raised her eyebrows to invite the couple to tell her their names. 'Sue and Michael,' said the lady visitor. 'We're just fueling up before going for a walk.'

Margaret, satisfied that formalities had been completed, explained, 'People are on their way to the church service which starts at 11:00 a.m. By splendid tradition Cobbles Café here opens an hour before the start of the service to enable we churchgoers to have a drink and buttered fruity teacake prior to the uh ...' - she looked around, then whispered - '... ordeal.' Like you, I'm fueling up. Though on a day like this, a nice walk in the countryside is a tempting alternative. Proceedings can go on a bit,' she said, pulling a face. 'Particularly the fortnightly communion, so a bit of fortification is required. One or two even partake of a little spiritual reinforcement.' She leant in closer and whispered again, 'A drop of whiskey perhaps.' She raised her eyebrows conspiratorially and winked.

'Besides which, the church's clunky heating system barely raises the temperature above ambient so patrons require fuel to keep warm. In fact, it's normally a good few degrees below ambient. Hence, Peter's toasted teacakes are perfect nourishment. Even on a pleasant September day like today the stones of the knave are chill. The biggest problem is the vicar tends to ramble on a bit. Nice lass is our Rachel, but if she could just make her point a bit quicker, there would be less achy hips and throbbing bottoms when we finally get released. But it's a lovely place to go, and we're among friends.'

Suitably refueled, the devotees head for the quaint, square-towered

Norman Church that squats up on the hill, fifty yards from behind the chemist. On this occasion, the usual number was swelled by one as Julia had announced over breakfast that she intended to join the congregation for the 11 o'clock service. Tony declined an invitation to join her but as he looked out of his window at around 10.30 he could see her chatting with fellow churchgoers. He was pleased that Julia was making friends independent of him. He spotted Arthur and Nelly Noble arriving on their golf buggy with Mrs. Marshall in the back seat. Arthur bought it from The Country Club when they upgraded their fleet. Unusually it's a four-seater so each Sunday they strap Mrs. Marshall in one of the rear, backward-facing seats and transport her up the hill to church. The old lady claims to be eighty-five but is thought to be a good ten years older. She looked rather forlorn just a few days after bidding farewell to Ivy. Despite her age she invariably walks home after the service, except when there's snow or ice about. It is downhill after all and she always has company on her walk home, someone to keep an eye out. In fact, she doesn't go directly home, she usually calls in The Bull for a 'restorative.'

At 10:50 a.m. Julia clambered into the buggy next to Mrs. Marshall and Arthur drove them all out of sight up the hill to the church. As the rest of the worshipers left the café for the final assault to heaven, from Tony's viewpoint high above they looked like a colourful snake bedecked in a floral coat. The Square was now quiet. Peter's young assistant was clearing debris left by their fleeting visitors and a couple strolled hand-in-hand, idly window-shopping as they made their way down towards the Bull. Ron and Lizzy open at 10:30 a.m. every day during the summer, serving tea and coffee and the occasional late breakfast.

Hello, Goodbye

Tony decided to treat Julia to lunch at the Bull so he phoned through a reservation for 12:30. He must have dozed off because the next thing he knew was the rattling of the key in the door. He'd been asleep for over an hour. Julia came up the slope from the door. Nothing unusual about that. What was unusual was that she had somebody with her; a woman - the one Tony had spotted lurking around the Square. She was small and mousey with round-rimmed steel glasses. Mid-forties, maybe. She stood there and peered at Tony like a frightened wild animal.

He looked at Julia. She looked pale as she leaned on her walking-stick and said, 'Just listen.' Then she pushed the woman gently forward, 'Go on, love,' she said gently. 'Tell him what you told me.'

She just stood there. 'Here,' said Tony, indicating the sofa, 'come and sit down.' He got up and she allowed him to gently lead her by the arm. She was a skinny thing wearing faded blue jeans, an oversize sweatshirt and Nike trainers. But she looked trim and fit.

'Thank you,' she said.

'I'll go and make some tea,' said Julia.

'No, wait,' said the woman. 'Stay, please.' She reached out her hand to Julia who sat beside her on the sofa. Tony wondered what the hell was going on. He went back to his chair near the window and turned it round to face them; he hoped he was far enough away not to be threatening.

The woman looked down at her folded hands in her lap and said, 'My name is Naomi Green. I've kept an awful secret for nearly forty years and it's time to let go.'

She took a shuddering breath. 'I was fostered as a child by a couple called Painter. Sally and Daniel Painter.' I looked over at Julia, who inclined her head and raised her eyebrows. 'I was with them for six or eight months at the age of seven. That was 39 years ago. I have no memory of anything before that time, only that they took me in. I remember them telling me that this home was temporary. I don't think I fully understood but I do remember being very scared. After a time I was sent to live with a couple in Ireland. I was taken over on a ship by a man in a car and we were met there, at the docks, by a man and woman. I remember huge cranes and many large trucks. It was frightening, even in the car, and the three of us drove for what seemed like ages before I remember passing a signpost for Cork. Nobody spoke the whole way, I remember that. I know now of course that Cork is in the south-west. We finally came to a stop at an isolated farmhouse. It was nearly night, grey and foggy. This was my new home. I would be there for ten years. Literally **in** there for ten years, except when I left the house to collect eggs from the chicken run. They used me. All this time, they used and abused me.'

'Jesus Christ,' whispered Tony.

Naomi looked at him. The mousey eyes had an underlying flinty look.

Over the following couple of hours her story emerged, interspersed by cups of tea and a nibble on a biscuit or two.

She had found Julia through a diary, one that Julia had completely forgotten about. It was hidden within a book collection at the Painters' house. They had had floor-to-ceiling bookshelves running most of the way down the hall. Within them, hidden in plain sight on the bottom shelf was a book with a plain blue spine. It had lain undiscovered for about fifteen years. It was a diary Julia had kept for a few months, then abandoned. She had forgotten all about it till Naomi had told her earlier that day. Naomi had met Julia at the church gate, and she'd looked desperate enough for Julia to forego the service. They'd walked round the church and had sat on a low tomb in the graveyard. The diary was long gone but Naomi never forgot it. *'Diary of Julia Carter'* was written on the inside fly-leaf. Towards the end was a section that included a brief account of Julia's trip to the bank in London and her discovery. The entries stopped soon after that with a final one, *'Who the hell am I?'*

Naomi smuggled the diary with her to Ireland, hidden within clothes at the bottom of her hold-all. It stayed with her throughout those awful ten years. Aged seventeen she finally plucked up courage and escaped. She ran away and made it back to England, where she lived on the streets in London for eight years. She eventually got a job as a waitress in a greasy café close to King's Cross station and earned just enough to rent a room. She could only afford it because she ate at the café, sustaining herself on one free meal a day, plus any biscuits or scraps left by the customers. It was a miserable time really, she said, but preferable to what had gone before. She went to night school, discovered she had a natural ability for mathematics, gained an A-level and studied book-keeping. After three years she still worked in the café but also started helping the owner with her books. Then she helped friends of the café owners and was soon making extra money with a collection of regular clients.

But over the years she never forgot Julia. Throughout, memories of her childhood kept ghosting into her present. She knew from the diary that Julia had studied modern languages and guessed that she may have used that to go into academia. She contacted teacher-training establishments and finally struck lucky with Bishop Otter in Chichester. It was a wildly fortunate discovery and one that Naomi considered an omen of sorts. She followed Julia from a distance and finally decided to make contact a week earlier. It was sparked off when she had read a newspaper story of a woman seeking her mother at a convent near Dublin. The story had followed the release of the film called *Philomena*.

'I know it's rather eerie but I followed your footsteps, as a teacher and lecturer, across Europe. Where you lived each time. I shudder to think about it and frankly am rather embarrassed. But ultimately I'm glad I did because when I was ready to contact you, I could. I knew you had retired to Keswick.'

She'd learned from Agnes that Julia was here in Thistledean, and had sworn her to secrecy.

'So here I am,' she said. She was fidgeting with her hands as if wringing out a wet cloth.

Tony looked at Julia and raised his eyebrows. Julia shrugged and pulled a *'you tell me'* face.

'What do you want to do, Naomi? He asked.

She looked at him, then at Julia.

'I have done what I wanted to do,' she said. 'I've shared. For the first time in many years, someone else knows.' And she lowered her head and wept.

* * *

Tony watched as an extraordinary friendship developed. Drawn together through anger, fear and isolation, they were united by hope, a chink of light in the distance. Through shared dismay they formed a bond as powerful as any and through that sharing they felt they would never be alone again. Tony lost a little of Julia that day. She gave a piece of her core to her new friend. He felt Naomi a better custodian than he, someone who could truly understand. He sensed a reluctance from them both to take on any more, but being able to unload, even a little, eased their own burdens. He had done his best but Julia's way forward would now be at the side of a kindred soul and she would be a little less lonely for that.

Naomi booked into the Three Seasons B&B and stayed in town for three days. She and Julia talked and talked, intensely private conversations; a 'Do not disturb' at the door of their cocoon. Then they left. Naomi could drive but had no car. Julia could no longer drive but had the cash, so they bought a car from Dempsey's garage for Naomi to drive. 'Teamwork,' Julia said to me, with a big smile on her face. 'Just like you and me.'

They'd told Tony over dinner the previous evening that they were to go in search of Naomi's parents. Julia understood that calling. The place to start was Uppermill and the Painters, or what was left of their clan. They knew their path would be rough at times, but Tony was sure they would endure; they'd each crossed rocky ground before. The difference this time was that they would have each other.

Julia hugged Tony tight with a tear in her eye. 'I've left my toothbrush,' she said. 'I'll be back.'

'You'd better be.'

'Thank you for everything,' she whispered, and kissed him on the cheek. She held both his hands in hers, looked at him with those beautiful eyes and smiled farewell. He felt strangely abandoned and, God forbid, a little envious of their fledgling friendship. He'd never doubted his affection for Julia but only realized how strong it had become as they drove off, past the church, and turned out of sight. He waved at the empty road and wished them God's speed with a lump in his throat as he thought to himself, 'I hate goodbyes.'

Reflection

As Tony sat in his window seat a few days later and snacked on a bowl of peanuts, he was talking to himself again. 'OK, now what? My dear old friend has staggered off into a bright new morning leaving me with a bowl of nuts. I'm an empty shell ... oh do stop it!'

He considered. Well, what did he do before? Pottered about town making a nuisance of myself, he supposed. Previous pottering can't have been too important because he seamlessly took a month or two out to live a vastly different life. He reflected back on that. A chance meeting and an unlikely friendship that took him to the Lake District and France. And Manchester - let's not forget meeting a high-level politician in England's second city (Birmingham used to second but he preferred the new one), In fact, through her stories, he was taken to Canada and the Himalayas, too. Quite a trek in a short time.

He re-focused and looked at his own reflection in the glass, something he rarely did. Surreal as the whole thing was, he'd actually helped somebody. Julia departed in a better frame of mind than when she arrived - at least she appeared to. He didn't do much; she did all the hard yards. She made the choices, faced whatever came, unravelled and accepted her past. But he did help, he know he did. He'd there for her to lean on. Could she have done it without him? Probably. But he thought that was because he was there that she actually embarked on her quest in the first place. She probably thought of him as her crutch. That didn't sound very nice. Was he her voice of reason? No, that couldn't be right either. He was just there when she needed him, that was all. Perhaps that was enough.

What would he have done without her stumbling into my life, he asked himself? Well, not much. At least not much different, certainly nothing new or exciting. He'd carry on being an extremely minor political figure in a very small pond and an indifferent golfer (to be polite).

Yes, he thought, meeting Julia was his light-bulb moment - confirming that meeting folk and getting to know them is officially interesting. In this case it had also been rewarding. He met people all the time, but it was so often fleeting and superficial. 'Hello. How are things? Kids OK?' That sort of passing-the-time of day stuff, done either out of politesse or because walking round someone would take more effort than saying hello.

So, he considered, what did he do differently on this occasion? Firstly, he didn't ignore her (he couldn't really because he caught her. The alternative was to watch her face-plant onto the footpath). Secondly, he took a genuine interest in her. It helped because she was interesting and engaging and polite and humorous. Not everyone is all of those things. He was a bit transfixed just by looking at her. Actually, she set things in motion by asking him to walk with her. Despite the fact that her reasons were perhaps egocentric, in that she wanted a tow up a steep incline, she asked in a pleasant manner and that all but guaranteed his assistance. Gratifyingly, she seemed to enjoy his company too, so that had given him a boost.

So, he sat there, boosted. Now what? It was drizzling, the first rain for quite a while - it would freshen things up. He checked the calendar to check which day it was - Thursday. He also noted it was now well into September. Blimey, he thought, he really must get into some sort of routine. He decided it was time for a stroll to the Black Bull. Well, it was a start. The pub is Thistledean's social hub, like a French lavoir but not as clean. But somewhere he should be able to understand the language, at least most of it. Actually, it was only *one* of the social hubs; the café would lay claim, too, as would the church and even the Internet discussion page perhaps - at least it was till it was disbanded after being hijacked by out-of-towners and the website manager got sick of constantly editing controversial stuff out. *Select All. Delete!* And it was no more. A hub, electronically wiped.

One positive thing thing he thought he could do was take more interest in the town's security; after all he did promise to get involved. So, with civic intent, he donned his official yellow 'security' gilet and set off down the left-hand (north) side of the Square, looking semi-official and feeling a bit of a plonker, particularly as there were so few people about on this damp day. Paul Broadbent waved from his first floor office, then stood and saluted. Tony saw him laughing so he stuck his tongue out in retaliation. Next door, on the ground floor, Paula had someone under a dryer while her assistant, whose name Tony didn't know, was washing a client's hair as they leant back into a sink. The lights were on in the café and the rain had driven customers inside. The rain was heavier now and it was gloomy grey - autumnal in September, which frankly felt a bit early. There was a crotchety rhythm to the pitter-patters as the rain dripped off the parasols onto the wooden tables and chairs. Peter Lord waved. There was no Sniffy about - he had more sense.

Felicity saw him coming. He was partly recognizable by his yellow gilet, which stood out in the gloom, and partly because his umbrella was bought from her shop. It was a large green one, almost the size of his golfing brolly, with Thistledean printed in gold on each panel. Rather nice, actually.

'Tony,' she called, popping her head out of the door, 'have a look at the website, will you? Let me know what you think. It's still in development but I've put some historical stuff on and a section for Polly's exhibition.'

He promised he would and said well done. They waved goodbyes. Julia might be heading south but, yes, he felt part of things. He couldn't imagine knowing no one.

Thistledean Pies are ever-popular, and a queue of three awaited their turn in Parkers, where Dolores was sharing a story with a customer. She waved at Tony as he walks by.

He passed the charity shop in which a couple of punters were rooting through clothing rails packed with unwanted shirts and pants - unwanted by those that brought them in, that is; for others they are a new beginning and a bargain. Lights shone bright in Frampton's Bakery. Dilys was serving a lady in a light-blue rain coat and they were laughing. Dilys was often laughing. What a nice character she is. The machinery used to mix, knead, and form the dough was idle. Visible through a broad hatch, it waited in half-light in the bakery behind the shop to be re-energized the next morning. Tony always enjoyed his early-morning visits. It was interesting to watch Mike and Dilys beaver away in the early hours, and the smell was always fabulous.

Tony called in Smith's butchers next door and picked up a pound of pork sausage. Archie was also cheerful, as usual, in his red-and-white-striped apron. There was nothing much going on in Tourist Information; a damp day and no coaches in. Mrs. Townsend was busy re-stocking a display stand and Sniffy the beagle was curled up on a big cushion by a radiator, no doubt sleeping off his elevenses. He had to work hard for his treats on rainy days ... or not bother. Perhaps it was best to re-energize by the radiator in preparation for the return of days of plenty.

There were quite a few cars on the car park and Tony wondered why. Turns out there was a meeting - Holdean Horticultural Society invade once a month to have a pie and pea lunch and chat about, well, matters horticultural. There are a dozen of them and everyone reckons they just enjoy a few hours out. They were probably celebrating the rain; it had been dry spell for sure. Finally, Tony arrived at the pub.

'Eh up,' said Monkey as he took a bar stool.

'Hi, Monkey. How's things in the murky world of bricks and mortar?'

'Quiet, thankfully. In fact I'm planning a few days away next week up the east coast of Scotland. A golfing trip. I've got to know a guy who lives in Cupar, Fife. He's a member of the St. Andrews Trust and reckons he can get us a game on the Old Course. There's actually a ballot to get on, but if we're not lucky there's plenty of other places to play. Do you fancy it?'

'It's a nice idea, thanks. But I have enough trouble coping with our little course down here. I don't think my abilities are suited to the challenge of those famous links.'

'You'd get your money's worth, shot for shot, if nothing else.' He smiled. 'And it would be a bit of a laugh for a few days.'

'Let me think about it. It's a nice idea but I'm sure you can find people who can actually play the game.'

'It's a bit of a last-minute thing, so not everyone can get the time off. Tell you what, I'll ask around and if I struggle to find someone I'll give you a nod.'

'OK, that's fair enough.'

To be honest Tony felt chuffed to be asked and quietly hoped Monkey wouldn't find anyone else. He was worried about spoiling his friend's golfing enjoyment, really. But he suspected they would enjoy it, even if they spent time rooting through gorse bushes for errant balls.

Ron came over. 'Did you, er, enjoy your lunch on Sunday, Tony?' he asked. Tony had completely forgotten he'd booked for him and Julia and then been waylaid by Naomi's arrival.

'Oh, blimey! Sorry, Ron. We got side-tracked.'

He smiled. 'Not to worry; we were busy enough.'

Monkey tut-tutted.

'You can shut up as well,' said Tony firmly.

'Anyhow,' continued Ron, 'while you're both here, have a look at this.' He held out a leaflet. 'I'm going to start running some Friday evening entertainment. Nothing serious, just some fun hopefully. It's cracking off with this,' he said, pointing to the flyer, 'a week on Friday. What do you think?'

The act highlighted is:

Des 'n' Norma.

Comedy Operatic Duo.

Tony laughed, 'Great name, at least.'

'They're supposed to be hilarious. Brian saw them at a golf day down in Leeds and put me on to them.'

'Oh, I've just got it!' said Monkey. 'Very witty.' He chuckled. 'Mind you, I'm always wary when something is described as hilarious, because it never is.'

'I know what you mean,' said Ron. 'Newspaper headline-writers have a different take on hilarious to most of us. But these two are supposed to be really good. Hope you'll spread the word for us.'

'Sure, of course. Sounds fun. I'll be here, and Monkey will too. Won't you?' Tony said, looking sternly at him.

'Wouldn't miss it,' replied Monkey, grinning.

'See you've got the Holdean diggers in,' said The Colonel as she strode in.

'Their monthly outing,' said Ron. 'They enjoy their scram but are a bit cautious where drinking my ale is concerned. In fact they never touch a drop, the lot of them. Orange juice is what they have. I get through gallons of the stuff when they're in town.

'What you might term a pith-up then,' laughed Monkey.

'Oh, very good,' said Joan as they all chuckled.

'They're probably even more cautious of drink-driving now we have our security force on the prowl.'

'Well done nabbing those two hooligans the other night, by the way,' Tony said.

'It wasn't down to me, but yes, it's good to get a result.'

'Nothing on a police follow-up, I suppose?' asked Monkey.

'Not yet. Even so, I hope the buggers will think twice about coming back. Keith told me that Charlie was itching to have a go at them. Wanted to give them a good hiding. He's still steamed up about Jess.'

'The irony is,' says Tony, 'is that the coppers would be here in a shot if Charlie walloped someone.'

'Is one of the new cameras going to be focussed on the road into town?' asked Ron.

'Yes, and it's about time too,' replied The Colonel, 'We should have had one there all along. Having said that, at present the quality is so poor that we couldn't read the number plates anyway. Hopefully after Monday it'll be different.'

'Probably have the bloody camera nicked,' said Rob the Tax, who'd crept in unnoticed.

'Watch out, look who's ghosted in,' laughed Monkey. 'It's under-the-radar Rob. Just in time too - it's your round, mate.'

'It's worth a tenner to feel part of such a pleasant, close-knit family,' he said, smiling grimly.

'I'll just have a small Jamesons',' said Tony. 'I need to be compos mentis this afternoon to plan the rest of my life.'

'Not like Monkey,' said Rob. 'He's compost mentis. Quite lucid most of the time, but talks rubbish.'

163

'Right, that'll be a large one then,' said Monkey in revenge.

'Half of what?' asked Rob.

'Anyhow, Fergus, did you actually plan the previous 60 years? If you did can I suggest you get some assistance with the next bit? You might get a recognizable structure instead of six decades of disarray.'

'Five and a half decades, thank you, Monkey my old friend,'

'Don't worry, Rob. I'll not let you down. I'll have a double,' said The Colonel, looking over at Rob who looked furious. Then she said, 'Large coffee, please Ron.'

Rob breathed a sigh of relief but muttered something under his breath.

'Have to nip into Holdean this afternoon ... have a row with the telephone people. I need my wits about me. This phone I've got is bloody useless; it's driving me crackers. Someone's going to get a right ear-full. I tried phoning them from the landline but sat waiting for 20 minutes. Useless.'

'You don't need too much caffeine by the sound of it; you're revved up enough already. I'd have a single if I were you,' said Rob.

'Don't be tight. Large one, Ron. And I'll have a bag of cheese & onion to go with it.'

'Why don't you just have a steak and be done with it?' Rob puffed out his cheeks. 'I only came in for a half; I'm going to have to go to the building society before I go shopping at this rate.'

'Oh do stop whining, Rob! Just think what The Colonel's done for you over the years.'

Rob looked incredulous. 'Bugger all, that's what.'

Tony drank up and left everyone chuckling.

Slate Mill Farm

Tony's apartment was quiet. Unnaturally so. He missed having someone else there. He decided that tomorrow he'd go and find the old man at Slate Mill Farm, Frank Lattimer. He checked the forecast, which looked promising. The rain was due to clear that evening and tomorrow the sun would return. He decided to walk. It was a decent trek, about nine miles past Tony's old farm, but he had all day and could take his time. He reckoned a total of seven hours walking there and back at a steady pace. That would be OK; he could take plenty of breaks. It was a while since he'd had a really good hike and the thought of it energized him.

He got that buzz you get when you have a plan and you're looking forward to something. An almost child-like enthusiasm. The great thing about living where he does is the opportunity to get up into the hills. Within half an hour you can be the only person in the world. He'd need some gear, so he dug out his rucksack and started planning.

He left his apartment at 7:30 a.m. and walked down to Frampton's Bakery where he bought a couple of morning rolls and a wedge of carrot cake. He got some sliced ham and beef from Smith's next door and packed it all in his sack with the bottled water, maps and extra clothing.

There is no direct road from Thistledean east towards his old farm, so if you're driving you have to take a circuitous route and it's nearly seven miles; but walking directly it's only a couple of miles. He soon clambered over the style out of the park and crossed a large meadow. Earlier in the year it would have been bright yellow with rape seed. He'd always hated that name until he read an article recently and discovered that 'rape' is derived from rapum, the

Latin word for turnip! To be honest, he never really trusted the stuff at all. It's grown in ever-increasing quantities worldwide and in its raw unaltered state is very high in erucic acid which can damage the cardiac muscles of animals.

Now we human beings, he thought, are an animal, so are we susceptible? Probably, unless we process the life out of it to get rid of some of the poison. These days we're told that over-processed food is bad for us so, for Tony, rape seed oil's a no-win on more than one count. It's also used as an additive in bio-fuel so it's used to power our cars and fuel our bodies – Tony wasn't sure he liked that combination, and since reading the article he'd tended to stick with olive oil and butter.

The stubble had long been ploughed back into the field; the soil was smooth and uniform as if it had been prepared and sown with a winter crop, wheat perhaps. Despite yesterday's rain, it was pretty dry under foot and it was a pleasant walk. By eight he'd crested the first ridge. He was now out of sight of town and on his own. He was heading into the morning sun, so donned a pair of sunglasses. The farm's new owners were a young couple who rented the property from a man called Freddie Lord, a local landowner, who'd bought the place from Tony. With the extortionate price of land, renting was likely the only way the younger generation could get into farming, unless owners' offspring carried on the business, of course. It's a hard life though, and many youngsters are drawn instead to the bright lights and technological miasma of the modern world, and other people.

Contracts between landlord and tenant vary, the tenant paying either a fixed fee or a profit share, while the landlord provides the land (obviously) and expertise, and possibly machinery as well. Whatever the arrangement, the tenant has respectable security of tenure these days, if they keep to the terms of the agreement. It also keeps fresh ideas and young people in the countryside, something of which Tony is very much in favour.

He crossed another style and began to climb into the hills. He descended and climbed once more before he was able to see the smallholding. After three quarters of an hour, he sat on a hill looking down on the farm. It was tidier than Tony remembered, and it looked like the barn had been re-built. But the most unexpected thing was the huge light-grey shed situated about two hundred yards below the house. It looked like a giant rectangular warehouse. He was about quarter of a mile away, but could see that the lower portion of the long side facing him was open and chickens were scrabbling about in an attached field which has a fence around it. He was looking at a massive new poultry house.

He was just packing his flask away when someone came up behind him.

'Hello,' said the stranger.

'Hello to you, too,' he replied, looking round to see a man of similar age. He was dressed for walking with sturdy boots, multi-pocket trousers and a lightweight jacket over a blue turtle-neck undershirt. He slipped a small day-pack off his back, took out a bottle of Red Bull and had a drink.

'It's a monster, isn't it?' he said, pointing to the metal shed. 'Horrible damn thing.'

'I suppose they call it progress?'

The man just shook his head. 'It ruins the landscape and I'm bloody sure it's not much fun for the poor chickens. Do you realize there will be about ten thousand birds in there? They only keep them a couple of years before they're sold off or killed - after that they're past their best. They're no longer economically viable because they don't lay as often. What a way to treat the poor creatures. It's cheaper to get rid and start again. Cruel, that's what it is.'

He took his baseball cap off and scratched his head through a mop of grey hair.

'You seem well informed.'

'I learned a bit about it when they were building it. Do you know that because the side opens up and the birds have access outdoors, they can call them free range? Inside it's pretty dark but there are timer-controlled lights that create false daylight to prompt the birds to lay. Fully automated too, apart from packing the eggs into boxes. These are the eggs you'll see stacked high in supermarkets.'

He slipped his day-pack onto his back and set off south with a cheery 'cheerio.' He was right, though - it was a monstrosity. Tony remembered a few sheep and milkers, and a scattering of hens foraging around the yard competing for meagre pickings with the odd duck. But someone had dragged the premises into the modern day. He realized it takes new blood and somebody prepared to take a risk to make it something other than a pleasant, if tough, way of life. The older generation had run its course and it was time for new generations of young families.

He carried on north. Within a mile he hit a Water Board service road, one of a series of gravel tracks that crisscross the fells, providing access to hill-top reservoirs and water-courses. He turns right and headed east towards Pike End Reservoir, marked on his map. In times past Tony had come up here with his mates Julian and Jenny. They lived at Grove End Farm a mile and a half from Tony's place. They were his only real childhood friends. Sadly their father, Mr. Stanley, died when Tony was fourteen and his friends moved away with their mother. He'd reached the age where he'd taken a fancy to Jenny, a pretty brunette girl with a giggly laugh. Tony had smiled when he recalled she was a great forager and always fascinated by worms and creepy-crawlies. She'd pick them up and examine them before showing the lads. To be honest he didn't share her enthusiasm and found it difficult to get revved up over a worm. She'd sketch them when she got home. She was a talented artist and had quite a collection.

Julian was a year or two older but Jenny and Tony were a similar age. They were both beginning to blossom as teenagers, becoming aware of each other. His fledgling love life came to a sudden halt when they left. He'd wept as he watched them drive away for the final time. He knew things would never be the same again. Despite attending a mixed school in Holdean, his interest in girls was suspended till he met Ellie ten years later. He'd often wondered where his pals ended up. He hoped that wherever they were, they were happy. He recalled some lovely times scrambling around the hills and swimming in Pike End during the summer. They were fun, innocent days before he had to blend into the real world - a time before alcohol began to savage his father.

He walked to the sound of birdsong and a breeze whispering in the tufty grass. Tony understood all too well that memories are best recalled superficially. Tony's better memories were recent and near the surface, but if he dug too deep or for too long then demons would appear.

He kept on, taking a track north up through a high valley. An hour later he had crested the high point between two rounded hills and was rewarded with a wonderful view. Hills and forest swept away before him, an infinite number of shades of green. The trees, fields, moors, sunlight, haze and shadow were all air-brushed on to an infinite canvas. He stood a while and breathed it in.

He had been over there before, a number of times in fact, but not for a good few years and never before in his mid-fifties. In truth he was glad of the downhill stretch; his heart was thumping a bit. Slate Mill Farm was still seven miles or so distant, still north but slightly off to the east.

He passed through a wood of deciduous trees then crested another hill and entered a pine forest. These were plantation trees that would be cropped when mature. He walked along a firebreak track, the soft crunch of his boots on the gravel and bark mix the only noise. He stopped by a gate blocking a track off to the right and had a cup of tea from his flask. He checked the map and figured he had another mile or so of the forest then a further two before hitting a small road that would take him to Slate Mill. He'd come eight miles from home and was feeling fine.

It was 10.30 a.m. and he was making good time. He was quite high, well over 1,200 feet, so when he exited the forest he found himself faced with moorland, a huge bowl in effect, which he had to cross. Ground birds sprang up before him, singing furiously, complaining at his heavy-footed intrusion. He had to jump the occasional stream, nearly dry after the hot spell, despite the recent rain. When he at last crested the slight incline across the far side of the bowl, he descended about 400 feet and hit the road up to the farm. About a mile to go.

The road ran gently uphill to the farm which was up at the head of a valley enclosed on three sides by hills. He was walking towards a *trough end*, the head of a glacial valley. So many places within striking distance of his childhood home were familiar, but this landscape was new to him. He had definitely never been there before. As he approached the head of the valley he was faced with a bank of evergreen trees. The only evidence of habitation was a windmill that poked up above the tree-line. The wind was still light and the three blades spun lazily. In effect, the only way to spot Slate Mill Farm from any distance would be from above; it was certainly well hidden at ground level.

The road entered the trees then deviated to the right at a slight angle. After thirty yards the road angled left again and only now was the house itself visible. This kink in the road appeared quite deliberate and it meant that anyone approaching would see only trees.

The farmhouse was two-story, stone with a slate roof. It was squat and solid, able to withstand the winter storms that would doubtless whistle through the valley. To the right was a barn, in front of which a few chickens scratched around in the dust. There were no vehicles to be seen; Mr Lattimer must have been out. Ruins of a large building lay off to the left. This was probably the original Slate Mill. In fact, as he moved on he could see evidence of a hillside dug away. Slate extraction? He presumed so. It was long abandoned and largely grass-covered, like a healed scar. Steep grass-covered slopes swept upward on three sides of the valley head.

Then suddenly from behind him, 'And who are you?'

He nearly jumped out of his skin.

'Jesus wept! You surprised me.'

It was a young man he'd seen once or twice in Thistledean.

'I'm Tony.'

'I've seen you in town,' he said. No smile, wary. 'What are you doing here?'

'I've come to visit Frank Lattimer. Is he at home?'

He appraised Tony for a moment. He was a short lad in his late teens, 20 perhaps, with black hair and sharp, shifty eyes. He squinted. 'No, he's out.'

'Oh. Do you have any idea when he'll be back?'

'What do you want him for? He's not keen on trespassers.'

'Trespasser? I don't think so. I met him last week in Thistledean, the day after his wife passed away. I thought I'd walk out and see if he's alright.'

'Aye, well. He's doesn't welcome visitors as a rule.'

'I've come a good way to pay my respects. Could you at least tell me how long he'll be?'

'That's him now.'

Tony couldn't see or hear anything so he just frowned as they stood in silence.

Fifteen seconds passed before he could hear the faint rumble of an engine. Then, a few seconds later, Frank Lattimer's old Land Rover appeared out of the trees.

'You've got good hearing, young man.'

He just stared at Tony. It was quite unsettling and Tony hoped that Frank could rescue him. The Land Rover parked in front of the barn 30 yards away and the old man got out and shuffled across the yard. Flat cap, jacket, string belt, old boots.

'Oh, it's you,' he said. 'What brings you all the way up here?'

'I've just come over to say hello. See if you're OK.'

'Aye,' he says, appraising me. 'Young Sam been looking after you, has he?'

'Well, yes, I suppose he has. I've only been here a few minutes. We were just talking.'

'He's our intruder alarm. Eyes like a hawk, he has.'

'His ears are pretty good too,' I said.

'Yes, I suppose they are. He's young - that helps.' He looked at Tony for a moment. 'You'd better come on up to the house then. You'll have a mug of tea?'

'That would be lovely, thanks.'

A wooden veranda had been added. It spanned the full width of the house and was nearly six feet deep. There were three steps up on to it from the yard. The right-hand end of the veranda dipped away in a gentle slope down to ground level. The ramp looked like a recent addition. To the left of the door were a set of four bamboo chairs round a tile-topped coffee table. An ancient black Labrador opened an eye and thumped her tail on the wooden boards.

'That's why we need young Sam as a look-out.'

Tony bent to stroke the dog, who thumped harder.

'Bella retired a couple of years ago and has hardly moved since. Take a seat,' said the old man, indicating the chairs on the porch. 'I'll make the tea.' He clomped inside.

He sat down and Bella waddled across to sit next to him. Tony tickled her ears, which seemed to be appreciated, He wondered, not for the first time, why he didn't have a dog.

He reflected on the oasis of a property. Hidden by trees in a bowl at the head of a valley, it was peace epitomized. The windmill behind and to the right was old and had a faint squeak, protesting its isolation. Every now and then an eddy of breeze spawned a dust devil that twisted and danced across the yard. Two buzzards drifted across the face of the slope to his left. When things are so quiet, such as then, you tend to notice an unfamiliar sound. First, there was a muted grumble coming the through the trees, then a more harsh chatter as a car crossed the yard. It pulled up close to the steps and a lady in a white uniform got out and walked into the house with a nod of acknowledgment and a slight smile. She looked like a nurse and carried a black leather bag.

Bella thumped the deck and followed the lady with her eyes.

Mr Lattimer emerged carrying a plastic tray with two large mugs, a bowl of sugar and a jug of milk; also a Quality Street chocolate tin from which he'd removed the lid to reveal some digestive biscuits. He put the tray down on the table, 'Here, help yourself.'

Tony added milk to one of the mugs and took a biscuit. 'Thank you.'

They were silent for a few moments before the old man said, 'My lass, Emma. Needs a bit of help just at the minute.' He inclined his head towards the dusty, blue car.

Tony just nodded.

'Emma is Sam's mother. They're staying till she's back on her feet.'

Sam came out of the house, crossed the yard and disappeared into the barn. There was a roar and a moment later a motorcycle sped out. It crossed the yard before being swallowed by the trees, which absorbed the sound almost instantaneously. They were left with silence and a faint haze of dust.

'It's hard for the lad, seeing his mother struggle. What with losing his Nan, too. It's a lot for a youngster to cope with.'

They sat quiet for a while. Tony was intrigued about Sam's mother but, for a change, kept his mouth shut. They finished their drinks and Frank asked if he fancied a turn round the paddock. The paddock turns out to be a large field behind the farm - at least five acres. Basically rectangular, enclosed by a by post and wire fence, three sides ran up into the hillside. There was a rickety old Dutch barn off to the right and just to the right of that a stream ran off the hill with a small channel directing water through a large stone trough. A dozen cows, milkers, peacefully chewed the cud. They were enclosed in an area about a quarter of the paddock, surrounded by a basic tape-style electric fence. There was a faint clicking noise from the batteries powering the fence. They leaned on a gate. Up above the field Tony could see a few sheep dotted around the hillside and the lazy buzzards had been joined by a third.

'He's quite a lad is young Sam,' said Frank Lattimer as he gazed into the distance. 'Found his mother living on the streets in Birmingham. He knew she'd been in some sort of nursing home or halfway house to supposedly recover, but she upped and left. She couldn't stand being closed in and did a runner.' He toyed with a piece of twine that was wrapped round the top of the gate. 'She'd been in the army, fought in Afghanistan. Got herself injured, shot she was, and came home to a welcome nobody deserves. It's a real mess, particularly when they stick their head above the parapet for queen and country. They looked after her physical wounds, at least for a while, but she was left in a terrible state up here,' he said, tapping the side of his head. 'She was ignored; cries on deaf ears. Or they heard her and ignored her. If they can't see it broken or bleeding there's nowt wrong. That seems to be the criteria for looking after their own. Her physical wounds are fixing slowly but her head is all over the place. Fine one minute, the next she goes inside somewhere. Neither me nor the lad can reach her sometimes. For Sam, it's really hard to take. Then there's the dreams. Shouting and screaming. It's terrible.'

They gazed out over his paddock for a while.

'You're having a really difficult time, Mr Lattimer. I'm sorry to hear it.'

'Frank. Call me Frank. Aye, it near broke my Nell's heart to see our lass suffer. Can't tell you how proud she was when Emma joined up, got her uniform and all. Then we heard she was wounded and sent home. We were both frantic. Went to see her in her nursing home. It wasn't too bad to be honest, and she put a brave face on it did Emma. Just for us, I think. We couldn't see what was going on inside. It reassured us a little to think she was being looked after. The next we heard was a phone call from young Sam. He'd been living with his dad after he and Emma had bust up. His dad was jealous, I think, her being successful and all, making something of herself. Couldn't stick it, so he moved out. When Emma went to the Middle East Sam went to live with his dad for a spell. Ryan he's called; he isn't much cop, to be honest. Can't hold down a job for more than a month or two.

'Anyway, Sam went to see his mum one day and she wasn't there. She'd upped and left with another lass. Nobody knew where they'd gone and nobody could find them. I'm not sure how hard they looked but, whatever, Emma had disappeared. Sam found her. She was living on the streets. He asked around and found her under a railway arch wrapped in a filthy duvet. Her friend was dead. Topped herself, I think, reading between the lines. Ended up in the canal, full of pain-killers. Anyhow, as I say, Sam phoned me and I went down there straight away to pick her up. I was in a right panic, I can tell you. I brought her here and that's where she's been for the past year or more.

'My Nell stared to get sick not long after Emma arrived ... 'er liver. What an environment for both of my girls to try and get better. It was hard, I can tell you. In the end I wanted Nell gone, she was so ill. Now she's gone all I can think is that I want her back. Wishing never got anybody anywhere.' He gazed off into the distance again.

Tony got the impression that the distance was somewhere Frank Lattimer spent a good deal of time.

'I don't know if Emma will ever be well again. That's a physiotherapist with her now and she's improving her movement. It's her leg that's the biggest problem. She walks out a bit and we push her in the chair when she's had enough. We have a woman counsellor too. Private, mind. We have to pay. Comes in once a week for an hour. She says Em's making progress, but if she is, it's mighty slow. I want to see her smile again, laugh, you know?' He looked at Tony.

Tony shook his head slowly. 'I'm so sorry to hear of your troubles Mr. L ... Frank. I really don't know what to say.'

'Nowt to say when all's said and done, is there? We just have to get on with it. The alternative isn't an option. Thanks for listening anyway.'

They walked back to the house. Tony said he'd better be setting off back; it was a good three and a half hours' walk. Frank offered to drive him but Tony declined. He would enjoy the trek. The blue car had gone.

'Just a moment, if you will,' said Frank. He went inside. Tony stroked Bella, who thumped her appreciation.

'Come and say hello,' Frank said, beckoning him inside.

Revelation

Tony felt he had little choice but to follow Frank into the house. They turned right, walked through the lounge and entered a room that may once have been a study. It was now Emma's room. A light-haired woman of around forty sat in an upright wingback chair, not dissimilar to the ones in Tony's apartment, but this one somehow looked medical. She looked healthy enough; the only evidence of her physical injuries was a bandage wrapped from the top of her calf up a few inches above her right knee. She wore a yellow T-shirt and a pair of blue shorts. She had blue eyes and mousy hair cut just on her shoulders. She looked physically fit, hard and lean. Within reach to her left was a wheel-chair and leaning against it was a walking stick. On her right was a side table with a glass of water, a book and a pair of glasses. Across the room an orthopaedic bed was neatly made and a triangular grab bar hung down from above.

'Thank you for coming all the way out here. It's very thoughtful of you.'

He walked towards her and shook her out-stretched hand.

'It's not a problem. I enjoyed the walk and I'm glad I came. I'm Tony, by the way.'

'Emma,' she said. 'I wish I could walk with you but that's a little way off, I fear.'

'I'm sure your overall fitness will help you recover.'

'I used to be fit for sure. Not so much now. This damn leg is taking an age to right itself. I do what I can but it's immensely frustrating. But that's enough of that. I want to have a word with you.' She looked up at Frank. 'Dad, will you give us a moment?'

Frank nodded and left, closing the door quietly behind him.

'Grab that chair and sit here,' she instructed, indicating the dining chair against the wall.

He sat before her, slightly to the side. She started without preamble.

'My son has had a difficult time. Sam has seen his dad take off. Then he's had me disappear abroad with the job and come back injured, and recently his grandmother died. He's 19 and an angry young man. He saved my bacon in Birmingham, you know.' She looked him in the eye.

'Yes, Frank mentioned it. It sounds like a very gutsy thing to do.'

'It was. Thoughtful and determined, he is. Wherever he is now I have to focus on the good things.' Tony wasn't quite sure where she was going with this.

'I was in a right old mess, I can tell you,' she went on. 'I'm on the right track now, I think, but it's been a tough time for all of us.'

He nodded.

'But, whatever has happened,' she went on, 'however much we've been through the wringer, it's doesn't excuse what Sam did.'

Tony was nonplussed. He'd no idea what she was referring to. 'I don't follow,' he admitted.

She sighed heavily and looked him in the eye. 'It was Sam who robbed the flower shop.' She shook her head. 'As God is my witness, I had no idea he was capable of anything like that. I couldn't believe it when Dad told me.'

'Jesus ...' Initially, that was the only word Tony could find. Eventually he asked, 'How did you find out?'

'My dad went to town a couple of days ago. He went for a cup of tea – he often does when he's in town. He was asked if he had seen anything suspicious on the night of the fourteenth. A guy in a yellow jacket told him that the flower shop had been burgled and a lady badly injured. My dad explained that we lived quite a way from town and he had never driven out that distance in the evening. It was only when he got home that it dawned on him that Sam had been going out on his bike in the evenings. He found £500 pounds in Sam's bedroom drawer and challenged him. Sam didn't confirm or deny anything; he just ran out of the house and shot off on his motorbike.

177

'He didn't come home that night. We were really worried, I can tell you. He did come back late the next morning and admitted to me what he'd done. Dad feels guilty, not only because of what Sam's done but also for going through his belongings. There's a big trust issue between them now, both ways. I'm not sure that will ever right itself. And of course I'm mortified. I can't believe he did it. He said it was for the money, to help me get better. He knows how expensive things are, physio and counsellor to start with. He was trying to help, yes, but there's his anger and the violence. That's the frightening thing.'

Tony just sat there. He didn't know what to say.

'I don't know how to make it right,' she said. 'What can I do? I can pay the money back of course. But what about the rest of it?'

Tony shook his head slowly and said, 'The logical course of action is to inform the police. That's the dispassionate thing to do, the clinical thing.'

But was the clinical thing really the right thing? Logically, there were no extenuating circumstances where such a serious assault was concerned. But in this case? The flip side was that this family had been through their own hell. They seemed to him a group of people facing up to all sorts of demons not of their own making. Was there a way round this without inflicting anything else on them? He needed to think.

He said, 'It's awful, Emma. All of it. But leave it with me for a day. Let me have a think.'

She sat quietly with her hands in her lap. 'Thank you. You must do what you feel is right. I can't change what has happened; I can only go with whatever happens and try to make amends.'

As he got to the door, she called him back and held out an envelope. 'Here. At least you can return this.'

He nodded and left. He said goodbye to Frank who was aware that they faced a situation that could make life even more uncomfortable for his family. He looked morose. There was no sign of Sam. Tony thanked Frank for the tea and told him he'd be in touch soon.

'I was going to come in and tell you,' he said. 'I'm glad you came.'

Tony nodded, shouldered his rucksack and set off for home. Bella didn't thump her tail as he passed. She knew something was up.

It took him three hours and fifteen minutes to get back. The weather was lovely and on any other day he would have thoroughly enjoyed his time in the woods and on the moors. He didn't want to be gloomy but he wondered how many more times would he experience the space and solitude of such a magical place. It was beautiful and special but relegated to his subconscious as the recent revelation came to the fore. It wasn't even his thing; he'd been thrust into the role of mediator, though he was forced to admit that part of the reason he was involved was because he'd poked his nose into Frank's business. Had it stopped with consoling him over his wife's passing he could have handled that, unpleasant though it was. But he didn't get to choose what came next. His association with Frank had developed and taken on a momentum of its own. It now included his family and it had all turned from unpleasant to horrid. With Julia it was a fun yet fraught interlude - more fraught than fun perhaps - but they both got something out of it. This situation was just plain nasty.

The fact is, though, that even if he hadn't got involved with Frank, the robbery would still have happened. As it was, he was in a position to help. By the time he'd let himself in to his apartment he had the seeds of an idea, but he decided to sleep on it. He jumped in the shower feeling bone weary. Then, while sitting at his kitchen table, aching from head to foot, eating his supper of pork chop, veg and cranberry sauce, his phone pinged. It was Peter reminding him to pop in and have a look at the exhibition room. He replied that he'd be there about 11:00 the next morning. Before that he had a visit to make.

Absolution

The following morning Tony entered Jess' shop at 8.00 am. She smiled her big smile and asked what on earth he was doing up and about three hours earlier than normal. He knew she'd be there. A florist's job is an early morning one, very early three times a week when she'd go to the market to buy fresh flowers. He knew that Saturday was one of Jess' market days so she would have been in Newcastle at 4.30 that morning and back at her shop before six. Large, flat cardboard boxes were piled against a wall, containing the flowers for her displays. There was an almost overpowering yet wonderful perfume.

He asked how she was. 'Fine, thanks, all mended.'

'Great,' he said. Then after a brief pause, 'Jess, I need to talk with you.'

'OK,' she replied warily. She took a large bunch of chrysanthemums from a box and put them on the counter. 'No problem. What can I do for you?'

He paused. 'There's no easy way to say this, Jess, but yesterday I found out the identity of the person who attacked you.'

She turned and stared at him.

'Well?' she asked.

'Here,' he said. 'Come and sit down.'

They sat side by side on an empty wooden bench she used as a display stand.

'He's a young man that lives on a farm about ten miles from here. I really don't know how to explain all this except by just telling you the facts. So please bear with me.'

'OK,' she said.

He told her everything, right back to meeting Frank Lattimer for the first

180

time in the café. He finished lamely, 'I'm very sorry, Jess.'

'Don't be sorry; it's not your fault. Thanks for telling me.'

She got up and stood with her back to him. She was quiet and began to arrange flowers. He said nothing. After a few moments she turned and leaned back on the counter.

'Can you leave it with me? I need to think. Then I need to discuss it with my Mum and Dad and then Charlie.'

Tony thought to himself that Jess might look younger than 23, but she acted wiser. It sounded like her brain was already processing the information. She had a determined look on her face. The first port of call was her Mum and Dad – that was good.

'Sure, Jess. Let me know if I can do anything. I'm always here if you need to talk. Just text or whatever.'

'Thank you,' she said again.

'Oh, here,' he said, passing her the envelope.

She looked inside and just smiled sadly.

'One thing, Jess. While you think about things, just bear in mind that we'll need to deal with the police and our helpers here in town. When all said and done that's perhaps a minor consideration but we need to decide what we say. We can say everything or we can say nothing. Perhaps there's a middle ground? It's for you to tell me; I'll be led by your decision and you have my absolute confidence. But again, if you need to talk about it, I'll be here.'

She walked over and gave Tony a brief hug and a peck on the cheek. 'Thanks,' she said. 'I'll be in touch.'

He left Jess' shop feeling lighter, as if he'd unburdened himself a little. That was tempered with having left Jess with her own burden. He was pretty sure she'd be OK but it would be difficult for a while. It was impossible to say for sure, but he thought he knew what he'd do in her shoes.

* * *

Being Saturday the market was up and running. There were no yellow jackets about but Peter Lord was exercising his pad and pencil, limbering up for another day of blessèd conflict. More slaughter than conflict, actually. It was right versus wrong but if a confrontation got to the point where Peter licked his pencil tip, there was no going back. Incidentally, Tony had come across a story on one of the websites he followed. It concerned scooter rider Karlos Dearman, who, in 2011, was given a ticket as he lay in hospital, recovering from injuries caused by another traffic warden. The 19-year-old ended up in hospital after a careless, off-duty traffic warden in a parked car suddenly opened his door in Sheffield while Karlos was riding along the road. His scooter was parked at the roadside while the guy was carted off in an ambulance. The scooter was ticketed by another warden despite the poor guy being in a hospital bed. Peter had chuckled when he told him. Quick as a flash his devious mind had analysed the situation. 'They were working together - it's obvious. Just another way to get the numbers up.'

Not everyone would have come up with that scenario; you need a scheming thought process and that was one thing Tony didn't have. They exchanged waves. Tony turned and saw Jess leaving her shop. The lights were off and she'd left a note on the door. She walked away down the hill.

Monkey had booked them in to play in the monthly medal at 1.30 p.m. He'd quipped previously that he deserved a medal just for entering with Tony's disparate swing - a swing he'd once described as *'a man attempting to free himself from a number of fast-moving snakes.'* Very unkind, Tony told him - but admitted it was funny, almost Pythonesque. *'That would be a man flapping away a swarm of parrots,'* Monkey countered. Wholly unlikely. Whatever the creature, the analogy was the same, Monkey had told him - where Tony's golf game was concerned he was a man with little apparent control of his limbs.

Tony had a coffee and fruity teacake lavished with butter in the café and scrolled through the news on his phone till he went a bit cross-eyed from the tiny print. He walked down the hill to have a look at the new exhibition room. He was a bit early but the door was ajar, so he went on up.

Access is via a pair of external stone staircases, one at each end of the building. He approached from the left. The door opens on to a small lobby and from there one pushes through double swing doors into the room itself.

182

It's a long room with a vaulted ceiling. Unpainted rafters and trusses are exposed and the spaces between painted white. It's actually the ideal setting for some sort of medieval banquet, where punters get sloshed on mead and throw gnawed bones over their shoulders. There are picture lights down each wall, around ten per side at a quick guess. Below each light is a photograph or painting of one aspect of the town or local area. There's a light down the far end with an empty space below it. The first one on his left actually shows the building that houses Tony's apartment, titled: *Former civic offices, High Street, Thistledean.* In addition to the wall lights there are numerous mini spots strung on steel wires from the rafters that illuminate glass-topped display cases.

One case houses a wonderful model of Thistledean as it was 150 years ago. It's not a great deal different as far as the buildings are concerned but the market is much more extensive and there are many more trees than today. It's a wonderfully realistic model. There are tiny representations of livestock with horse and carts weaving through timber-framed market stalls. All in miniature are caged hens, goats, and other livestock, vegetables, textile, meat and cheese stalls.

Peter came over, inclining his head. 'Well, what do you think of our set-up?'

'Superb,' Tony replied. 'Nothing less. It's much more extensive than I expected.'

'Yes, we've lots of stuff and it's good to see the place brought back to life. In fact we've plenty in storage that we can't display. There's no point stuffing it so full that we overwhelm people. We'll rotate it so folk can come back again and see something fresh.'

'You've worked hard. It's great! Well done.'

He smiled. 'Not just me, it's Barry and the rest of the helpers who've really got stuck in. The heating will be up and running by next weekend so we'll be green for go. The installers, a firm from Holdean, will register it all with Building Control to keep it all kosher. We've had the fire officer in, too, and everything's OK from their perspective. Just need some punters then, eh? Oh, we'll need to upgrade the insurance too. Shouldn't be too much - I'll let you know. Can't have any mishaps with the senior visitors, can we?'

'Indeed not.'

'We've even talked about getting a lift installed from the Tourist Office downstairs, but we'll see. I'm getting some costs as a start so I'll keep you posted.'

Barry Townsend strolled up.

'I heard you. We'll get enough people through, mark my words. There will be plenty of folk sent up from the tourist office down below. My misses will make sure we're not idle up here.'

'There's a spare slot over there for a painting by Betty Millard, Polly's artist,' said Barry, indicating the blank space below one of the picture lights. 'Should be arriving any time – she's sending one up by courier, I believe.'

Tony asked who was going to staff the place.

'There's me and three others who can give a lot of time to it,' said Barry. 'At least till we get everything up and running. And at least another half-dozen folk have promised to come in part time. I think we're covered on that. To be honest, there's not that much needs doing. All the displays are pretty much self-explanatory, just answer a few questions, perhaps, and point folk towards the loo. We'll need a minimum of two staff on at a time for the insurance, but I'm sure we'll be fine.'

'Brilliant job,' said Tony. 'Good on you all!'

He wandered through the room, having a quick look at the displays. He'd have a closer look another time; he had to get organised for his latest golfing catastrophe. He waved goodbye and walked back up the hill to his apartment.

He was up near the pet shop (5:00 p.m.) when Jess called from behind him. She ran up, slightly out of breath. 'Can we talk?'

'Sure,' he said. 'You want to go to your shop or come up to the apartment?'

'Your place, I think.'

'Fine, come on up.'

He made coffee while Jess waited at the kitchen table.

'OK,' he said. 'Shoot.'

She took a sip and looked up.

'I've spoken with everyone. Anyone important, anyway – Mum, Dad and Charlie – and between us we've come to a decision. Basically, we all want someone to pay for what happened but, if what you say is right – and we've no reason to think otherwise – we don't want that family to suffer any more. At the end of the day, no lasting harm was done. Charlie was mighty angry, I can tell you. He was all for going to find them and lynching the lad. But even he calmed down when I told him about his mum.'

She was quiet for a moment and Tony let her pause.

'I've just read a book. It's about abuse within a family over three generations.' She looked over and could see Tony's look of distaste. She smiled. 'Don't worry, it's not as gloomy as it sounds. Actually, the message is one of hope and redemption – and unpleasant though some of it was, it actually taught me a lesson. That's the point of the book, I suppose. In essence, the family's third generation was heading the same way as the previous two until the main character, the second-generation mother, recognized the signs in her son and turned him over to the police. She was grief-stricken and conflicted about turning in her own son but realized that the only way to change the generational cycle of misery was to physically break that chain. It's much more convoluted than that, but that's it in a nutshell. I likened it to the family involved with my attack. If we prosecute this lad, chances are he'd be jailed. What would that do for him? What would it do to the family? Chances are that if he was prosecuted and sent away, which is quite likely, it could tip him over for life. He sounds angry. I'm not surprised to be honest. The world is giving him a really tough time and he's lashing out. I want to try and help him break that cycle.'

Jess sipped her coffee. In a way it was what Tony had expected. He wasn't surprised she'd come to this decision, difficult though it must have been. She was a bright, decent person with no malice in her. Without question, the decision would have been hers. She would have convinced her family to follow her.

'But I'd like to meet them, Tony. Would that be possible?'

'I'm sure it would. Should I phone them now? I have Emma's number here.'

'Yes, please.'

He spoke to Emma who said the sooner the better. Her military training was telling her to sort this out as quickly as possible then move on. He told her that Jess didn't want to take the matter any further. She wanted to draw a line. They arranged that Tony would drive Jess over at five that same afternoon.

He phoned Monkey to cancel the golf. Something's cropped up, he told him. *'Good,'* he'd replied. *'A day off from your off-putting escapades.'* He said he hoped everything was OK. Tony reassured him and said he'd see him soon.

They arrived at Slate Mill Farm just before five. Frank was sitting on the deck with Bella at his feet. The old windmill squeaked in the background and Tony's pair of buzzards was soaring on the evening breeze, looking for carrion. Frank stood and came down the steps to meet them and shook hands with Jess. He nodded and smiled briefly, nervously.

Tony introduced Jess and they exchanged hellos.

They went into the house and turned right into the lounge. Sam stood up from the sofa as they walked in, also looking nervous. Emma was standing before her wheelchair, leaning on a pair of crutches. She walked awkwardly towards them and introduced herself to Jess. 'Thank you,' she said.

Jess nodded and shook the proffered hand. She smiled and said, 'I'm pleased to meet you.'

Emma stood back. Sam took two paces forward. With his head bowed he said, 'I'm sorry, miss. I'm really sorry.' Tears streamed down his cheeks. 'I don't know wha ...' But that was all he managed before he ran out of the house into the yard. He sprinted away and we saw him get swallowed by the trees. I guess he felt safe in there. Nobody could see him, nobody could hear him scream.

Emma sighed and invited Jess and Tony to sit down. Frank, visibly shaken by it all, turned and went to put the kettle on. 'I'll do us some tea.'

Jess immediately broke any tension, any awkwardness. 'You've had an awful time, all of you,' she said, looking at Emma. 'I know that what happened can't be undone, but we can park it. I don't need revenge, I don't want any form of compensation, certainly not money. My reward will be to see you back on your feet, fit and well. In fact, I feel awkward to be in this position, to be able to give something back when you have done so much more with your life than I have. But we are where we are. From my point of view it could have been a lot worse, though I have to say it wasn't pleasant. But there is no reason to make things worse for you guys when you've had a packet already.'

Emma smiled thinly. Tony suspected that she wasn't used to being on the receiving end of any benevolence.

'Right,' Jess chuckled. 'I sort of prepared that little speech and now I've done with it I feel like a total berk. I hope I don't sound patronising. I don't mean to be; I sincerely wish you well.' Jess left the room and went outside. She returned a minute later with a large bunch of flowers from the car which she gave to Emma. 'Here,' she said, 'just to prove that there are some nice things in this world.' Then sternly, 'But these are the last you'll get from me until you come in person to my little shop.' The two women exchanged smiles.

'Thanks,' said Emma. 'I'll do my best to be there soon.'

We left after drinking our tea. 'Say goodbye to Sam for us,' said Jess. 'Wish him well. Tell him he's forgiven.'

We drove the first part of the trip in silence, consumed by our own thoughts.

'I'm very proud of you, Jess,' Tony told her. 'Your family should be, too.'

She patted him on the arm and thanked him for guiding her through it. He smiled and nodded. 'I really had very little to do with anything apart from making the discovery by chance.'

'You gave me the opportunity to do the right thing, Tony,' she said. 'That is definitely not nothing.'

'I think we should tell the yellow-jackets and remaining Junta members where we're up to. They've all done their best to help me so they deserve to know. I'm sure they can be persuaded to keep it between ourselves.'

'I think you're right,' Tony said. 'Again.'

He dropped her at her mum and dad's place on the way into town.

Later that evening while he watched a film on TV, Jess' mum called to thank him for helping her daughter through a difficult time. Once again he demurred but as he put the phone down he was secretly quite pleased to have helped someone. Poking his nose in, he thought to himself, can be beneficial after all.

A short time later, though, he would discover that although some things go well, others can go horribly wrong.

Mrs. Marshall

Tony had Mrs. Marshall on his arm. She had just visited the chemist and, while walking, welcomed the company. 'Yes,' she said, when he had suggested a pit stop at The Bull. 'Splendid idea.' Whether eighty-five or ten years older, she walked freely with an upright gait. 'Though I'm somewhat limited on distance,' she warned.

They joined Robert the Tax who had spread out a broadsheet newspaper on a large round table. 'I'll fold this up again then, shall I?' he said after his peace had been disturbed.

'Quite right, too,' said Mrs. Marshall with mock sincerity.

The two men had pints of Old Peculiar and Mrs. Marshall had her usual Talisker - 'a large one please, with just enough water.'

'Secret to a long life, you know,' she said, holding up her glass.

'What? A tot of whiskey?' asked Rob.

'No, staying alive!' she chortled and they laughed with her.

Tony told her the news about Polly and her excitement about landing Betty Millard, famous artist. Mrs. Marshall shamed Tony by knowing exactly who he was referring to. 'I have a keen interest in art. Actually painted myself in my younger days,' she explained.

'You painted *yourself*, did you?' asked Rob with a smirk. 'Body painting? Self-portrait?'

She smiled. 'You daft so and so! I attended London's School of Art in 1940 for a couple of years. In fact, I was there with Lucian Freud, if you've ever heard of him. Dark soul he was, I might tell you. And a secretive devil. Never did totally trust him. They were an interesting family, though; his father was

189

Sigmund and his brother Clement. An eclectic mix of personalities if ever I saw one.' She smiled at her memories. 'But yes, I remember reading about Betty Millard painting the Belgian royals. Well, well, I look forward to seeing her. I must give Polly a ring and congratulate her.'

'Do you still paint?' asked Tony.

'No, no. If I'm brutally honest, I realized I wasn't much good. I left the stage vacant for those who actually had some talent. I made a far better midwife than painter and have no regrets on that score.'

Mrs. Marshall qualified as a midwife at the beginning of the Second World War and worked till 1982 when she retired at the age of sixty-two. After she retired, she did make the odd 'guest appearance,' as she termed it. When things were busy, or when someone made a special request to have her in attendance, she'd don her uniform and help another child make their entrance.

'Yes,' she mused, 'I have some wonderful memories, particularly of dear Ivy. When I look back now I realize what energy we must have had. You have to remember we both started in the days before the National Health Service. That wasn't born until 1948, to coin a phrase.' She smiled. 'There wasn't a great deal of support for us midwives to begin with. They were hard but wonderful days and I felt privileged to be with so many people at such a crucial time for them.'

'It was extra-special,' she continued, 'because, although we were employed by the county council and paid a fair wage, we'd regularly come home with some lamb chops or other treats - cheese, butter or half a dozen fresh eggs, for example. They were real luxuries after the war. I'm so glad I was a midwife back then. It's so different today.'

'How so?'

'Well,' she said, 'the war mainly, of course, and all that brought with it. But back then we did the very best we could with what we had available and that was enough. Sadly things did go wrong, of course they did, but despite people's grief and anger they ultimately knew we'd done our best. I remember the little souls who perished all too clearly, but I console myself when I see those I helped bring into the world going about their daily business. I was, and still am, very privileged. These days it's all so high-tech and regimented. Of course the midwives still do their very best and they do a wonderful job. In addition, medical and technological advances mean that more sick or premature babies survive, which is wonderful. It just seems to me that the system within which they work is created by people in offices with no real handle on reality. The miracle of birth itself is swamped by bureaucratic flim-flam. And sadly, in today's litigious world, one's best is sometimes not good enough. It's a responsible enough job as it stands, so the extra pressures must be enormous. I'd hate it, I think.'

'In my younger days it was the war that united us. Not just locally, but nationwide too of course. But I think maintaining a sense of community is so important. Particularly these days when so much appears to centre around individual needs. I always thought that if the whole community thrived, individuals found their place within it, and the whole prospered. Conversely, it's not possible to create a real sense of community when people's first thoughts are for themselves. It's about giving, I suppose. I was fortunate to make a good living while adding something to the place I lived. I sincerely believe that giving is more fun than receiving.'

Mrs. Marshall offered to buy a drink but it seemed enough was enough. Tony announced he would go for a walk in the hills. Rob unfurled his newspaper again as Tony piloted Mrs. Marshall to the door and on her way home to her cottage just behind the pub. Tony then collected his walking boots from his apartment and set off past the church. He was heading for Myn Tore, a large hill to the west of Thistledean. He decided to go up the eastern side and down the west, then return home alongside the banks of Myn Tore Reservoir, named after the hill that feeds it. It was about a three-hour trek taken steady, but not too arduous. He enjoyed a walk and wouldn't spoil it by rushing. He reckoned he'd be back around four-thirty. Home for a cuppa and a nap.

Despite it being a Sunday and the weather fair, there were very few other walkers about. He could see a couple near the distant summit but that was all. Tony loved the fact that whichever direction he took from home he was off the beaten track. There were some lovely walks and plenty of peace and quiet. He mused that, for many, a gentle walk was the salve for a busy life. But for him, the walk was the busy part. The rest of his life was a sort of idle potter around town. He smiled to himself. He'd rather have it that way.

More often than not he saw deer on distant slopes. Birds of prey hovered and swooped and sheep grazed on the rich grass. He felt blessed to live in a delightful part of the world.

As he stood on the summit fifty minutes later he could see Keilder Forest (Keilder Water and Forest Park to give it it's Sunday name) up to the north. It shimmered in the afternoon sunshine. If people went for a hike in this area it was more often than not to Keilder. It's a wonderful place to be and a great base from where to explore Northumberland, Hadrian's wall et al. It's a huge area in total - a hundred and fifty-thousand acres or thereabouts. Tony prefers to visit Keilder in winter - there are less hardened tourists about and he prefers the peace and quiet.

Almost due north is Sighty Crag, a hill located in the southern region of Keilder. It's supposedly the hill furthest from a road in England, the remotest from civilisation. He smiled to himself at this dramatic factoid. Mind you, Monkey John told him that piece of information so perhaps he should verify it! Actually, his friend did offer him a further bit of hilly education - he told him about Marilyns. Tony thought he was having his leg pulled at first, but he checked and sure enough a Marilyn is a hill, specifically in the British Isles, with a minimum height of 150 metres. The name was coined to contrast the Scottish term Munro which is a hill or mountain in Scotland of minimum 3,000 feet. Apparently there are something over fifteen hundred Marilyns in the British Isles and he was standing on one of them.

He descended the west ridge meeting not a soul and headed back along the banks of the reservoir. He walked along the north shore along a track covered in wood chippings, his hushed footsteps muted further by the thick pine woods around ten metres to his left. A lone canoeist was paddling west on the flat calm water; his craft was red-hulled and he was propelling himself along with a bright yellow paddle. He was heading towards the afternoon sun, leaving an expanding 'V' in his wake. 'Boy,' Tony reflected, 'what a wonderful way to spend an afternoon ...'

The canoeist rested his paddle across his lap and waved. Tony acknowledged as the ripples from the canoeist's wake made the gentlest sigh as they landed on the rocky shore.

Tony looked out over the water as he sat on a wooden bench to have a breather and take in the view. Apart from the canoeist, it felt like there was nobody else in the world.

Often when he found a peaceful spot such as that, he thought of the words of Kurt Vonnegut, who said, *'Enjoy the little things, because one day you'll look back and realize they were the big things.'*

Right there, sitting on the bench, Tony knew he was experiencing one of those little big things. Then, for some reason, he thought of his ex-wife, Ellie, who'd disappeared about five years ago. Not disappeared in the sense of anything sinister – she just up and left, taking Bernard, her Shih Tzu, with her. Awful bloody dog, a real yapper – but Tony did miss Ellie initially, at least her cooking. He remembered he had the feeling she needed to *'re-discover'* herself and was weary of the muddy life on the farm. In a way he couldn't blame her.

He'd only moved off the farm relatively recently. It was getting a bit of a struggle and, despite enjoying his own company, it did get rather lonely at times; particularly over winter. He now enjoyed being at the heart of things. It was probably just coincidence that Ellie had just won a tidy sum on the National Lottery a month before. Tony reckoned she was beguiled by those TV programmes about living in the sun. She'd probably gone south to Manchester, or some such place. He invented that little nugget with a bitterness that surprised him. Monkey once asked him if she would ever come back. 'No,' he'd replied, 'not if I have anything to do with it.' He realized that ultimately he was better off alone. He had plenty of friends and acquaintances in town and he was quite happy. The end of Ellie signaled the end of part one. That's how he looked at it. Part two, now well underway, was rather enjoyable. 'Just look at today,' he thought to himself. *'I do what I like whenever it pleases me. How about that?'* That, he concluded, was just fine.

A Bad Dream

I t was now the third week in October, and the world had lost a little lustre. The days were cooler and the distant fells had muted to light brown. Every day the morning sun, when it put in an appearance at all, crept over the hills a little further to the south each day. There was even a whisper of Christmas as cards appeared in the newsagent. The last Sunday in the month would see the clocks change and winter would be officially unwelcome.

Wonderful little things can become big important things, sometimes nasty little things that become big important things. When you hear something unexpected and shocking, the expression often employed is, 'it makes your blood run cold.' How accurate is that? Well, when you analyse it, some say not at all. In fact, it's quite the opposite. Instead, it's like the opening of an oven door or a furnace. There's a blast of heat accompanied by an adrenaline rush. A flush of panic as our hearts hammer. No, it's definitely not cold.

Tony was having breakfast when his phone rang. It was Inspector Birch asking if he could come and have a word. Certainly, said Tony. He expected to be asked a few follow-up questions about Julia's break-in and poor Nick's attack. He told Tony he would be there in an hour. So, he showered and did some tidying up.

He buzzed the Inspector in and Tony could tell by his expression when he opened his apartment door that something was amiss. He bid him enter and offered a cup of tea or coffee. 'Neither, thank you.' He was accompanied by Sergeant Appleby with whom Tony had had a bit of a falling out in Keswick, so their greeting was cool. She didn't decline a drink because she wasn't offered one.

They sat round the kitchen table and Tony asked what he could help with.

Inspector Birch asked, 'Have you heard from Julia Carter, Mr. Mason?'

'Not recently, no. She stayed with me here but left last about three weeks ago. A Saturday, I think. What's this about?'

'She hasn't contacted you since then?'

'No. What's going on?'

He motioned to his colleague who passed over a handbag.

'Do you recognize this, Mr. Mason?'

'I'm not sure. Possibly. I suppose it could be Julia's, if that's what you're asking me. I can't be sure, though. How did you come by it?'

'Have you by any chance taken any road trips recently, Mr. Mason?'

'I've travelled locally, if that's what you mean.'

'You haven't had cause to travel on the M6 through Cumbria?'

'Not recently, no. The last time was when we last met in Keswick. Getting on for a month ago, I think. Tell me what's going on.'

'Ms. Carter is missing, Mr. Mason. Her handbag, this one,' - holding it up in case he was in any doubt - 'was found at Exelby Services on the M6.'

That was the point when his blood didn't run cold. The inspector ploughed on. 'We got the registration of the vehicle from your garage here when we started looking into Ms. Carter's disappearance. A search flagged it up at the service station. We saw Ms. Carter in the company of another woman on the station's CCTV. We saw them go into the building. When they exited, the drove across the car park where the other woman appeared to throw something over the boundary hedge. We sent local officers to search and they found the bag. All this was about a week after they left here. This was found inside.' Tony held his hand out and his sergeant passed him a clear plastic bag. Inside it he could see a small piece of paper with *'Tony. Courage'* written in black felt tip. Inspector Birch said nothing, waiting for Tony's reaction. If he been expecting him to hold his hand up and confess to something, the police officer was disappointed. They just stared at each other. One angry, the other scared.

'Does that mean anything to you? What does she mean by that?'

He shook his head. 'I don't know.'

He stared at Tony in silence. A silence Tony eventually filled.

'Really, I've no idea.'

'We are concerned for her safety,' the Inspector said finally. 'If you know anything about her present whereabouts, I'd ask you to tell me immediately.'

His hot flush had settled but he was left with a heart rate that threatened to burst the damn thing out of his chest.

'I've no idea,' he managed. 'Really, I have not seen nor heard from her for well over a fortnight. Why would I not tell you if I knew?' The inspector held his hand out again and Sergeant Appleby passed him another photograph, this one blown up to A4 size. It was a choreographed double act where the junior officer kept producing white rabbits on demand.

'This image is from CCTV footage taken at the Exelby Service Station.' As he said it he was looking at the photo. 'This person was seen by a witness with Ms. Carter on the day we're presuming she disappeared.'

He passed over the photograph. As Tony had assumed, it was Naomi. His heart jumped again.

'Do you know her?'

'Yes. Well, I don't know her really, but she did come here to my apartment with Julia.'

'And what name did she go by and how did Julia know her?'

'She's called Naomi Green. She and Julia met ... well ... outside the church, I think. Then they came here and she told me her story.'

'And what was that?'

Tony sighed. 'About her being fostered and her life somehow mirroring and intertwining with Julia's. It was a sad tale, equally as miserable as Julia's. Worse even.'

The Inspector looked at his colleague who pursed her lips.

'I have to tell you, Mr. Mason, that this woman is a very nasty piece of work. She has been on the police radar, here and abroad, for at least fifteen years in connection with a number of crimes, including extortion, murder, you name it, across Europe.'

Tony sat there in disbelief.

'So why the hell are you asking me if I've got anything to do with it when you know the answer perfectly well?'

The inspector ignored him. 'You know her as,' he looked at his notes, 'Naomi Green. In fact, she is German and her real name is Eva Mayer. At least we presume it is – she has more aliases than enough. She was formerly high up in the German intelligence service, the BND, or Bundesnachrichtendienst. She left after she was suspected of selling state secrets, military stuff she had high-level access to. Disappeared rather than left. She knew she was compromised so buried herself in one of the identities she had created for herself. That was fifteen years ago, since when she's cropped up all over the place causing carnage. She's worked for a number of individuals and organisations – basically anyone who can pay her enough. She is highly trained, utterly unscrupulous and, needless to say, extremely dangerous. We're working on the assumption that her paymasters on this occasion are involved with people-smuggling. It's big business and very lucrative. I regret to say that Ms. Carter may have tangentially touched some raw nerves while doing her own looking. We strongly suspect she was responsible for the attack on Nick Saxleby in Keswick. That will be a murder charge if we ever find her. More immediately and alarmingly, we fear that Julia Carter may be Eva Mayer's most recent victim.'

'This note with your name on it. That's personal. What's it about?' Sergeant Appleby spoke for the first time.

'I've no idea. Really. It could be some sort of cry for help or it could have been written at another time altogether. I just don't know.'

He stared at the photograph. 'She was here.' he whispered. 'In my house.' Inspector Birch nodded.

'I saw the woman a couple of times in town, in the days before she and Julia met. That was slightly peculiar, but nothing really untoward.' He shook his head. 'I can't believe she wasn't exactly what she purported to be,' I said.

'Which was what?'

'A woman in distress. Her awful childhood, awful life to this point.'

'She is known to play the long game,' said the inspector. 'She plays her part. She is very good. Very convincing. She is well rehearsed and patient.

Not least because of her diminutive stature. It has fooled many bet ... many people.'

'You were about to say better than me, weren't you? Well, let me tell you, the story she told was utterly plausible. Julia fell for it. I fell for it. And they drove away together. I let them. I enabled it, for Christ's sake!'

Tony was quiet for a moment. He stared at Sergeant Appleby. 'She's not just better than me is she? Not if she's been giving you lot the runaround for fifteen years. So don't go making insinuations against me when it's you who have allowed her free reign.'

'OK, calm down Mr Mason. We're doing everything we can to find Ms Carter.'

'Well go and try somewhere else, because she's not here.' He sighed. 'She told us such specific things. Julia's diary that she'd found, for example. How the hell did she know about that if it was all make-believe? All that stuff about Ireland?'

'Mayer is certainly no fool. She combines lies with bits of truths and half-truths. The Painter's house was broken into last January. Their cat was killed. It's neck broken. We presume that is when she found the diary. She's ruthless and very thorough.'

Tony shook his head in frustration. He felt sick and useless. More anger would come later. He wasn't of a mind to forgive himself; just for the moment he needed to use the self-pity to punish himself.

* * *

A week went by. Each day Tony woke up his first thought was of the mess he'd created and his heart thumped. Finally, he got angry with 'that bloody woman.' He knew deep down he wasn't to blame, at least totally. How the hell could he have been so easily duped Throughout this time there was one tiny ray of light, like a single bright planet shining in a black sky. Hard as he looked, he couldn't see Julia actually blaming him for anything. He tried to envisage a glare or an accusatory frown. But all he could see was that sparkle. That damned sparkle. Amazing and mocking at the same time. But what it came down to was this: if he hadn't poked his nose in, she would be alright.

He had to get out of this. Think. Would Julia have gone looking for her family without him being around? Possibly, yes. Their meeting was the catalyst but it's likely she would have searched anyway, just from a different starting point. Would somebody else have dropped everything and gone to France to help her out? No idea, but Tony didn't have anything to drop so he was able to go. In fact, he wanted to go and he knew she appreciated it.

So, he tried to think it through. Who was this Naomi / Eva woman working for? Or working with? Birch mentioned people smuggling and the most obvious was the highest profile person - the politician, Marie Batiste. But they'd ruled her out because she had too much to lose and frankly she was very credible when they'd met her. Plus, as smart as she was, Marie Batiste couldn't have been in two places at the same time. Marie Batiste's star was on the wax; she wouldn't risk damaging her ambitions.

There was the organisation 1919, with whom she had familial links. Could 1919 be behind it, unbeknownst to her? The only reason for them to be involved was that they might fear exposure if they were still active. Was it all tied in with people trafficking? It was probably very lucrative and potentially thousands of targets from the world's conflict zones. He did a little research and there was a market for people wanting to take on anonymous children, for reasons most of which were little short of barbaric. They included the sex industry, slave labour, child begging, domestic servitude, child soldiers, even organ removal. Just in the UK there were estimated to be well in excess of 10,000 victims of trafficking a year, around a third of them children under 18. And the UK was a minor player in the worldwide racket. With huge sums of money involved, the crooks had a big incentive to protect their 'business.' Had Julia and Tony inadvertently poked a sleeping snake?

Julia's mother was spirited away to England, probably. And possibly by the group 1919, or at least somebody affiliated with it. That was to protect the reputation of Julia's alleged father. The trail then went cold apart from the brief note and photograph found among family keepsakes. He made a note to chase that up. So, did Julia's mother inadvertently become entangled in the whole mess?

Then there was Julia's 'uncle.' Duncan was undoubtedly a very unpleasant character but did he have links that stretch to the present? He'd be long gone but did he leave an organisation behind? He was involved with, at the very least, manipulating the adoption system. Then there were the Painters in Uppermill. Julia and Eva (Tony had to start thinking of her as Eva from now on) said they were setting off in search of answers, and first call was to be the Painters. But that would have been part of Eva's great con. All that stuff about being shipped to Ireland would have been made up, total guff.

So, he basically had to ignore anything Eva had said. He couldn't ignore her completely, of course, because the deceitful mare had taken his friend. 'Taken.' What did that mean? Abducted, kidnapped, killed? He was getting himself worked up and realized he wouldn't find any answers dwelling on what might be. The police had all this information and if they couldn't get to the bottom of it what chance did he have? Did Tony have what they didn't? He couldn't think what.

He looked out over the rooftops and tried to draw some inspiration from his beloved hills. Tony always felt to be at his best when doing something positive, however much merit it turned out to have. It's certainly fair to say that he was at his worst when sitting around working himself into a stew, like he was now.

He called Julia's phone, which unsurprisingly went straight to 'leave a message,' which he did. He rang the police to ask if there had been any news. No. Also not surprising. Both hopeful stabs in the dark. One thing that disturbed him as much as anything was that Julia would leave him a message if she could. A phone call, text, even a letter or note. The only thing was the scrap of paper the police found in her handbag - with his name. Presumably a cry for help - or it was a way of saying that she was OK? At least she was when she wrote it. Unless somebody else wrote it!

Half past five. Bugger it! He opened a bottle of Merlot.

A Peculiar Story

T ony has parked his troubles with Julia. It had taken a concerted effort to get out, but today was an important day. Betty Millard, star artist, was in town. Polly, painter and potter, had been a bundle of nerves recently while planning her exhibition, but the day had finally dawned. Attention on her had been mitigated somewhat because her show coincided with the opening of the town's exhibition in 'The Long Room'.

There was a bouncy castle centre stage in the car park, surrounded by market stalls. The historical exhibition overlooked the town square, giving a nod to the modern world.

'You watch,' said Monkey, 'our parking führer will have a ticket on the bouncy castle by close of play. He's almost slavering at the mouth with all these strange cars in town. Look at him leaning on that tree all nonchalant; he doesn't know whose day to ruin first.'

It was a busy Saturday and thankfully the weather was kind. Dry but overcast - a decent early October day. Walking past Polly's gallery, Tony could see it was busy so he wandered down towards the exhibition. The Bull was doing good morning coffee trade and dear old Sniffy looked to be setting off on his daily round - it was going to be a profitable day. Tony could see the marauding mutt sloping off in the direction of the café. He envisaged him practicing his hangdog, doe-eyed expression, perfected over the years to win maximum treats.

The exhibition looked very classy. The display cabinets were brightly lit by their overhead spots and the features and paintings round the walls individually lit. There was a couple having their photo taken in front of the painting Betty Millard had donated to the town. Though renowned for her portraits, she had painted a view of Thistledean. It was the perspective Tony has when looking back as he walks towards his old house - as if looking from afar over the roof of the building he's currently in. In the painting, he could pick out the top two-thirds of the market square and see his flat above the chemist. Also, the church peeping out, top right. It was really good actually, and made him stop and pause a moment; which he supposed was the idea.

Barry Townsend was standing beside a glass-topped wooden display case housing the scale model of the market square. He was beaming and fielding visitors' questions with wry humour and enthusiasm. He was also handing out scrolls - buff-coloured rolls tied with a red ribbon. Felicity Winstay, local philosopher and gift shop proprietress, now writer too, had penned an introduction to Thistledean. It was something to hand out to visitors as a gift and keepsake. Damn good it is, too. It reads thus:

Thistledean - An introduction and a peculiar story
By Felicity Winstay

Old Mr. Porter, the chap who looked after our communal gardens until his retirement, decided to cheer somebody up by sending them an anonymous bunch of flowers. Being springtime ... but wait, we're getting ahead of ourselves. We need a bit of background here. So, let's start with who we are and where we are ...

Well, our town is called Thistledean, situated way up in the north of England. It's also a place suspended in time. Somewhere in the distant past it missed the omnibus to the future. It sits obstinately in a cocoon at the foot of the Northumbrian Fells. As the world spins manically by outside, Thistledean is quiet and still, a liniment for the strain of modern life, a balm to an itch. To use an oblique analogy, Thistledean is a bit like Aunty Marion's old biscuit tin, the one that makes a periodic appearance when she wants to impress visitors. On the lid is a fading picture of an idyllic thatched cottage framed by a tartan border. It's not easy to get the lid off these days as there's a touch of rust about, made more difficult because Aunty's fingers are a bit rheumatic. But with some huffing and puffing she manages.

The interior is that metallic gold colour that looks reassuringly expensive. Quite suitable for the high-quality, buttery shortbread from Scotland's capital, some 75 miles to the north. The original contents have long gone but the tin was too good to throw away, so has been re-employed. It has aged gracefully, slowly maturing into an object of familial familiarity.

Unfortunately, the (non-chocolate) digestives on offer today have less appeal since Aunty declared that she wanted her ashes interred in her tin after her demise. We chuckled at that and pointed out that a) if we put her in the tin prior to her demise there may be questions asked and b) she was being rather morbid and c) such comments could easily prejudice today's enjoyment of our afternoon tea.

Over time her comments have augmented the legacy of the tin and added another brief footnote to its history. Sadly, in years to come people won't remember the countless happy tea parties; instead they'll focus on Aunty's ashes. Yes, our town is a bit like Aunty's tin. At first glance it looks great but it's weathered around the edges and contains some relics. Some of our residents have grown tatty with their town, as if they've wrapped it round themselves like a threadbare old dressing gown. Both tin and town were conceived somewhere back in the mists; both have a certain allure but both could perhaps do with an overhaul.

A cobbled, elongated rectangle (that we perversely call a Square!) defines the centre of our town. Two-storey buildings look on, hunched over, peering malevolently at goings-on below. The thrice-weekly market is scrutinized, as are regular busloads of visitors that come and soak in our ancient charm for a spell.

One day, in the café that overlooks the Square, a lady was sitting beneath a parasol enjoying a latte and a lump of homemade fruit cake. Life rumbled by on the nearby cobbles as she witnessed a sequence of events that may be considered unusual elsewhere, but not here. A brown and white, floppy-eared beagle dog sat by a visitor and politely asked for a morsel of cake. The man, probably a dogist, nudged the mutt away with the toe of his boot. The hound looked at the café owner and in the blink of an eye the man with the offending boot was ordered to leave. He was barred from the café for life. Despite protestations of innocence, the man was punished for assaulting our town's mascot. Sure, he was hard done to, but mess with our town's treasures at your peril.

So beloved and influential was our beagle that the café's menu had a doggy theme for a while. It offered a Great Dane-ish (XL bacon sandwich), an Earl Greyhound (a quick cup of tea) and a LeonBerger (in-house, all-in, quarter-pounder). Thankfully the Shih Tzu Surprise was discontinued – in fact the entire menu was re-hashed when trends 'vegetarianised' and meat took more of a back seat – or rump, as it were.

Just a few feet from where the lady sits, a golf buggy with a flat tyre is being issued with a parking ticket. It seems a bit unfair really but, according to our local traffic officer, rules are rules and illegally parked vehicles will be treated as equals, whatever their provenance. 'The fact that this one,' pointed out our warden, 'is owned by an old duffer who can barely walk past the extent of his own stomach is incidental. It is contravening highway regulations and will be ticketed.' A man not to be messed with is Peter.

During the writing of the ticket, the owner of the buggy staggers up with a jack and spare tyre and commences a furious discussion with the warden. The exchange is witnessed by the lady in the café and recorded for posterity by a tsunami of Japanese photographers who are flooding by. The oriental snappers are in turn under the watchful eye of a fierce-looking lady wearing a yellow road-mender's waistcoat. She's known as 'The Colonel' and is a particularly intimidating member of our local security patrol force.

There you go - very briefly, that's a snapshot of our town. Where incidentally that mystery I mentioned earlier unfolded a couple of years ago. Here, let's start again ...

Old Mr. Porter, the chap who looked after our communal gardens until his retirement, decided to cheer somebody up by sending them an anonymous bunch of flowers. Being springtime, he picked a lovely bunch of dewy daffodils. He chose two letters of the alphabet at random - 'B' and 'G', opened the phone book to the Gs and took a random stab with a pin. He landed on the name Garrity. By chance there was only one Garrity with a 'B' first name - Garrity, B.L. 12 Park View, Thistledean. There was no reply to his knock so he left the flowers on the front step.

He walked by the following day and the flowers were gone so he allowed himself a smile. Two weeks went by and a letter arrived at Mr Porter's home address, post-marked from Trondheim, Norway.

Dear Mr Porter
Thank you for my flowers. They are beautiful and remind me of home in times gone by.

The letter was unsigned, no date, no return address. Just that distant post-mark. Perplexed, Mr Porter wrote a short note which he left in a water-proof plastic bag on the doorstep of 12, Park View. It read:

To whoever it may concern.
Thank you for your letter.
Who are you? Are you really in Trondheim? If so, why?
Finally, I left the flowers anonymously. How did you know my name and address? How did you know to thank me for the flowers?
Yours faithfully
George Porter
Gardener, Retd.

A further ten days went by before another letter arrived, also post-marked Trondheim.

Dear Mr Porter.

I lived in Thistledean many years ago. I was a nurse during the war and sent to Norway. The field hospital where I was working took a direct hit, so here I remain. It's quiet now, too quiet. And it's lonely. Your lovely flowers adorn my grave.
  How did I find you?
  Oh, just a random stab with a pin in the telephone directory ...

Enjoy your visit to Thistledean. Please come back.
  Felicity Winstay

Tony wandered round the market and bought himself a treat to accompany his evening meal - his favourite mild, creamy Lancashire cheese. He popped his head into the gallery and caught Polly's eye. She waved and beamed and pointed to the rear of the room. Someone was sitting under a spotlight while Betty Millard sketched a charcoal portrait. He gave her a thumbs-up from the doorway.

Do what he may, his thoughts kept drifting to Julia. He had to consciously think of other things to improve his mood. But without doubt he was lifted by the success of the day. There was enough misery in the world, and he got a genuine buzz to see people happy. He decided that tomorrow he, too, would be happy. For a start, he would go for a good walk.

Pride and Pain

He was up early, ready to go for his walk. He turned on his laptop to check for messages when his heart skipped a beat.

By Email: PS E.M. Appleby, Hertfordshire Constabulary, Welwyn Garden City

FAO Tony Mason

To inform you that Eva Mayer was captured three days ago and arrested in a hotel room in Reims, northern France.

Police received a call from an unspecified female which led to Mayer's arrest.

During the call, the name Naomi Green was repeated a number of times before the caller fell silent. However, the call remaining connected, and as a result police were able to track the location of the phone. The phone was subsequently discovered to belong to Mayer herself.

The policeman who took the call remembered Europe-wide alerts regarding Eva Mayer, including her various aliases.

Mayer was found unconscious in her room and was taken to hospital. The cause has not been made public. She has subsequently been released from hospital and is in police custody.

I am pleased to report that Ms. Carter was found in the same room in the adjacent twin bed. She had been secured to the bed frame by means of handcuffs and a length of steel cable. She was dehydrated and confused. But she is alive. She was taken to hospital where her condition is described as poorly but stable. The exact location of the hospital is being withheld for security reasons.

Mr. Mason, I know you. Your inclination will be to charge to France to 'help' your friend. Please do not. She is in a secure private hospital. Secure and private for a reason! Leave this to the authorities. Ms. Carter will be interviewed by specialist officers and her mental and physical heath carefully assessed.

I assure you she is receiving the best possible care and I will update you on her condition as soon as possible. Meanwhile I took the liberty of asking the hospital pass on your best wishes. If you are in any doubt about the severity of the situation and potential danger she may be in, bear in mind how easily Ms. Carter was abducted.

It appears Ms Carter unwittingly got too close to the wrong people. The day following Mayer's arrest, a report appeared in the French regional newspaper, L'Union. A transcript of extracts from the article is attached.

Yours faithfully

Extract from the journal L'Union

"Marie Batiste, charismatic leader of the French Communist Party, was arrested in Paris last night. She was taken into custody where she is being held on unspecified charges. The move marks a devastating fall from grace for the brightest star in French politics. The party she leads was expected to make huge gains in forthcoming elections.

In a simultaneous operation, her father George Batiste was arrested at his home in Saint Quentin, Hauts-de-France. The nature of the charges against him are also unknown.

Very few details have emerged, although their timing is political dynamite with elections due in three weeks. One claim to have emerged suggests that the arrests centre on George Batiste's membership of the radical group '1919' (Dix neuf dix *neuf). It is well documented that Mr Batiste's father, Jean-Claude, was a founding member of the nationalist organisation. For many years 1919 was implicated in acts of aggression, some of which were even termed 'acts of terror' by certain commentators. However, very little, if anything, has ever been proven, and the group has even achieved near cult status in some quarters.*

1919 was formed at the end of the Great War following the signing of the Treaty of Versailles when a number of influential individuals believed the agreement to be largely ineffectual, leaving France vulnerable to future incursion. The organisation decided to take matters into their own hands.

In a further twist, there have been allegations of historic links between 1919 and the French Communist Party.

L'Union asks: Is it mere coincidence that the PCF (Parti Communiste Français) was formed in 1920, just one year after 1919?"

This was one of the few days Tony wished he had a partner. News like this, received out of the blue, was suffocating and needed to be shared. Relief mixed with concern, but an overwhelming desire to protect. To be frank, he never expected her to be alive, not the way the police portrayed her abductor.

Questions buzzed around in his head. Mayer unconscious, but how? The phone call to the police. Where had they been these past weeks? He decided he needed to let them know that he would look after his friend, financially and emotionally. He would do whatever was necessary. And he knew where she could go, at least in the short term.

He replied to Appleby's email. Be polite, he thought to himself ...

FAO Sergeant Appleby

Thank you so much for the information.

I can't tell you what a relief it is to hear she is alive.

I will respect your wishes and wait to hear from you. I will not interfere. As you would probably say yourself, I've done enough damage already.

I have a suggestion for somewhere for Julia to go when she is strong enough to travel.

I understand the sensitive nature of the situation, so suggest that the best way is for me to call you direct. (A face-to-face meeting is difficult due to the distance involved.) Please let me know.

Thank you
  Tony Mason

Twenty minutes later, after he had stomped around his lounge venting his frustration and calming down after the adrenaline rush of relief, he phoned Agnes Duckworth.

'She's alive Agnes,' he said, 'she's in hospital in Reims, France. She's poorly but the signs are good that she'll be OK.'

They talked for a few minutes then exchanged sighs and comments of relief and Tony said he would call her again when he knew more.

He sat at the kitchen table processing what had happened.

He would still go for his walk, but the route would include one extra stop.

Dad

Down past the bottom of the Square to the left, the road splits. The right-hand fork turns sharply and eventually joins the access road to Thistledean. To the left a sign, *Private Road. Harmer Hall.* Tony took the road to the left. For a quarter of a mile, the single track lane was dotted with passing places, and terminated in a large set of iron gates each hung from its own stone pillar. Right and left of the gate, a wrought iron fence curved away.

The driveway to Harmer Hall is flanked by rhododendrons and ancient, mature trees, primarily beech and oak. The road passes in front of Harmer Hall. It's an imposing two-storey, brick edifice, cornered by stone quoins, fronted by an impressive portico where horse-drawn carriages would have offloaded their charges in times of plenty. Today the hall looks tired and in need of attention. The lower floor was latterly a hospice, but that closed a year ago because a brand-new, state-of-the-art one was opened in Holdean and rendered this one redundant. The hall's custodians are discussing various ideas for the property's development but nothing has been decided to date.

However, the road continues past the front of the hall, turns to the right and a hundred yards further on is a large detached bungalow which has been transformed into Thistledean's retreat. There are four suites, each with bedroom, bathroom and 'living' area including seating and a small open-plan kitchen.

It is very secluded and surrounded by large trees and high hedges on three sides. It is open to the front with extensive views over fields and copses far across the Northumberland countryside and on towards the fells. Tony walked under a new entrance canopy and pressed a bell-push to the right of double sliding doors. There were two cameras on the front corners of the canopy covering the drive and one camera above the door itself. Tony looked up at that one as the doors slid open with a whisper.

He was greeted by Caroline Spears, the Retreat's Director.

Tony replied to her welcome and followed her into her office where he inquired about the possibility of Julia coming there to recuperate when she was deemed fit to travel. He knew he was perhaps jumping the gun a bit, but he was keen to do something positive as he blamed himself for his friend's woes.

'Providing the authorities are happy, there's no problem with her coming here. We all realize she must have had quite an ordeal, so it will be a pleasure to help get her back on her feet.'

'The one thing we must do,' stressed Tony, 'particularly for now, is to keep this between ourselves. I know the police will be concerned about security and, due to the nature of what she's been involved in, discretion is certainly important.'

'Well, I can assure you that privacy will be no problem.'

'I'm sure. One idea, should it be required ... could we reserve one other room for a guard or whatever? Whoever it is could live in as a resident.'

'Blimey, it is cloak and dagger. But yes, I see no reason why not.'

'I don't really know what the police are going to request, or stipulate, but if we show some initiative it might not do any harm. The other thing is, don't worry about the cost aspect. I will cover that.'

They bade each other farewell and Tony donned his ruck sack; he left feeling more relaxed than he had for ages, happy in the knowledge he had something positive to offer Sergeant Appleby. He could now look forward to his walk, which would take him to Slate Mill Farm.

Throughout three and a half hours of sunshine and showers, the fells were first embracing, then malevolent, then occasionally malicious. Being high up it was possible to see the squalls approach and take measures. For the darkest, angriest blasts, those that score a direct hit, Tony cowered behind dry stone walls under a waterproof cape and hat. Other downpours drifted by and somewhere else got a soaking. They looked like a curtain of mist being drawn across the land, sometimes multi-coloured when the sun was refracted. He arrived in sunshine, dazzling and warm in the rain-washed air. Surfaces gently steamed and, next to the nearby barn, water dripped onto a tin bath - ting ting ting. The windmill creaked.

Frank Lattimer and Tony leant on the gate by the paddock. It seemed to have become their go-to spot for a chat, like their gateway to the past. Pleasantries were exchanged before Tony asked the question that had been on his mind for years. 'You lived close to us when we lived on our smallholding but I'd never heard of you. How did you know my father?'

Frank smiled a wistful smile.

'It goes back quite a way. Although we lived quite close we saw each other rarely and I never actually met you as a youngster. But I knew of you.' He gazed up the hillside. 'Your father and I were at college together in Newcastle and frankly we were pretty bad lads. We got up to some stuff that wasn't exactly within the college rule book - in any damn rule book if the truth be known. It's nearly sixty years ago but it's still fresh. We messed around with drugs - LSD primarily. We experimented ourselves and progressed to selling it around the college to make some pocket money. In act, it became rather more than that. We were dealers, I suppose, but we only considered it a bit of a laugh at the time. Until it went wrong. A girl died. We weren't sure if she took a bad lot or whether she just reacted badly to it. Whichever, she jumped off the college roof. Probably thought she could fly. Who knows. Nineteen she was, called Faith.'

Frank shook his head sadly.

'Boy do I wish I could rewind and change it all. Barely a day goes by. Poor lass. I remember her parents coming to the school. Her mother's face was haggard; she looked destroyed. I'll never forget. I watched them arrive from a classroom high up in the building from where she fell. Or jumped. I saw them pull up in a VW Beetle, cream-coloured it was. The mother held a handkerchief to her mouth as the father looked up towards the roof. I swear he saw me and looked me in the eye. I nearly keeled over, I can tell you; I was terrified he knew. There was no chance he could see me, of course. I actually checked later, stood down there and looked up. At worst, I would have been an indistinct blur at one of a hundred imperfect window panes. It was my imagination, or guilt, that spooked me.

'We, your father and me, got away with it to some degree because we weren't the only ones selling the stuff. Nobody could prove that we were directly responsible, otherwise it could have meant criminal charges. Even so, we and four others, were booted out of college. It was a shameful time. Shame is what I felt, anyway. I always presumed it was the same for your father. He was harder than me in many ways, somehow less forgiving, but I always believed that the girl's death weighed on him. Though he never said, he kept his thoughts to himself.

'Just occasionally we would meet up, once a year perhaps, usually in a pub in Holdean, sometimes further afield. We'd talk about our farms, about anything but the girl. We'd done all our talking about her over the years and latterly she just sat there in the background, haunting and taunting, daring us to ignore our consciences. I think your father got more angry as time went on, frustrated with himself really because the mistake he made all those years ago still affected him. He was a fairly easy-going soul to begin with at college but he became increasingly surly as he got older.'

'Did you two take drugs/ Could that have changed him?'

'We experimented, that's all. I'm not sure how much your father did. We never sat round stoned or anything. Perhaps he did more than me, but I have a feeling it wasn't the drugs that affected him.' He shrugged his shoulders. 'Who knows? Whatever caused it, he just sort of soured.'

We gazed out over the hills for a while and Tony laughed bitterly.

'Yes,' he said, 'sour and surly, that's where I came in. That's the man I remember. There wasn't a great deal of affection in him, for me or my mum. In fact we'd both be on the wrong end of his fist every now and then, or a belt. I always suspected there was something dragging him back. My mum never mentioned anything, probably fearful of a pasting. In the end he dragged her down, too. She became almost as miserable as him. You'd have thought he'd have been able to park those past memories, particularly as they were so long ago. Made for a miserable childhood; that's why I spent so much time roaming the moors. But I'm still amazed I never came across this place. I thought I'd covered every inch of grass hereabouts.' Tony sighed. 'Surely he could have made an effort for his family?' Rhetorical question, of course, which neither of them tried to answer.

They were quiet for a while before Tony asked, 'How come you ended up living so close to one another?'

'Chance and fate, I suppose. We were studying mechanical engineering in Newcastle but after we got expelled we were at a loss as to what to do. It was your father who came up with the idea and we both ended up at agricultural college. There was a weird synergy about our lives. Both of us had inherited some money, too much too young perhaps, and neither of us really felt the need to knuckle down and study. So we got into trouble together instead.' He shook his head and sighed. 'It was almost inevitable looking back; we had no defining direction. I think we both felt a bit of security in each other's friendship.' Frank chuckled sourly. 'Rebels without a course, with apologies to James Dean.'

'Then one day, not even a year into his studies, your father announced he was buying the smallholding where you grew up. I panicked a bit thinking I was going to be left behind so I started looking around. Then this place came up. I gather from others living hereabouts it was quite a profitable little quarry at one time. But the guy who owned it got old and the business went downhill as he lost interest. By the time the guy died there was little left but bare bones. So I bought it, not because I had any interest in the business; no, it was the location. The whole thing was run down, including the house. Rotten windows, roof collapsed at one end, so because of that and the fact that it's pretty isolated I got it cheap. There was a bit of escapism about it, or running away. Your Father married your mum and you came along almost immediately. Me and Nel married a year later but it was twenty years till Emma arrived.'

There was something not quite ringing true to Tony, but they were interrupted by Emma calling from the house. She had put lunch together, a 'surf and turf' salad she called –cooked ham and beef and some fresh salmon with plenty of greens. 'If I have to eat healthy, you can join in, too,' she said. They sat and talked about nothing much, but they all had plenty of thoughts bubbling under - some of them could be referred to as excess baggage.

Tony supposed that was what Julia had been doing while digging away at her past; trying to shed a load. She and her younger self had been tethered by a yoke to an unfathomed past. Like a muddy geyser whose surface is calm most of the time, just every now and then a memory bubbled up from below and broke the surface tension as gloopy bubbles escaped. Then the image would disperse and things would be calm again for a while. But they always seemed to come; there never seemed to be long-lasting peace.

'How often in life are things perfect, even for an instant?' Julia had asked.

It was a great question.

Night at the Opera

There was a late-season tourist coach in town. They were scaling down now it was near the end of October, so it would be among the last of the season. This was a group of Far Eastern holiday makers who may have visited historic Roman sites in London, Chester and York, before heading to Thistledean. Now lunchtime, the visitors were happily chatting away while seated at two large tables awaiting their meal.

'Did the Romans actually come to Thistledean?' asked the lady in charge of the group of twenty visitors. It said *Miriam Dove - Historic Tours* on a badge on her jacket. 'You can tell me,' she winked and smiled at Felicity.

'Actually, it's inevitable. Hadrian's Wall is close by and there is plenty of evidence of them down the road in Holdean. They wouldn't have come to Thistledean, per se, because the Romans were here before the town existed, but there was likely some sort of settlement here. We've just had a pile of artifacts donated, some of which are Roman. The name Holdean, that's the town down the road, is thought to be some derivative of Danum, which is actually Doncaster, but whether that's just something conjured up by historians, nobody is sure. It wasn't me anyway, creative as I am.'

Rob looked on grinning. He is a mixture of a man. Sometimes studious and thoughtful, traits well suited to his former employment at the tax office, at other times he is forthright, as if trying to escape his starchy persona. He enjoys his golf, in a solitary, introspective way. He is often seen wandering around the golf course, head down, muttering about his own shortcomings. It is like a self-administered torture, as if he is thrashing his own psyche with a horsehair whip.

217

As he searches for balls, often launched into a bank of heather or a paddock of knee-high grass, he is regularly seen from the waist up because the rest of him is hidden by foliage. He battles through the undergrowth with red admirals and cabbage whites for company. In fact, as Monkey pointed out recently, 'If he wore a camouflage jacket nobody would ever notice him.' In his more candid moments, he passes judgment on out-of-towners.

'I tend to keep out the way when an 'Orient Express' is in town,' he says. 'It gets rather busy at times. Lots of chatter in a language I can't understand, excited visitors showing each other various purchases, taking photographs of everything and everybody. But they always smile before they poke a camera in your face. Invariably well-mannered.' He sighed. 'If only Monkey was as well behaved.'

Rob can actually be quite amusing, particularly when expressing opinions on various friends in a light-hearted manner. Recently discussing Cobbles café with a visitor, he slandered Peter Slattery's Eccles cakes, which he called 'Keilders,' 'because they taste like the mulch you find on a forest pathways.' He also accused Peter's Black Forest Gateau of 'tasting like the bark from a damp tree, and his scones should be called stones for obvious reasons. But don't listen to me,' he said to the mystified visitor, 'go and sample his wares yourself. If you're struggling, you can borrow some teeth from Tombstone, our local dentist.'

There was an extended group of Far Eastern visitors gathered round a couple of dining tables in the pub. They made a colourful, eclectic addition as many were wearing expensive outer garments accompanied by trainers and gaudy caps or visors, some with the name of the tour operator writ large on the peak. Ron and Lizzie tried to make them feel at home by stocking a selection of oriental drinks such as Sake, Amazake and Kuroshu from Japan and Chinese rice wine. 'Never thought I'd be serving Lancashire Hot Pot and Amazake, I can tell you,' said Ron, laughing.

There was laughter and chatter as a man and a woman showed off his-and-hers animal slippers. Others were chuckling, peering suspiciously at their drinks. That day they had a fixed menu with a choice of hotpot or vegetarian stew. The vegetarian stew was basically the hotpot without the meat, but people seemed to be tucking in heartily. They were happy, and in holiday mode in faux-Romanesque surroundings among a peculiar race of northern Englanders.

'I enjoy having them here,' said Joan. 'It's great really; they're just a bunch of folk having fun. It's pretty extraordinary. Tomorrow it may be Edinburgh or Chester, next week home, probably doing the gentlest Tai Chi in their local park at sunrise. What a wonderful world we live in. I wonder sometimes how they'll describe us to their friends and family back home.'

'Very peculiar, I would think,' said Rob.

By 1.45 peace largely returned as the visitors departed the pub and headed back to the shops to forage. All except one man. An elderly chap was sitting alone at a table fiddling with his telephone. Ron went over and asked him if everything is OK.

'Yes, please,' replied the man. 'No like shopping.' They all laughed and the old man smiles sheepishly. Ron gave him a complementary drink and offered words of sympathy. The man seems to understand and bowed his head reverently.

* * *

Most people went home but returned later in the evening to see *Des 'n' Norma*, the comedy operatic turn engaged to launch Ron and Lizzie's Friday night specials. A 'meal deal' evening was put on. Fish and chips or pie and chips plus a drink and the entertainment for five pounds. Denzyl, Prawn Broker had done Ron a deal on fifty cod fillets and Parkers' butcher had done similar with fifty pies. The brewery had donated a barrel of ale. It all added up to a good deal for the punters. 'An 'introductory' deal, as Ron points outed numerous times over the evening. 'Special price, introductory offer only', 'a one-off price this evening only.'

The regulars wound him up mercilessly. 'Good deal this, Ron.' 'It'll be difficult to up your prices next time.' 'Very difficult.' 'Particularly if old *Des 'n' Norma* are a bust.'

'Will you all shut up?' Ron looked increasingly flustered as the pub filled up. They ran out of pies, but only for the last few people to order - and they were happy with the fish, so no damage done.

Des 'n' Norma did go down a storm. By the time they took to the makeshift stage everyone was full of good grub and most had downed at least a couple of drinks. It turned out they were both professional opera singers in their day, but parts were hard to come by and singing in the chorus wasn't that well paid. So they formed their double act, singing songs and telling tales about life in the closet world of the opera.

Their finale was a spoof love story between two unlikely characters - Potty Rava and Poo Cheeny - with lyrics and a dance routine that had the audience in stitches. Each had a love rival, Pava Cheeny and Poo Rotty and they got themselves in a frightful muddle trying to sort it all out. Hilarious and imaginative. The dance aspect was clever, particularly as they had to work within the confines of a small stage, but their sighs and frustrated shrugs told of their long-suffering difficulties within the world of international opera (or even Yorkshire Opera, a branch of the genre which had really yet to take off.)

Ron and Lizzie looked as if they'd been through a particularly fierce battle as people drifted out approaching midnight. They wondered whether it was really all worth it. Yes, they decided, it was. Besides, they'd already provisionally booked a magic act that was getting rave reviews. They both agreed that one party night per month would be plenty.

Twice Removed

The revelers had gone home and the town was quiet. A little after one in the morning, an unmarked private ambulance drove up Hall Road, across the bottom of town behind the shops, and made its way sedately up the hill to Harmer Hall. No fanfare, no advance warning. Apart from the two-person ambulance crew, the only people aware of this special delivery were Caroline Spears, Retreat Director. Joyce Melling, carer, and Tony Mason. All five people were sworn to secrecy.

She looked tiny wrapped in blankets on the stretcher as it was lifted out of the ambulance. With a metallic clunk, the stretcher's legs unfolded. A liver-spotted hand escaped the bed covers and grabbed Tony's wrist. He smiled down at his friend. Her white hair was spread on the pillow and she looked weary, but she turned her head, looked up and mouthed, *'Thank you.'* There was a mischievous sparkle in her eyes.

'I've come back for my toothbrush,' she whispered. 'Told you I would.' Tony knew at that moment that she would be alright.

The stretcher was wheeled across the smooth concrete forecourt and disappears inside. It had been decided that Joyce would be Julia's primary carer, providing the two ladies took to each other. Caroline and Tony would be there when needed - they anticipated Caroline would manage the practical side of things and Tony the emotional; but they'd agreed that things would just have to play out and they would see where it led.

They all agreed to leave Julia to settle in for at least twenty-four hours. Give her chance to draw breath and acclimatize a little. So, it wasn't until Sunday morning that Tony got the chance to really sit and talk with his friend. She looked surprisingly good, sitting up in a comfy chair, not unlike the wing-backs in Tony's lounge. Julia, smiling, said as much. 'Home from home.' She looked cozy, wrapped in a pale blue shawl with a thick cream blanket over her legs. They smiled and hugged.

'Gifts,' Tony said, handing her a toothbrush and her sheep slippers.

'Perfect. Help me on with the slippers, would you?'

'Now, at last, I'm home.' She smiled and patted Tony's hand.

Joyce came into the room. 'I have to take your pressure and pulse. Excuse the intrusion.'

She went about her business as Tony looked out of the window, down the garden and over the fields towards the fells. The lawn and beds was now showing signs of autumn, despite having regular attention from a local gardener. 'It's a heck of a view,' he said to Julia.

'After a month, or however long it was, of hotel room walls, any view is a bonus.'

She looked out over the garden. 'But yes, it's a lovely spot, isn't it?'

Then she said to Joyce, 'So, how am I doing? Will I live to eat my lunch?'

'Possibly even dinner.'

They all chuckled. Joyce left.

'She's nice.'

'I'm glad you get on. She should be retired but keeps going by popular request. She's obviously doing something right.'

They paused before Tony said, 'I'm sorry to have put you all through this.'

'What on earth are you apologizing for? It wasn't your fault you got tricked. We both got taken in - it was as much my fault as yours. Probably more, as I wasn't as emotionally wrapped up as you. I should have seen through her.'

'I don't think so. She was convincing though, wasn't she?'

'She was evil. Still is. Evil.

'Yes. But there was something else.'

Tony looked at Julia. She avoided his gaze and looked out over the garden.

'It sounds extraordinary, but we ended up with a kind of Stockholm Syndrome.'

She went quiet. Everybody and everything paused for breath and at that moment, faintly, they could hear the church bells start to ring across the other side of town. They looked at each other and smiled.

'I can see fancy hats, smart suits and a golf cart. Normality in a world of madness. I look forward to attending. I have a few thank yous to say.'

She paused, gathering her thoughts. She needed to talk.

'I realized pretty quickly that all was not as it had appeared with Eva. We stopped on the motorway to use the restroom. When we got back in the car, she drove to the far end of the car park where she took my handbag and threw it deep into the bushes. To say I was taken aback was an understatement, I couldn't believe it. I asked her what she was doing but she wouldn't say a word. My phone was in there and purse. I knew then I was in trouble.

'I'm not going to tell you everything that happened, save to say it involved a number of changes of vehicle and one small boat that crossed the channel, or the North Sea, I'm not sure. We'd spend a few days at a time in various places, either small motels or isolated country houses.

'It's like a dream, really. We were disguised as we travelled, or at least at borders or when we stopped in towns and cities. Different wigs, clothes, scarves, glasses sometimes. In a small town in Germany, I can't even tell you the name, she said, 'This is where I'm from.' She said it with venom and she looked at me with manic, angry eyes.

We set off again and she began to talk about me; about my being 'displaced.' That's the term she used. Intrinsically about me having no proper roots. She knew quite a lot about me. I just listened. I learned that she was also an orphan or, more accurately, Eva is also an orphan. She's alive, in custody. She'll never be free again. Actually, that's not true, she will be free when her time comes, but it may be a while. She's still quite young after all. Being orphans, we shared something, had something in common. I could see her fighting inside, wanting to share something of herself. As if she had to battle to break something of herself free. I knew we needed to talk so I could try and gain her trust. I had already seen the impulsive, irrational side of her ... think handbag.

It all changed in one moment. It was when I said, *'I understand.'* Those words seemed to unlock something in her. As if they illuminated a time in her life when everything was alright. I'd sparked a memory.

She looked directly at me, as if trying to fathom whether I was on the level or fooling with her. She made her choice and looked away. We just seemed to accept that as a starting point of our, what can I call it, relationship? It wasn't friendship; kinship perhaps - the sharing of the small part of each of us that we had in common. Two wandering stars isolated in a big sky.

It was quid pro quo. I would give a bit, then she would respond. I told her the basics about my rootless life, my foundations of straw, my travels following my non-relative, my many journeys and adventures with ghosts as travelling companions. I was confirming much of what she already knew about me, so I had to tell it exactly as it was.

She told me that at one point, she didn't specify where, a switch had tripped and she disappeared deep inside. Towards the end of her teenage years she became what she is. She was intelligent and trained to work in security. The nature of the work meant it was somewhere she could pretend and hide. She never told me the bad things she had done, nor the reasons, but she knew I was aware that she'd done some despicable things.

There were many quiet times, too, when I had time to think. In our younger years, we had both lived another reality - she went one way, I another. Perhaps I was just lucky to go down a benign path. I've wondered since how close I came to taking another road. What stopped me seeking revenge on those who displaced me?

There's an unfathomably complex miasma of neurones, DNA, perhaps even something spiritual, that go into making the basis of what we are. Left to our own devices we'd probably do OK, but sadly adults and peers get involved and exert influence, tell us what to do. They insist on telling us how to behave, what to believe in, who to believe in, where to go, who to associate with. The problem is we can only influence some of these things as we develop. Fragments of these influences stay with us. Ultimately, it may be just one of these things that shapes us. If we're betrayed, for example, or abandoned. Both Eva and I were betrayed, I think, but something in me prevented me turning into a monster. That something simply wasn't there for Eva. Or maybe her betrayal was worse than mine. I imagine it as a tiny electrical impulse triggering a fragment of DNA which is enough to change things forever. It's a game of chance and luck whether the wrong switch is triggered.'

Julia asked for a glass of water.

'Hydrate, the doctors told me. Must do what I'm told.' She smiled, momentarily breaking the intensity. She went on, 'Eva told me she had lived a large part of her life in the shadows being someone else, or hiding behind someone else. She went there because she couldn't face the real her, nor where or what she had been. She knew that by continuing to do what she did it would make her past deeper and darker. Despite this, she wasn't able to stop. Whatever was deep within her kept driving her on.

As we travelled, she would disappear from time to time. I mean physically. I would be tethered to a bed or chair, but with water and food. She'd return and would be quiet for a while. I wondered what she'd done. I didn't ask, and she never said.

For the last couple of weeks before we arrived in Reims, I got the impression she was making one final pilgrimage to what was familiar. Places she'd lived, for example. After Germany we went to Switzerland, Austria, Italy, even Turkey for a spell. She became more thoughtful. Not friendly as such, but less combative. Amazingly, I felt pretty safe. I felt she was trying to make a decision.

'One thing that really disturbed me was poor Nick. I asked her about it. She told me that, although she had been in my flat, she wasn't responsible for his death. What could I do but believe her? I think I do believe her. When we met in Thistledean there was a flint in her eyes, but I soon came to see there was an evil and a madness. It was only when she opened up that she softened at all. Not all the time, but I could see glimpses of pre-madness, or however I can describe it.

'We entered France again and headed north and to that hotel in Reims. We were quite close to where my past was at least partially resolved in Saint Quentin. I think it was her choice that we ended up as close to my reality as she would allow. She wanted some resolution by proxy.

She did say that we were both twice removed. Firstly, from family and secondly from reality itself. We had both had lived a parallel life clothed in a fake persona. She looked me in the eye and said, with regret I believe, that both of us had lived very different alternative realities.'

Julia sighed and closed her eyes. Tony thought for a minute she'd gone to sleep.

'Imagine living for years without meaningful human contact. Not talking, sharing or laughing. I have my unusual history but at least I've interacted over the years through my work and friends. In fact, through teaching and lecturing I made sure I had contact - and with young inquiring minds that kept me on my toes. Eva has been totally isolated.'

She turned her head and looked at Tony.

'She meant to die in that hotel room, you know. She said she had made her own choice to lay down and finish it. She asked me to delay phoning anyone till she was gone. She put the phone on the cabinet between us within my reach. She looked at me, then took handful of tablets washed down with water. Then she lay down and curled up, wrapped up in the duvet like a baby in the womb. I waited two days, but she clung on. Her breathing at one point was barely discernible, but then it grew a little stronger and I realized she would live.

'Was there something within her, a tiny percentage, that held her back from taking enough pills? Had a crack of light from her past unconsciously willed her to live? I think it did. An ultimate fear of dying too, perhaps. I can't forgive or forget what she has done, but I can go a little way to understanding. And for that lost portion of her, that shred of decency, I was willing to help her leave this world on her own terms. But she was to be denied.

'The awful irony, that after all the terrible things she's done, she failed to end her own life. I was pretty weak by now so I made the call. She had even pre-programmed the phone for the police station. That told me, that as she lay down, she trusted me with her death. That's as big a responsibility as trusting someone with their life.

'She lay unconscious on the bed next to me and the police eventually came. I was somewhat tired so it's all like a peculiar dream. As she was restrained on a stretcher and carried out I realized that I had seen a little flicker of light in the darkness that is Eva Mayer; something I suspect nobody else has seen, at least for many years. When I go, I'll take that chink of light with me and her dark will be absolute.

'Eva Mayer was not her real name by the way. She did tell me what it was, but asked me to tell no one. I'll honour that and not even tell you, Tony. It means that Eva will always keep a little something that truly belongs to her. I feel I owe her that.'

Julia's head lolled back against the headrest and she closed her eyes with a big sigh.

'Wow,' said Tony. 'That is some tale.'

'Isn't it? But, despite me knowing quite a bit about her, I couldn't tell the police very much. Vague locations and the approximate routes we took, but she never told me anything of what she did. I'm thankful for that, of course, but you would still have thought I'd have been able to help more. I'm glad she didn't share. I wouldn't have wanted the burden of her memories; I saw what they'd done to her.'

Then Julia smiled and her eyes sparkled. 'Inspector Birch came to Reims. He came into my hospital room looking utterly English.' She shook her head. 'He asked me if I was alright, then sat on the edge of my bed like he was an old friend. Then he burst out laughing. He went bright red and the nurse who was taking my pulse looked very alarmed.'

She laughed.

'I asked him if he was alright.'

'Of course,' he said. 'I knew it. I knew you'd solve the case. I bloody knew it. We've been after her for years, then along comes Miss Marple with her size four shoes and a walking stick.' And he laughed some more.

'I told him I take a size five actually, and he laughed again. I like the man. It's good to allow yourself to be human every now and then.'

Tony smiled and said he was amazed she had come out of the ordeal with any sort of amusing memory.

'The reason I got involved at all is because I poked my nose where it wasn't welcome. Not on purpose of course, but I did nevertheless.'

'Yes,' said Tony, 'I know a thing or two about that.' Then, more seriously, 'Are you not frightened that her partners, or associates or whatever you call them, will come looking for you?'

'No. I'll be quite safe.' She lifted her chin defiantly. 'Eva won't say anything; she will want me around to preserve that ray of light. I believe she'll look after me. She trusted me with her death after all. I choose to trust her with my life.'

Tony shook his head in amazement at his friend's positive attitude. Julia looked out of the window again, deep in thought.

'The other thing is that I refuse to be incarcerated here longer than necessary. If there is to be a trial it won't be for months, and I'm not living under lock and key. They said I might not even need to testify, as they've got plenty of evidence already. Inspector Birch said I need to lie low, so I'm in here partly for my own protection. And only here specifically because he had someone check the place out. They reckon, without physically locking me up somewhere, this place is as safe as anywhere. Besides, I'll be back here properly before too long, so I want to make the most of things. This latest episode has focused my mind rather. I'm nearly seventy after all.' She grinned.

'I think your long-term memory is on the blink.'

'Cheeky blighter.'

She took his hand.

'I thought of you a lot, you know. Leaned on you at times. There were some precarious moments when I imagined you with me, just like when you caught me off that bus. I had time to think and during the darker hours I wondered what you and I had, or have. It's a bit more than friendship, isn't it? I came to think of it as a sort of wrinkly love affair, at least on my side. I looked forward to seeing you again so much.' She squeezed his hand. 'Remember just after we'd met and I asked how many times things are just perfect? Well, when I finally arrived back here, that was the second time in as many months. I think that's pretty extraordinary and it makes me very lucky.'

She paused. 'I would like to see Mrs. Marshall. Do you think she'd come?'

'Don't you need to clear it with your Inspector friend?'

'No, I don't. I'm not a child. What can he do anyway? Arrest me?'

'I see your point. Sure, I'll ask her.'

'I could do with some adult conversation.'

'Now who's a cheeky blighter?'

She smiled.

About the Author

Jo lives in Lancashire with wife Jan and dog Tache.

He began writing monthly articles for a canal magazine in 2007. Catastrophically (for the magazine!) following an 'editorial misunderstanding', they parted company. Jo began to chronicle their travels which ultimately resulted in his three 'At Large' books beginning with A Narrowboat at Large. Jo describes the books as huge warm memories on which he and Jan can draw both during long winter evenings and in their rocking-chair years. Magical times.

After destroying the UK's canal infrastructure on two Narrowboats and rearranging a fair amount of continental waterways heritage on a rusty old Dutch Barge, their boating days came to an end in 2015, to everyone's relief except theirs.

Boating days behind him, Jo's new challenge is an e-bike. However, to mix metaphors, it's not all been plain sailing. Ordeals on Wheels sums it up quite nicely.

Twice Removed is Jo's third novel. It sits proudly (ahem) and nobly (ahem again) alongside stablemates, Operation Vegetable and Flawed Liaisons.

You can connect with me on:
 https://jomay.uk
 https://www.facebook.com/JoMayWriter/?ref=bookmarks

Also by Jo May

My writing is a mixture of non-fiction ('done it') and Fiction ('might be nice to do it')

A Barge at Large

A Barge at Large is a light-hearted account of what happened when Jo and Jan May bought a 100-year-old Dutch barge. The engine barely ran, the heating system didn't work and the rusty patches were growing like fungus on an old loaf. With professional help generally unaffordable they learned to do things themselves, including kicking numerous bits of misbehaving equipment in an attempt to make them see reason. Gradually, things improved to the point where they could at least have lunch without an alarm going off. Traveling from the north of Holland to Burgundy in France, they had less space, but more freedom, less cash but immeasurably richer. There was no keeping up with the Jones' – if anyone started being pompous they could untie the ropes. We'd go elsewhere to experience the pleasures and quirks of new countries and a wacky assortment of people who'd also drifted into a watery existence from any number of directions. We endured misbehaving lavatories and dribbly windows, but also delight tin the wildlife, windmills and wine.

A BARGE AT LARGE II
Looking Back, Moving On
JO MAY

A Barge at Large II

This volume continues Jo and Jan May's European adventure on their old Dutch Barge, Vrouwe Johanna.

Using skills learned as a baker in years gone by Jo transformed a neglected, scruffy boat into something fit to live on, at least for a couple with low expectations.

For two years they cut their teeth in Holland, remodelling their boat then learning to handle it on large lakes and quiet canals (where they couldn't do too much damage) before moving on to rearrange the infrastructure of the French waterways. According to their mate Dave, they finally reach the 'not totally incompetent level where other boaters at least had half a chance of returning to port undamaged'. They eventually run out of people to annoy in France and move on to Belgium where they find a new collection of victims.

Incorporating further boating tales, a short road trip and a shambolic introduction to camper vans this episode sees them expand their horizons and begin an uncoordinated search for a life after boating.

'I have always believed that you only get the chance to do something special for the first time once. Don't bother what is round the next bend, that will come soon enough, try and make the most of now because once you've turned the corner it's too late. All we have to look back on is today, so make it count.

Did we make the most of it? Very nearly.

Would we do it all again? No, it would never be the same.'

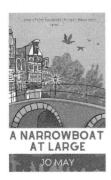

A NARROWBOAT
AT LARGE
JO MAY

A Narrowboat at Large

is the first of three best-selling boating books in Jo's At Large series.

'So why did we take to the water? My wife can't swim, the dog hates it and I prefer beer.

The main reason is that my wife's doctors had told her she was in real trouble so we developed a different perspective about the future than many people. We needed to get on with things.

We knew nothing about narrowboats and how we would cope being cooped up together – particularly when it's minus five and the nearest shop is miles away. We had a mountain to climb – which you can only do by using locks - and we'd never done a lock.

A more accurate analogy is shooting the rapids. Our venture took on a life of its own and we were washed down stream on a tide of enthusiasm and ignorance. We had to make it work or the people who had laughed and scoffed that we were mad would be proved right.

Well, make it work we did, and we boated for twelve years – first on narrowboats then an old barge on the continent.

It was marvellous and it possibly saved Jan's life.'

A Bike at Large

When he was overtaken by a jogger on a borrowed mountain bike, Jo knew it was time for drastic action. Welcome to the world of a man in his 60s and his new e-bike.

His first injury occurred within one foot! Setting off for his first practice ride round a car park, he misjudged the width of the handlebars and scraped his hand on the cycle shop's stone wall.

'You'll go places you'll never have dreamed of,' said the shop owner. Prophetic words indeed. Eighteen hours later Jo was embedded in his neighbours hedge due to a clothing malfunction. Fortunately, before setting out he'd put his ego and self-esteem in the top drawer in the kitchen.

With the emergency ambulance on speed-dial, Jo climbs a steep learning curve on a series of mini adventures throughout the north of England, mercifully with a diminishing distance to injury ratio.

By calling his e-bike a 'Lifestyle Investment', it took his wife's mind off the cost. At the time she needed some new slippers, so it was a sensitive issue. Asked whether he was searching for eternal youth? 'Not really,' he said, 'more trying to keep out of my eternal hole in the ground.'

Fuelled by red wine and optimism, off he goes.........

Flawed Liaisons

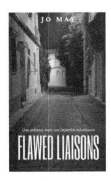

Harry Dunn is an ordinary man living an ordinary life. But a series of events turn his world upside down. His life implodes and he is forced to run.

He is on the ragged edge when a surprise inheritance offers him a lifeline. But it's a poisoned chalice.

He hides away in the underbelly of a prosperous market town among the destitute where he befriends Mary, a woman tormented by her own demons.

Both are forced to confront their pasts as they try to unravel the mystery at the heart of Harry's downfall. What they discover is evil from the past that refuses to die - depravity carried through time in black hearts.

Harry and Mary forge a bond, a liaison born from the misery of their pasts. They have both suffered but find that others have paid a far higher price.

Operation Vegetable

Deep in the English countryside is Watergrove marina, home to a group of unlikely characters living on their narrowboats.

Life is carefree until a local land-owner decides he wants to build three luxury houses on the resident's vegetable plot.

Step forward Judy, a lady of physical substance, fierce determination and jocular disposition, who leads our ageing boaters in a counter-offensive code-named 'Operation Vegetable'.

H.Q. is the local pub and it's here that our ageing boaters raise a creaking battalion.

The boaters find help from an ageing rock star and a TV Gardening programme. Skirmish follows skirmish until one of the boaters is severely injured and the stakes are raised.

Has the despotic land-owner, a man of few morals, driven by power and greed, finally met his match?

Can the boaters overcome this scourge - or have they simply lost the plot?

Printed in Great Britain
by Amazon

25587584R00142